Above the Houses

Also by Susan Engberg

Pastorale

A Stay by the River

Sarah's Laughter and Other Stories

Above the Houses

SUSAN ENGBERG

Delphinium Books

HARRISON, NEW YORK • ENCINO, CALIFORNIA

FIRST EDITION

Designed by Jonathan D. Lippincott

Library of Congress Cataloging-in-Publication Data
available upon request.

ISBN 978-1-883285-30-2

For Simon and Eliza

I would like to express my gratitude to the editors of the following publications, in which certain of these stories originally appeared in slightly different form:

Above the Houses—The Iowa Review, Vol. 35, No. 2, Fall 2005

Moon—Threepenny Review, Fall 2004

Beginning—Sewanee Review, Vol CXI, No. 1, Winter 2003

Time's Body—The Sewanee Review, Spring 2008

Fortune—Michigan Quarterly Review, Vol. XLII, No. 3, Summer 2003

Reunion—Southern Review, Vol. 39, No. 4, Autumn 2003

Rain—Southwest Review, Vol. 88, No. 1, 2003

For essential help in bringing these stories into the world I give thanks to Wendy Weil, agent; Christopher Lehmann-Haupt, editor; Meredith Watts, photographer; my brother, John Herr, microbiologist; and my husband, Charles Engberg, architect, musician, and generous heart.

Contents

Above the Houses

❧

YOUR fingers test from the smoldering, plum-colored center of impact down to the eyebrow, the swollen lid. It's just a bruise, one more thing. Reaching for your toothbrush, you grimace at your mirrored self: shiner, spiky new haircut, the shocked face of upheaval—in short, a sight.

He appears behind your image. Even now, in his gray sixties, your husband's face is fresh, like a precocious child just up from a nap. "My God, what happened to you?"

Two weeks ago, just before the move, he said the same thing about the hair.

You decide not to dwell on damage. This is his first morning on the new job, and you feel how his thoughts are already pulled elsewhere toward new colleagues, new corridors, physics in yet another academic hothouse. For you, for now, gravity is made of boxes and more boxes, a locksmith, the plumber's return, a carpenter if you're lucky.

You tell him you walked into a wall in the night. You shrug. The bedroom was dark, the door wasn't there; your body forgot you'd changed houses, that's all—nowhere near the end of the world.

"Oh, poor head." He places a gentle, salubrious kiss. "What was that story about someone's visiting relative who fell down the stairs?"

"Sally's uncle."

"Terrible."

"I suppose I'm lucky."

As you bathe, you are gentle with the contusion, gentle with yourself in this context of extreme change, but you are too smart to complain. You argued your case months ago; now you have agreed to do this with him. Yes, you have left behind an intact, harmoniously functioning life—city, job, friends, neighbors, doctors, stores, garden, buried pets, the works—but presumably not your wits. Your eyes widen lopsidedly at yourself in this different bathroom mirror.

Sally's old uncle got up in the night in his daughter's house; he stepped toward what he must have expected to be the same level but fell through what was not, never regained consciousness, and died within a week.

The bruise throbs.

"Tom, do you think the heat is more humid here than at home?"

"This *is* home now."

"Please answer my question."

"Yes, all right, maybe. But pretty soon it'll be cooler."

Then you remember your dream: a job offer, to be editor of a magazine, called—was it really?—*Core and Correlative.*

You tell him.

"Joan." He looks searchingly at you, holding your shoulders. Then he tells you that you will become reestablished here; you will find a new life, he promises you will; it's only a matter of time.

You are supposed to be reassured; perhaps you are.

A few minutes later, clean, you sit beside him on the bed to meditate, each at your pillow station, not touching yet locked like molecules. Together you have raised two sons. Together you are living on earth now. You close your eyes, breathing alone, yet with everyone.

Your litany of losses is a useless scrap of grocery list on a table somewhere else; you've already bought that food, eaten it, *moved on*. Shelters change, you tell yourself. Everything changes but what does not. What does not is why you both sit, like this. One must be ready, you have been told, *to take the final leap*.

Nearby a crow gets riled up, then another and another, flaps of sound.

It's too early for the barking of the shut-up dog next door on the north, but the woman across the street is calling her cat again—*Nammo*—something like that. Houses here are so close the outdoor spaces feel almost like communal rooms. After only four days, you're already wondering about the neighbors, their lives, why this woman, for example, calls her large yellow cat so many times a day. *Nammo, Nammo, Naam-mo!*

At breakfast your husband looks stoked with anticipation. The different city and house, the boxes, the nighttime wall, your promises, your children, the never-ending education of your heart are some of the consequences of loving this man. From him today you extract a promise to get the name of a good carpenter. Without more bookshelves, you insist, neither of you will be able to survive. The fervor of your small request makes you feel somewhat better.

When his car backs out the narrow driveway between houses, the crows start cawing again, out there in the busy world rooms where you may or may not still have a part to play. In the kitchen is a hot, skewed stillness, everything stationary but out of place, and nothing will be set to rights without your energy. It is a chaos you have ordered five times before, for him and for the advancement of Physics into ever more subtle realms, which funnily never changes what is always left to do, here in the kitchen where the molecules appear so big and adamant.

In your former kitchen you argued that you didn't know if you could do it again. You said to him that after a certain age trees were too old to transplant.

He said humans had legs for a reason. This was a calling.

For *him*. For you, everything would have to be put together all over again.

He said you were being called: *he* was calling you.

Then you looked out the window, not this present one cheek by jowl with the people next door, but into that former modest vista of flowers, linden tree, honeysuckle hedgerow. You saw the cardinal's flying flash of red to the sunflower seeds. You were crying by then. You saw Sally helping Jim, home from chemotherapy, walk from the car to their back door. Tom came up behind you and wrapped his arms around your waist, his face in your hair—the long hair you recently had. You were crying for all the lives you had learned to live near over the years, who made the great web that held you to your task, some for decade after decade, others only for a moment, like that baby who had been toddling alone down the sidewalk in diapers in May—how it was you, you who rushed out to him, scooped him up, saw the small handprint of blood on the bottle of juice. You covered his ears as sirens ripped the sky. It was for him you were crying that day in your old kitchen, and for his murdered grandmother, and for the students who every night all summer pushed themselves who knows where on the porch swing of love across the street, and crying, too, for the new widow with the light burning all night in the window of the upstairs room, and for Sally and Jim, good friends, good neighbors, and their long ordeal.

Welded against your husband, you were splitting apart. You were everywhere. You were missing your own children as if they had left only yesterday, a raw, wrenching loss; you didn't know how you had ever managed to part with them. You grieved for the gone cat who had slept like a sandbag across your feet and the setter whose ashes had felt like an atomized replica of the old living dog, bones and silk. You were crying for the young bird, flashing back and forth like a red shuttle in the air, and for you yourself, who had moved over and over to new places, new people, each time locating yourself all over again in the mesh of life, from which someday you will necessarily be released. There was nothing left of you that day but feeling, and it had lost all of its containing walls.

You said to him, your husband, the one who was asking you, again, to do it all over again that, all right, if you were going to go, you were going to scoop up the whole compost pile and have it taken along in the moving van; you'd worked on it too long to leave it behind. Did he hear you? This was non-negotiable.

Without more than a face-down nod to you at the back door, the burly plumber from yesterday heads straight for the basement. Over his shoulder he tells you damn if he didn't lie awake all night over your venting problem. What a mother. People want to do all these fancy modern things upstairs no one ever heard of when the house was built, and then he's the one who's got to make it happen down below. Maybe he's getting too old for all this.

You follow his squat figure down the cellar stairs into cooler air. The last time you were his height might have been in sixth grade.

Yeah, he says, he's getting too old to take the headaches—they didn't used to keep him awake like this. The old houses are the worst, and the inspectors! They don't give a damn what you're up against. But anyway, he thinks he's got this one worked out in his head, and he's going to be pretty proud of himself if it looks the same in the light of day as it did in the middle of the night.

He purses his lips and breathes heavily through his dark nose hairs as he shines his flashlight up along the cobwebbed network of ceiling pipes, angled every which way among the rafters, a rough filthy grid that supports the whole enterprise above, where in trust you slept, showered, sat on your pillows and closed your eyes, holding to nothing, assuming you were upheld. He paces slowly, beaming his light here and there, face tilted to the heights, an astronomer kept awake by the myriad problems in his dirty heavens.

"Well goddamn, Ernie," he mutters, "if you don't still got what it takes." Then to you he says, "Okay, missus, we're in business. I'll go get what I need outa the truck." But he stops and holds the flashlight out to the side of your face. "Hey! What happened to you since yesterday?"

You tell him about the wall.

"And that's it? I don't need to worry you're in trouble, do I?"

Gratitude spills to your eyes. To be cared for by Ernie—astronomer, gnome, squat god of wakefulness on your behalf!

Music rises in your mind as you fill the kettle and several pitchers with water to tide you over while the main line is cut off: Bach, phrases of girding order. Yes, what this house needs is music, music to tell its bones who's living here now, music to tell yourself you can be alive anywhere. So the boxes you'll open first this morning will contain CD player, speakers, discs, but now do it *adagio, adagio*: the swollen eye is reminding you to be deliberate in your work, girded with order.

With your good eye you catch a glimpse of the chunky nine-year-old from the house next door to the south as she comes again through her gate and across the shared driveway, fourth day in a row, this morning in a pink leotard, feet bare. Why has she apparently attached herself this way to you and your boxes? Her name is Lily. She disappears alongside your house.

Only last week, from your former window, you watched Jim sitting in his backyard in this same late August sun, his legs folded one over the other like useless parallel walking sticks, his stick fingers lifting a cigarette to the purple crack in his cadaverous face. One of these mornings Sally will call you long distance to say the medics came again in the night, but this time there wasn't a cell of remaining space into which breath could be pumped.

You set the containers of water on the counter and cover them with a clean towel.

Lily arrives at the back door just as Ernie returns from his truck with some lengths of pipe.

Lily says, "Here I am again."

Ernie says, "Can you get that door for me, sweetheart?"

After he disappears down the basement stairs, she asks, "Why did he say *sweetheart* to me?"

"Well you must be a sweetheart. Is that what you want to be?"

"Yes!"

This child is sweet, though with her thick little body and gappy front teeth and one droopy-lidded eye, she hardly seems to belong to her mother, Margot, who is startlingly, casually, opulently beautiful.

"What's that on your head?"

As you tell her, she puts a hand reflexively to her own forehead, above the droopy eye. Lily has already told you she is to be

operated on for her "defect." Any opulence she has inherited from
her mother shows, so far, in her cascading brown hair and the lux-
uriantly lashed eyes.

She comes closer. "Can I touch it?"

"All right." You bend toward her.

The tips of her fingers are like hot sunshine. "Does it hurt?"

"I'm living with it."

"I have dancing today."

"I see you're dressed for dancing. Do you like it?"

"I don't know. I guess. Mom says I have to do it for grace."

"Really! Well. I've heard it's good for that."

"What's this thing?"

"That? It's a sweet red pepper. You have peppers at your
house, don't you?"

"No. All my life I've wanted to eat a red pepper."

"Well! That's a long time. Do you want a little taste now?"

"Okay. Please. I go back to school on Monday."

You watch her biting into the first red pepper of her life—can
it be?—her wide-open eye surprised, her drooping eye secretive.

"Do you like the taste?"

"Yes," she says, determined.

"If you don't want it all, you can put the rest in the sink."

"Mom says Dad eats like a cowboy."

"Oh? How do cowboys eat?"

"They only eat what has legs, nothing with roots."

"Pepper plants have roots," you say.

"I knew *that*."

Lily's father, Larry, the first day you met the family, let his
wife manage the conversation while he stood wide-legged and
conspicuously masculine beside her in the driveway, allowing his
insistent daughter up onto his back, a good-humored horse for an
overgrown rider, evidently an old game. Margot, you've been

told, is in the art department at the university—film, video, something like that.

"Look!" says Lily at the sink, standing on tiptoe. "You can see right into our kitchen!"

"I know. When you're in your house, can you see into ours?"

"Yes."

"Weren't you ever in this kitchen before we moved here, Lily?"

"Nuh-uh. But I wanted to all my life."

It does seem as if she has been waiting a lifetime for your arrival, you and your boxes and red peppers and who knows what else. What are you going to do with this spontaneous trust?

"Romeo and Juliet," reads Lily as she takes another disc from the box. "I've heard of them."

"That's ballet music. Shall I put it on for you?"

Off goes Scott Joplin, on goes Prokofiev, and the expression on Lily's face gets more complicated.

"What have you heard about Romeo and Juliet, Lily?"

"I don't know. Was he her brother?"

"No, but they loved each other very much."

"Why?"

"Well . . . because nothing was more important than that, I guess. It's a sad story, though, because their parents didn't want them to love each other."

"Why?"

Why. How to tell a story that is so much larger than the size of itself it seems it could contain at least one way to look at all of history? Meanwhile, Lily's arms are lifting away from her torso, which is like a stubby piece of pink pipe, her heels are lifting, she's pointing her toes for one step and then another. In the welter of the living room you have only, it seems, begun to live in today, Lily now makes a tiny leap and thuds to the maple floor. Your heart lurches. She is like yourself. You're nine, you're fifty-nine. For you she's dancing, stepping off into air, smiling a gap-toothed smile. Her arms come together and again extend, her face collecting itself, as she leaps once more and lands in a heavy graceless barefooted slap. Young Juliet at play, before the great love of her life.

The music continues, but all at once Lily stops. Then you see what she has seen, the beautiful woman on the other side of the front screen door, her mother, who is shading her eyes, peering into the room.

"Hello, hello? Lily, is that you? Come right away, please, or you'll be late for your class. Hello, Joan, how are you getting along? I hope you don't mind your helper—she insisted you needed her."

"And so I do, it seems. Come in, Margot."

"I'm sorry to be in such a ridiculous rush. You wouldn't believe the kind of day I'm having. Hurry now, Lily, here are your sandals." She slides the shoes across the floor to her daughter.

You press the button that sends Prokofiev back to Moscow, Leningrad, St. Petersburg, back to the years before the war, the war that in taking your father shot away part of your childhood, which in its absence feels sometimes like the loss of one of your own dancing feet. You became what people called *a somber child*.

"I got tied up on the telephone," says Margot, her glance circling your mess. "It was Berlin. These international calls, you've got to take them when they come, there are so many other obstacles as it is—oh please, Lily, don't make this one of your dawdling days!" Margot is wearing blue jeans and a linen jacket whose sleeves she now scrunches higher above her silver bracelets.

Lily has sat down on the floor to buckle her sandals. Her cheeks are almost as pink as her leotard. She's taking her own sweet time, you're pleased to see, but you're also anxious for her.

In the absence of the music you hear banging from the basement, metal against metal, and now that muffled barking again from the house on the north side, same as yesterday and the day before and the day before, starting about this time and continuing off and on for the rest of the day, the dog that is evidently shut up alone. You're about to ask Margot about this other neighbor and the poor dog, but she is stirring the air with her hand to hurry the stolid pink child on the floor.

"Seventeen minutes, Lily, that's all we have." Then she notices your face. "Whatever happened to you! What a nasty bruise—are you all right, Joan?"

You tell the story with utmost swiftness.

"How unfortunate for you—not exactly something you need, right? Lily! I'm telling you this is not the time for the slow-motion game." Margot slides the sunglasses down from the top of her splendidly messy mane of hair. "By the way, your haircut is fabulous," she says. "I should do something radical like that—not that I believe it would actually simplify this frantic life of mine."

Adagio, neighbor, adagio. You're remembering Jim and his sucking breaths, the baby with the bloodied bottle dangling from his mouth. You breathe in. Out. What is your job to be now in this world?

Up from the basement come heavy steps, and in a minute Ernie in his work boots, wrench in hand, is peering in from the threshold of the kitchen. "Could you come take a look, missus?"

He looks down to Lily. "You leavin' us, little lady?" Then he nods awkwardly toward beautiful Margot in her sunglasses.

Lily quickly finishes buckling. She scrambles up and plants herself in front of Ernie and demands of him in a bold, excited voice, "How come you didn't say *sweetheart* to me this time? Did you just forget?"

Several hours later, the locksmith is telling you a story about folks one street over who didn't think to change their locks when they moved in and one morning someone calling himself a carpenter turns a key and walks right in with some fancy excuse about coming back for his ladder and a few lengths of board.

"But I desperately need a carpenter right now!" you're saying as the telephone begins ringing, ringing.

"Not like that you don't," says the locksmith as you get up to answer, remembering that the murdered woman hadn't changed the locks either; the estranged husband still had a key. The baby must have seen it all.

It's not Sally on the telephone, as you guessed, but Margot again, still rushed, also perhaps a bit apologetic, with an invitation for tonight, a very informal, very last-minute gathering that she is throwing together. You run your fingers through the strange harvested field of your hair. You thank her. You say you'll call and ask Tom.

"Oh, and I've been hearing such marvelous things about your *Tom*!" She says his name as if it were the title of the latest blockbuster. "What a treat to have you with us!"

After her call you wish the plumber and the locksmith would get out; you don't even want any carpenters to show up now; you don't want neighbors to appear; you don't want to be nice to anyone's children. Alone, you want to be alone.

Before long the locksmith is indeed done, then Ernie. From their efforts the laundry machines stand ready to be loaded; the dishwasher fills and empties; the refrigerator belches ice, a piece of which you slide now and then over your bruise; and you are the only one possessing workable keys to this house. Just let anyone try to intrude: you're safely locked in, you here with strewn possessions and over there next door—yes, there he goes again—the barking dog, a deep imprisoned *boof*.

Who would keep a dog locked up alone from so early until so late? Well, you've met him: Willard, a lawyer, and he appears perfectly sane, except, of course, that he seems to be working insanely long hours.

You go back to knifing open boxes, pulling out wadded papers, things and more things. This box says TABLE LAMPS/ LIVING ROOM.

Boof! boof! Let me out!

Look at your hands, so nimble and quick, so admirably industrious: boxes today, who knows what wonderful job tomorrow!

Boof! boof! boof! boof!

You sink down onto your knees. The next box must have been labeled by a zany twin: VARIOUS USELESS OBJECTS. What a joke— who but yourself did you think would unpack it and be amused?

Boof! boof!

Folded over now in child's pose, head to knees, you are just an object, washed up with other junk, listening to the tide going out, feeling dry, feeling everything, waiting for the next wave of your small life, which seems as if it might never, this late, come again.

What? You're crying? Boof! and yet again boof! Oh, come on, don't pretend you're crying for that dog, the dog you may think is barking for you; he's not, he doesn't know you exist. You're separate. All you want is for the unhappy sound to stop. You're not responsible for that dog over there. You cover your ears, and now the barking comes as if from a faraway tomb. How compact you've made yourself—why, you could be packed into this very box! PRAGMATIC FEMALE OBJECT/VARIOUSLY USEFUL/PACK LAST/ OPEN FIRST.

Buried alive.

All at once you're in motion. That dog is suffering. You stride over lawns to the neighbor's door. What are you doing? You know he's away at work. You ring the bell, wait for nothing, open the screen, try the latch on the inner door. Ah! for an instant the barking stops; then it returns, not with the steady, beaten-down anguish of before, but in hopeful frenzy, and the dog appears, clawing frantically at a window near the door. Woof! Woofwoofwoofwoof! You've made things worse!

He's a black-and-white mongrel, with a fringed, upturned tail. You've seen lawyer Willard, still dressed in his dark suit, release him at night into his backyard. You think you've heard the dog called Harry. Hairy? You lay your hand on the glass, over the nose of the undistinguished dog.`

He scrabbles his front paws against the slippery surface. Look, he's smiling at you! Oh, there, there Hairy Harry.

You glance around, see no one, not even the woman calling Nammo the yellow cat. The next logical step, now that you've taken the first leap, is to try the back door, and you are of course logical and thorough; your calm attention to sequence and detail was praised in the Office of Admissions, your last job, in the last city, the last life, where people appeared to consider you perfectly competent and sane.

The back door is also locked. Harry, who must have raced through the house, sounds as if he is hurling his whole body springily against the inside wood panels. Next door, beyond the fence slats, your own house presents to the afternoon sun an innocent domestic rear, and the four very large galvanized steel garbage cans of hauled compost are lined up neatly at the edge of your new, very small yard.

Lawyer Willard's house has the same kind of outside basement access as your own, slanted metal doors over a sunken hatchway.

Only a few days ago yours were pried open so the movers could trundle down your washer and dryer. Afterward you had to struggle to slide shut the rusty, misaligned inside bolt, but you finally got it—all battened down to do the same old laundry in a brand-new place.

Now Harry moans and claws as if his nose were at the bottom crack of the door, snuffling for a whiff of rescue from your shoes. Then he howls, Ow-woooo!

You back away. Boowoowoowoowoof! Oh, the outrage of being almost but not helped!

You feel like howling. You go over and yank the handle of the cellar hatch, which should be bolted as yours is from the inside, but it comes up easily. Sunlight rains down wooden steps. You descend into a smell of rodents, dank stones, earth. You'll have to tell Willard about his unsecured hatch. No, maybe you won't. You step down *adagio*, remembering Sally's old uncle. Are you in your right mind? You turn the knob and push against the inner door to the basement, expecting firm logical resistance, but it swings toward the dark nether interior.

In you go, past washer and dryer, stacked firewood, boxes, then up and up stairs to a door behind which Harry sounds so excited he's probably peeing all over. Self-abandonment, both of you.

You crack open the door to a kitchen—linoleum tiles, table legs, a stack of newspapers, a pair of running shoes.

You're here! Harry barks, wags, whines, moans, runs in circles, barks again. You've come! Yes, it *is* you he's been waiting for.

But the thrill is too much, too much, he's all over the place, he'll have a fit, oh you'll never be able to handle him.

"Harry, come!" you say in a sane and commanding voice and start back down the stairs. He races past you so fast he nearly knocks your legs out from under you. At the bottom he lays nose

on paws, wags hind end in air, and moans up at you. You catch
hold of his collar. "All right, Harry, come along." Crouched over,
you walk him across the basement and keep him restrained as you
climb to the outside. The yard gate, you see, is closed. You let
him go.

Flying joy! Bounding relief! Pee here, pee there, back to you,
thank you, thank you, off again, pee smell pee, race with joy.

You keep yourself mostly hidden in the hatchway, dog's-eye
level. Willard's yard is a baked, scruffy mess. He could use some
of your compost and a few sturdy, dog-proof shrubs.

Harry's over in a far corner, digging energetically at the base
of the fence. "Harry!" you say in a hoarse whisper. "Harry, come!"
He keeps digging. You whistle; he turns to look at you. "Come,
Harry! Come! Come here!"

All at once he's alert to something else, and a moment later
you hear the siren. By now Harry is racing back and forth along
the fence, stopping to howl, ow-woooo, again, again. The windows of your new world peer down. Who on earth are *you*? Just
act as if you belong wherever you are; climb out of the dungeon;
walk calmly across the yard; pretend you know exactly what
you're doing. That's the way. No one else needs to know how you
have improvised your entire life as a woman.

The point is, the point in the potent momentous present,
which is all you've got, is that, well, right now you've to get the
dog back inside.

You're close to him now. He throws you a companionable
look: Isn't this fun? Actually it is, now that you're in the open,
just doing what needs to be done. Come on, boy. You take a few
playful running steps toward the hatch opening. You pick up a
little stick and waggle it at him. An odorous bone would have
been better, but this is what you've got, and haven't you always
been given enough right at hand to put together a life?

Harry is undecided, but you're focused; you're powerfully patient; you have full attention and a magic stick, which, at the charmed moment, you throw a short distance in the direction of the open hatch. Success! Harry bounds toward it, you run after and slide your hand under his collar. Teeth clamped on the stick, tail wagging, snappy eyes watching you for what comes next: he's Harry your new friend.

You're careful with yourself on the stairs: apparently, there's going to be more for you to do after all in this interesting world. You release neighbor Harry back into his kitchen with the magic wand still clenched in his grin.

The lips of your husband touch your forehead, just shy of the bruise. "Sorry I couldn't get away sooner." His energy feels like, well, like his energy—or, no, not quite; there might be a slight static.

For now, you only nod to him from your pillow station; eyes closed, you're already on your way, going nowhere, doing nothing, taking care of everything you can.

Nammo!

But, listen—no barking from a discontented dog! You smile to yourself.

Tom eases himself beside you on the creaky bed that has borne you both through all your adult changes. He sighs, his breathing slows. His energy adds to your energy, each of you now heading to the same core.

When you think again it is to think that sitting together like this, agreeing to be quiet, agreeing with the quiet, is like another way of being married.

Now clothes flap fleetingly across your mind, what to wear tonight, a thought with a tail of quick imaginings, and then adornment fades, silky even in its passing.

Nammo! Nammo!

With what sweet longing the woman calls for the yellow cat, over and over, calling him home.

In Margot and Larry's entrance hall you're waylaid by the glossy oak dresser at the foot of the stairs, its drawer pulls of carved oak leaves, on it a brass lamp with glass lamp shade stained in blue irises and a rather large black-and-white photograph, matte finish: it's Margot against an ornate headboard, shoulders bare except for her dark shawl of hair, bedsheet loosely gathered in her right hand just over her breasts. She's looking directly at the camera. On her lap is an open book. There are other books and newspapers at the foot of the bed. Tucked against her left side in the chiaroscuro of her arm is a diminutive Lily, age three or so, her eyes trained on her mother.

"That was out near Missoula," says Larry's voice over your shoulder. "Where Lily was born. And conceived. Up there in the mountains."

You turn to face his considerable height, barrel chest, thick dark hair, large handsome face.

"That seems like a lovely beginning."

"Great air."

"You miss it?"

"You bet I do. I'm working every day on getting my girls back there."

Already he has spoken twice as many words as he did the day all of you first met in the driveway, when Margot seemed to be talking for everyone.

"So tell me," he says to Tom, "how did you get this lady of yours to follow you around?"

Tom can almost always be counted on to be amiable in company, courteous, equable, even though you're pretty sure he would be just as happy, or even happier, to be alone and undisturbed in the refreshing universe of his mind. "Well," he says pleasantly, then looks to you. "How exactly did that work, Joan?"

Probably only you can hear the slight interference in his energy tonight. You look back at him steadily. "This time the deal maker was the compost pile."

For having made it easy for both of them you are rewarded with laughter.

"Well, come on and meet some folks," says Larry.

You glance to your left down a little hall, where people gravitate toward a candlelit table. No children. "Where's Lily tonight?"

"Somewhere in the corral, upstairs most likely." Larry leads you to the living room, where Margot's voice spikes above the others.

As you draw closer to the group gathered around Margot in her red-orange summer dress and recognize the story she is telling, you hope that Lily is not only upstairs but safe in her room with the door closed and her head clamped between earphones full of her favorite music. Margot has come to the moment when Lily demands that Ernie call her *sweetheart* again.

"Will someone please explain to me how I could have produced such a retrograde daughter? I mean, what *is* this? What is the point of revamping womanhood no pun intended if your own girl child can't wait to trash all your efforts? Does she think I'm going through all this for *myself*? And then on top of everything she tells us tonight that she wants to be Juliet when she grows up. Juliet! Please, will someone tell me what's happening here?" Margot is laughing. Her face is flushed, shining. With both hands she rakes up her hair, shakes it out as if to cool her neck, and lets it fall again.

Then she catches sight of you and Tom. "Well, here's Joan, she was there, she'll tell you—Joan and Tom, everybody, our new next-door neighbors. Who was that gorgeous ugly man anyway, Joan?"

"Ernie, the plumber." Heads turn to you and you feel even more the burn of your naked bruise, the prickly gamin shortness of your hair.

"My progressively raised daughter, romanced by Ernie the plumber!" Margot pretends to sigh. "Is this a chaotic world or what? Help us, Tom, you're the scientific expert. Should we reformers just throw up our hands?"

"Well, no," says Tom, and you feel him struggling to repack what he knows into the partygoing moment. His gaze lifts slightly as if he were at this very instant formulating the equation that would roll up his beloved ten dimensions into a recognizable four. Then he takes a deep breath, perhaps, yes, a slightly tired breath. "Aren't we all a bit like the blind people trying to understand the elephant? Even what seems like chaos could be just a segment—"

"Oh, don't you just love it—a cosmic elephant!"

Margot is more drunk than you realized.

Then you notice Larry, his broad stance, his look that says *steady now, we've handled this before*, like a man with a lasso, possessing his wife with his eyes, gauging, playing the rope. You can almost see these two in their lovemaking, grappling with questions of hierarchy, a little roughly perhaps, then his hand coming down over her mouth, all her bravado reeled in, under.

Now Margot's audience is dispersing into buzz. A moment later a predacious nasal voice nips at your side, as if singling you out as the most vulnerable ruminant on the edge of the herd. "And so what do *you* do to justify your existence?"

You turn to a stubby man with popping eyes, a wide toothy mouth, a shirt of bilious green, three pens in the pocket, bulky arms akimbo, stubbornly squared up too close to you.

"Right now I'm listening to you—does that count?"

"Ha, ha," says the man, neither laughing nor backing off. "Seriously, though."

Where's courteous Tom when your life needs saving? Over there, involved; he's involved. And tonight he does look—well, older. You try to catch his eye.

You take a breath, but amazingly it's your smoldering bruise that speaks out. "Seriously? Seriously I'm exhausted because we've just moved and also right now I'm seriously parched. I must get something to drink."

Your knight stays on the other side of the room.

The short man edges closer. "My wife's not here tonight. She says she can't stand to go to parties with me anymore."

Your astonishing bruise speaks again. "Then why don't you come in two cars in case she needs a fast getaway?"

"Ha, ha. I can tell you've thought this one out."

"Not seriously."

"What happened to you anyway? Who did you knock heads with?"

"I can assure you it is not an exciting story."

"No? Well, I've been teaching public high school for twenty-seven years. You can't surprise me with anything."

"Twenty-seven years, that's dedication."

"My wife should hear this. Dedication sounds better than insanity. I'm walking out the door tonight and what does she say to me? She says I'd be better off in general if I didn't open my mouth. What does she know? Let me ask you something. Are you aware that democracy does not, I repeat does not, work in the classroom? I challenge you to prove that it does. And you can't tell me it works in marriage either."

"Democracy? Democracy. I'm afraid I really must have a drink of water before I can talk any more. Do you suppose you could point me in the direction of the bar?"

"Ha, ha, very clever. Don't worry, you have not succeeded in offending me. I only give offense. Go through that door. You are hereby released."

Abruptly he lurches away, he who must also be part of Tom's immeasurable cosmic elephant, along with you and everyone else. For one moment you imagine calling him back, lonely, narcissistic little man, salving him with kindness, but you really must head first toward saving your own life.

At last you have it, water lovely water; you drink and drink and then hold the glassy coldness against your battered brow. No, not *battered*, come on, you whose man has never lifted a hand against you, whose only failings toward you have come from preoccupation and partial sight.

The grandchild of the murdered woman wasn't even crying. His teeth were clenched around the nipple of the bottle. His eyes told you nothing, everything.

Across the congested dining room you now notice the keeper of your hairy friend Harry, lawyer Willard, gesticulating, his brow furrowed, as he makes a no doubt very important point. Oh, the cares of the world, and who looks out for the elephantine whole of it, who remembers the mongrels shut up alone while the public work goes on?

You sidle out of the possible line of Willard's vision. You graze on some green and purple grapes and then attach yourself to what appears a benign group. You're missing your old friends so much you could weep, those dear friends in all the places you've lived who are not here, who knew you, who know you.

It was Sally who helped you with the toddler while the bodies were carried out and the lights flashed and the yellow tape was pulled from tree to tree. The crowd grew. Word passed from mouth to mouth. He shot her, he shot himself, restraining orders don't restrain, he was crazy, she asked for it, he used his own key, incredible.

Listen to this, you should have told the locksmith today; listen, citizen, and weep.

Someone is asking you how you like it here, in their fair city—but isn't it daunting to move in during the dog days?

"Dog days?" Your pulse skips. "I haven't heard that expression in a while." You glance across the room at the back of Willard's head.

Just wait a few weeks, you are told, September and October are often the nicest months of the year here.

A light flashes peripherally. A woman in a tank top and overalls is taking photographs. She approaches your group, not talking, just clicking adjusting clicking, a young woman, tan strong arms, streaked short hair, coming closer, clicking. Now it is you she is focusing on, the side with the bruise, the flash coming nearer and nearer, no questions, just documentation.

All at once your hands fly to your face.

"Sorry," she says, touching your shoulder. "I get carried away. That's a beauty you've got. I'd love to back you up against the wall and take it straight on. Would you let me do that?"

"It was a wall I walked into in the middle of the night."

"Really?" She's thinking about her photograph. "Over there. Please, it will just take a minute. Do you have any idea how marvelously dramatic you look?"

She's about the age of your beloved sons; she's just trying to make her way in the world, seeing small things and wanting to show something larger. You shrug. "All right." You let her line you up against the white wall of the hallway.

"Beautiful, beautiful." She clicks again and again. "Now turn your head just a bit that way, that's it, that's it. Wonderful. Let me tell you I hope I look as great as you when I'm old. So, a wall? Then you haven't learned to walk through them yet?"

"No! Is that something old ladies are supposed to know how to do?"

"Sorry. I've got some far-fetched ideas about the age of wisdom, I'm afraid. What is your work, by the way? You look as if you've done interesting things."

"My work? Ah, yes. My work." But now your willful bruise has nothing to volunteer. It's up to you: self-characterization, which feels impossible.

"Hey! Sophie!" A woman calls from the other end of the hallway. "Hurry, we've got something for you."

"Oh, I'd better run see." She holds out her hand. "I'm Sophie. Obviously."

You say your name, you shake her firm young hand.

"Joan," she says. "Thanks *so* much. I'll try to catch you later." She gestures above her head. "Go on up if you want to see some of my prints—tell me what you think."

Black-and-white, minimal, rising by steps as the stairs rise, the photographs frame close-up bits of the vegetable world in contiguous harmony with cropped segments of man-made objects, natural and crafted, arranged to go together but also revealed as if discovered for what they are. Stem, thorn, leaf, frond, petal and petal, flower; spindle, knob, mullion shadow, mirror, spoon, leaf of book, book: a few pieces; enough.

They're very good photographs. You don't care anymore about having been used. Anyway, what better for old ladies than to be found good for something?

You're eye level now with the upstairs hallway; obliquely across, sitting splay-legged on the floorboards of a bedroom, still dressed in the pink leotard, is Lily, her hair in a wild, messy ponytail. She's not listening to music but making her own vigorous singsong.

"Good girl, Dolly. Now you can eat; eat this, Dolly. Chompy, chompy, chomp. All right! That's enough, you'll get fat. You'll get too fat to jump! Stop now, *bad girl*. Go to the stable!"

She doesn't notice until you lean in the doorway and speak. "Hello, Lily. What's your horse eating tonight?"

"Oats and cookies."

"Did she go over all those jumps?"

Lily nods. The obstacle course is made of Legos. A dozen or so plastic horses are nosed up against the bed skirt. As you come closer you scent warm child skin and hair, redolent little girl crotch.

"How was your dancing lesson?"

"Okay, I guess. I don't like it very much."

"Oh? Well, that's important, how you feel."

Lily is looking at you more intently. "Did Mom cut the cake yet?"

"I didn't see a cake, Lily."

"I'm supposed to get a piece. She said I had to wait—she always says that."

"I see. Well." You pick up a horse. "What's the name of this one?"

"Brucey-boy. I'm going to get a real horse, did you know that?"

"You are!"

Lily nods. She rests her head sideways on the bed. Fiery-cheeked, she looks exhausted. "Dad says when we go back out west I get to have one of my own."

"Oh! You're moving away? When's that going to be?"

"I can't know that."

"Well, I would miss you, Lily, if you went away."

Are you telling the truth? You miss your own children. You miss those fecund, packed years, the bliss of sleeping that close together, the clarity of the work of keeping everyone together under one roof.

You smell the living heat of this child. You hear party sounds rising through the floorboards, up the stairs.

All right, what's your job, right now, with this child of another man and woman?

All at once Lily bends her knee toward her chest, flexing her toes upward, and then, glancing toward you, slides her heel quickly, too quickly, along the floor and into the row of plastic horses. Sideways they fall, each into the next, clattery, clattery, clack. The bed ruffle flounces over some of the heads. Then, like a battle, it's over.

Again she rolls her eyes up to you, one pupil almost lost under its droopy lid. Her look tells you everything, nothing.

A man laughs at the foot of the stairs, and a woman—yes, Margot—keeps talking.

It's as if Lily has challenged you. All right—but—you step to a window where, in front of a nighttime view of houses and trees, a gauzy curtain panel has been gathered into a knot in the center of the glass. The fine white material falls into a knuckle of itself, loops back into hiding and spills out again like the end of a sash girded around a waist.

The call comes from outside the window, away from the party.

"Oh, Lily, listen to that. Have you ever made friends with the cat across the street?"

"No," she says, not diverted, not moving—she has already made her move; now she's waiting. You see now how difficult a child she can be, how needy. Shouldn't this family be left to itself?

Once more you face the window. Directly across the driveway is one of the guest rooms where Eric and Andrew, perhaps soon with wives, will sleep when they visit. The very names of your sons recall you to their essence, but the day-by-day stories of their lives, which once you and Tom thought you knew so well, come to you now in dribs and drabs, like books with pages, even whole chapters, missing.

"Where do you think that cat hides, Lily?"

Lily does not move. The horses lie where they have fallen.

Nammo!

The flow of love toward your children is as native to you as the simple flow of your own blood, more natural, in truth, than the long cultivation of love for your husband.

"Well, I think the cat hides under the porch. I'm guessing he has a secret place where he goes in and out."

"Why?" demands Lily, and as you turn to her you see she has picked up the horse called Brucey-boy and is walking him, clop, clop, across the floor to her lap, which is a start, anyway, a new beginning.

But all at once Margot's voice is calling *just a sec*, as if to someone below, and footsteps are hurrying on up the stairs, and then she is bursting through the doorway of the bedroom like a flower made of hair and skin and jewelry and red-orange cotton with a plate in her hand, a plate of cake. "Okay, Lily, here is—Joan, you, too!—I should have brought more—oh God, my head." She slides the plate onto the nightstand and then in one motion collapses sideways on the bed.

"These parties. Why do I think I have to keep putting together these everlasting *occasions*? What do I expect—something *life-changing*? Dream on. God, I'm dizzy, I'm swimming, I'm falling apart. What heaven it is up here—so quiet!"

For a moment you are all held in that quiet. You see the awkward beauty of the child on the floor and reclining behind her the full-blown beauty of the woman.

Then Margot props up her head in her palm. "Lily, you're not in your pajamas yet, what have you been doing? Phew! You need a bath—do you know that? Doesn't your mother take care of you?" She frees Lily's ponytail and begins to stroke the back of her head, playing with the disorderly mass.

"Can someone please tell me what this thing is about parties? Why do they always seem so redundant? It's like they're over before they even start." Margot's not looking at you, but talking as if to no one, or to her daughter's hair. "Not that they're not dangerous, anyway. I don't know why I put myself through all this. I've got no skin anymore, I'm losing my nerve—me!" Absently she lifts a handful of Lily's hair and lets it fan downward. "What a waste."

You feel like no one, just a stranger at the nighttime window. You don't know if you can do it again: city, neighborhood, lives and more lives, your own, again.

"Don't think I don't know what they're saying about me," says Margot. "I do, but I simply refuse to identify with what other people say." She draws a veil of Lily's hair over her own face, dramatically. Lily does not resist.

Then all at once Margot brushes away the hair and sits up. One foot knocks aside the body of a horse, but she doesn't seem to notice the tumbled stable. "Well, all right—what they're saying is that I don't really know anything, that I've just taken *their* materials and sexed them up. Can you imagine anything so silly? As if the idioms aren't there for the taking! It's hardly stealing, and it's not just rearrangement, either: it's alchemy. They have no idea what it takes, the heat . . ."

She snatches the plate of cake and begins to eat, one frosted forkful and then another. "I use the vocabulary, I submit it to the fire, call it whatever you want, the point is they're afraid of it, I'm not the same kind of player they are so they think I can't play at all—"

"Mom! Mommy!"

Margot is eating cake with a vengeance: sugar, sugar, and to hell with everything else. Her legs below the froth of red-orange skirt are spread out like slender tanned bridges over sleeping or dead cavalry, her sandals are slipping off.

"They say I'm merely suggestive," she says with her mouth full. "Well, *of course* I'm being suggestive, that goes without saying, that's the *whole point*."

You are nodding. You open your mouth to speak.

"Mom!" Lily is knocking her horse against her mother's leg.

"Up to now," Margot goes on, "I've always thought that what I had inside was so much stronger than anything that could happen to me from outside that all I had to do when the going got rough was use my own strength on myself first, get juiced up all over again, but now it's like I'm losing my nerve, I can't get to what I need to get to anymore—*what* Lily? Stop it! Damn it! Why are you pounding on me?"

"Mom, you ate all my cake, you ate it! Brucey-boy and I are *mad at you*!" Holding the horse by a rigid foot, she bounces his head up, up, up toward her mother's face. "We are very, very disappointed in you!"

Irritably, Margot pushes down the horse and then looks as if for the first time at the plate. Her expression changes. "Oh God, Lily, I'm sorry, what am I doing—well, look, it's gone, I'm sorry. Be a trouper and go get yourself some more—tell you what, bring some for all of us, we'll have a sweets feast up here, just us girls. Go on down, Lily, there's tons of cake—go on, go on!"

With a bared foot Margot tries to pry up her daughter's pink-clad behind. "Go *on*! This isn't the end of the world, and you know it."

Finally Lily hauls herself up and still carrying Brucey-boy by one leg trudges from the room. *Done this before*, says her thickly disappointed body, *done this before and before and before*.

"I'm a maternal delinquent," says Margot, with a kind of shudder. "I should just let him take her and go back out to his everlasting wide open spaces; they don't need me, they'd be better off, the two of them, you can't believe how much alike they are."

"Surely they need you. Of course they do! How could they not?" You realize you are wringing your hands.

"No, trust me, I'm redundant."

No, you're drunk, you want to protest—you don't know what you're talking about! But maybe she does. You are silent. Your bruised forehead pulses. It feels as if the whole world is streaming into you through that most tender place, and you don't know what you're supposed to do with it.

Sitting slumped on the edge of the bed, Margot is like a boneless cloth doll. Her hands lie loosely in her lap. "You want to know something?" She raises luminous, dark-rimmed eyes. "When I was pregnant with her, it was *him* I felt invaded by—honestly! And when she was born, you can't imagine what a shock it was to look at her and see an exact tiny version of his face. How did he do it? I said to myself. I'm erased!"

You do not contradict Margot to say that she appears to be the least erasable of women.

"It's like the two of them were born for each other. Neither of them sees *me*. So I say to myself, all right, I can be independent—I've already had to be incredibly independent in my life—but you know what? It doesn't work that way. I'm so tied up with them I don't know who I am anymore—it's like something essential is being sucked away. My creative work is suffering, and he doesn't care. All that is totally secondary to him. He wants me here when he gets home. And he says I'm getting fat—me!"

As if noticing the fallen horses for the first time, Margot bends over and sets one back on its feet, and then another and another until the whole line is back in formation at their invisible feeding station.

"I'm afraid I'm going to have to live away from him, Joan. He doesn't have my best interests at heart, he really doesn't, and I can't go on losing myself like this. It would mean leaving Lily because he couldn't exist without her, I know he couldn't, but I could adjust if I had to."

Suddenly she stands up and shakes the cake crumbs from her skirt. "This is ridiculous. I'm so sorry. I've got to stop talking and get back downstairs. What on earth is taking Lily so long? Oh God, I've got to stop drinking, I know I do, I know it weakens me, and I need my strength, I'm going to need all of it."

"Yes, that's true, I feel the same way."

"About what?"

"Strength."

"Yes," she says, nodding. But does she sound disappointed? Did she want you to say that you, too, even at your age, feel that you must leave your husband in order to be yourself?

Margot goes over to Lily's dresser and brushes her hair vehemently in front of the mirror. She rubs her front teeth with a fore-finger. "All right, I'm out of here." Then, armored once more, she meets your eyes.

"Don't look so shocked, Joan. This is not the end of the world."

You find the bathroom, close the door, and try to collect yourself. If only, you think, breathing itself were enough.

Over the washbasin is a broken mirror, a network of random cracks radiating from an off-center point. The kaleidoscope of yourself looks as startled as if the shattering were just now occurring. Once upon a time, maybe like that, the world was created, and now—now is it really left to itself, the created ones left entirely to the mercy of one another? You run cold water over your hands and press them against your flushed face. No shard of glass, you notice, has fallen; all still are held within the one white frame.

Downstairs the entrance hall is empty. The eyes of Margot in the bed in the photograph do not see you, but only show her wanting to be seen.

Corralled on her father's lap in an easy chair in the living room, Lily licks up the last bites of a piece of cake. Brucey-boy lies in her lap, his four plastic legs stiffly in the air. Lily's own dirty bare toes curl up; she holds her plate close to her chest.

Next to Tom on the couch is a space the size of you, to which you home, molecule to familiar molecule; he lifts his arm for you to lock into place against his side. You wiggle your fingers in greeting to Lily and overhear her father say the word *gun* to an attentive young woman on a hassock near his knees, but you know it is not the sort of gun the estranged husband carried when he unlocked that door in your old neighborhood, the old key in the old lock; no, Larry's gun would be fired legally across a wide outdoor space toward the brain or the heart of a wild animal.

Next to you Tom is listening—patiently, good teacher that he is—to a bearded young man who is tipped forward in a rocking chair.

"Then the dualities you say are like lenses?"

"That's it." Tom is nodding. "You look through the math and what seemed different is now actually shown to be the same."

"That ought to give me something to mull over while I'm working." Now the bearded man smiles at you.

Tom says, "Joan, this is Douglas, and you're going to be extremely pleased to know who Douglas is."

"Okay. I'm ready to be extremely pleased."

You're keeping half an eye on Lily, who wipes her forefinger through the last blob of frosting and then holds it in her mouth, sucking. Her eyes are glazed.

"Douglas is a carpenter, a cabinetmaker really, and he's said he can help us."

"What a godsend! Oh, I am pleased." You hear yourself describe the desperately needed shelves, while you notice that with no more sugar on her plate Lily now looks slack and combustible.

Larry, trailing his fingers up and down her back, seems as absentmindedly devoted to her as he might be to a dog: he likes her there in his lap, you think; he likes his lap full of the heavy pink sensation of his daughter while he keeps on being listened to by the rapt young woman on the hassock—guns, whatever. Yes, you are right: his arm tightens around Lily as she starts to get up with her empty plate, he pulls her back, tickling her.

"Where are you going, girly girl, just where do you think you're going?" he says in a loud voice, tickling her until she collapses back against him.

Conversations around them taper off.

"More cake!" Lily shrieks between giggles.

"Then you'll have to get some for everybody. You'll have to bring back the whole goddamn cake." Larry keeps tickling until Lily is gasping for breath.

As if from air, Margot alights on the arm of Larry's chair and pulls the plate firmly from her daughter. "Enough, both of you!"

Tom nudges your shoulder. "Aren't you tired?" he whispers hopefully.

You see the battle that is on its way, the horses just cresting opposing hills, thundering down on the chubby, pink, over-wrought princess who is about to be torn limb from limb.

"Just a sec," you say to your husband, and in that second you're on your feet with your hand held out to the child.

"Could I possibly borrow Lily for a minute?"

Surprised, Larry loosens his grip. Still balanced on the arm of the chair, Margot holds the empty plate aloft, over all their heads. Lily struggles to get her weight up on her feet, and then, still clutching Brucey-boy, she takes your hand.

"What?" she demands in a high, excited voice.

"A project, Lily." You speak quietly as you lead her to the front door. "I'm going to need you tomorrow."

Behind you the party buzz starts up again. Someone else is insisting on cake—more cake! Finish it off—Margot's voice—get that wretched thing out of here!

Glancing back, you see that Margot herself, collapsed red-orange poppy, has slid bottom-first into Larry's lap. She swings a casual leg close and closer to the hassock where the young woman is still perilously stuck.

What a relief to shut the screen door behind you! Outside a warm creamy nighttime light coats the neighborhood. There are stars enough to comment on to Lily, a mango-colored moon in the blue-black sky, and across the street in an upstairs window the large yellow cat lying like a sphinx beside a lighted table lamp.

"What project, where are we going?"

"Just my backyard. Be careful in your bare feet."

Together you walk down the shared driveway where only a few days ago you first met Lily and Margot and Larry. You see the heads of people through the windows, then the flare of a flash. Someone laughs loudly, but out here the sound is smaller.

Lily still holds your hand. She makes Brucey-boy gallop through the air beside her. "Do you know what? I could have a real horse back here. There's way enough room, but they won't let me."

"What would you name a real horse, Lily?"

"Romeo!"

"What if it's a girl?"

"I don't know."

"Juliet?"

"No, I get to be her."

In the dusky yard that is now yours, you lift the cover from one of the garbage cans. A heavenly smell rises. "All right, here we go. Do you know what this is?"

Lily reaches in. "Dirt."

"Sort of. It's compost."

"What's that?" She reaches in again, sort of dreamily, and lets the dark stuff sift through her fingers.

"Compost is like black gold. It makes a garden do wonderful things. Do you want to help me spread it?"

"Yes!"

"All right then. We have a deal. First thing tomorrow."

"You could have a horse in your yard, too," she says as you walk together back toward the front of the houses. She's wiping her hand on the belly of her leotard.

People stand talking on Margot and Larry's porch and sidewalk. The party is dissolving. All at once you hear a familiar barking, and the dog comes tearing down the driveway toward you.

"Harry! Harry, where are going? Harry!" It's lawyer Willard on his tail.

Harry's nosing all over your legs now, quivering his fringed tail, smiling up at you; he's all but calling you by name.

"Well, for goodness sake," says Willard, stopping short.

"Hello there, doggy, how do you do?" You reach down, and Harry buries his wet nose in your cupped hands.

There are no messages on the answering machine, no bits of story from the lives of your sons or your friends. This day is almost done. You are alone with your husband, who says, "Aren't you coming up now?"

"I only need a minute to walk around down here and talk to the house."

"Talk to the house?"

"Humor me, Tom, I'm new here."

The objects in the dim living room look mildly out of place, like pieces of luggage in a way station. The music plays without sound. A back window has been left open. As you cross to close it, a breeze pushes toward you, laced with threadlike currents of the coolness to come. Otherwise, the air is still laden with summer's sweaty work of churning out the end of itself, all that vegetation finishing its cycle, transpiring silently, a great dark animal at night, wakeful, efficient, forever optimistic.

You lower the window and turn its lock. You make sure the back door is locked, and just then a feeling of relaxation spreads through you: the heaviest part of this move is accomplished now;

you're once again in a place, toiling in the present. The house is a good house. You can do what you need to do anywhere.

You turn down the hallway from the kitchen and see that Tom is waiting for you at the foot of the stairs, one hand on the newel post, his thoughtful head bent, his shoulders uncharacteristically slumped. He stands as if in the future, at the end of a passageway, by stairs you, yes you, will come to climb alone night after night. Wait! you want to beg. Not so fast, not yet! But of course it's not yet. The long view is kindly shuttered off. You mate is holding out his arm for you, and you slide into place. Doubly you climb, in near unison.

He says, "That was okay, wasn't it, as far as parties go? I'm glad we found a carpenter anyway."

"Mm-hmm. He seems smart. And trustworthy. I liked the beard."

"You did?" Tom's steps are heavy.

"You sound tired."

"Aren't you?" His arm on your shoulder is heavy.

And suddenly you are remembering what Sally confided to you, just before you moved, about the last time—which soon became evident would really be the last time—she and Jim made love, how all the elements miraculously came together, almost as if the illness and any difficulties between them had been left in a different room. Jim even had some moments of thinking that he was going to get well. It was amazing, Sally told her, it was like accepting, so briefly and at such a late hour, the gift of ease.

You say to Tom, as you are undressing, "If it weren't so late, I'd call Sally."

Slowly he unbuttons his shirt. He pulls off a shoe and lets it drop. Then half undressed, he lies back on the bedspread. He doesn't move; his eyes seem to be fixed on the featureless ceiling.

"Tom?" You lie down and curve yourself around his head. "Something happened?"

"Not exactly."

You wait. You are watching his broad forehead, his eyelids and fine cheekbones, the bridge of his nose, the stubbled curve of his upper lip. Now he rolls to face you. "Tell me you're all right, Joan. Tell me it's all right we came here."

"What are you saying? Is it all right for *you* to be here?"

"Yes, I guess so. Just talk to me a little while. Humor me. Tell me anything."

"Well, all right, you want to hear a shaggy dog story? Here's a real one."

When you are finished he says, "You did that?"

"I confess."

"You sure had yourself a full day."

"Now your turn, you talk."

"I could go to sleep—just like this. You smell good."

"Not yet." You nudge him. "Start talking—what happened today?"

He sighs. "I think I must be getting old. Everybody looked so young. And ambitious, so ambitious. Are we old?"

"Yes. No."

"Maybe I should grow a beard—how d'you think I'd look in a beard?"

"Keep talking, get beyond the beard."

"Long day, long day. It started when I walked into my new office this morning. I couldn't believe we'd actually picked up and come here. Everything looked, I don't know, flat, a little drab, sort of bureaucratic."

"The people are all right?"

"The people are fine, the setup is fine. It's me. It's as if I've pulled back from things. Does this make any sense to you?"

"I think so."

He's quiet. His breathing slows.

"Tom, don't go to sleep yet."

"What's happening to me?"

"Maybe at this stage some dispassion is all right?"

"Yes, but why did it have to be on the first day! Couldn't I have enjoyed a little bit more glory first?"

"You're a piece of work, you know that?"

"Yeah, well you, too, but you're a prettier piece."

You stroke your hand down his cheek, along his shoulder, his arm, you take his hand in both of yours and hold it against your breast.

And just then, as the tips of your own fingers happen to touch, your two hands covering his, there's a little jump of recognition between them, like a deep avowal, as if long-estranged beings had been tapping from both sides at once of a door that has simply dissolved, the skin on one side sure now that it is the same as the stuff on the other.

Moon

❧

SHE was a bride, but since her marriage the summer before Nina had lived more or less alone. Her new husband, in his medical residency, often slept at the hospital, or left early in the morning, or came home long after she'd returned from work, eaten a simple meal, taken her now habitual evening walk, read for a while, and gone to bed. Sometimes he raided her sleep. Such coupling in dark, unidentified hours could feel primitive, as if she were being thrust deep back to an ancient topography in whose crevices immemorial rites were still enacted. In the morning, with Phillip's pillow already empty, these enthralling performances might pass for dream.

Once more the surface of her world would have resumed its fleeting, precarious twenty-first-century enchantment. The mourning dove, now that it was nearly spring, cooed from the balcony railing; the city traffic streamed in orderly lanes; her laminated badge admitted her to the staff door of the art museum. All proceeded as if it were real enough, herself as discrete as the elements around her. An assistant in the museum, she cultivated donors and organized events; she edited development materials; she participated in meetings with colleagues who were friendly but none yet true friends. Her closest friends were back in New

York. She'd left them and come to Wisconsin because she loved Phillip; they'd promised to be each other's bedrock friend.

He wasn't always gentle; he could forget to be gentle; sometimes when he entered her he thrashed this way and that, face contorted, eyes closed, as if forgetting her, and she would have to work to keep herself from subtle damage. It was the exhaustion, she thought, that reduced him to such rude needs. During this year he had become paler, his eye sockets sooty. What an unbalanced, unhealthy way, she thought, to be trained in the art of healing.

One Saturday a month Nina volunteered at a nearby hospital, not the one across the city where Phillip was training in surgery, but at least she was putting herself somewhat inside his world, seeing some of the same things he saw every day. Wearing the blue smock of a volunteer, she would push new patients from the admissions area to one of the nursing stations. She made conversation with them and with their families. Now and then people came in alone; they got themselves somehow to the hospital, walked through the doors with a few effects in bags, and were trundled down hallways to face by themselves whatever they had to face.

On nights alone she took walks. Their apartment was much larger than her former efficiency off Amsterdam Avenue, but nevertheless she often felt drawn to escape these rooms into roofless evenings. She walked in all weathers; she walked to ask herself questions; she had walked toward the depths of winter darkness and now was walking out into another spring. A year ago in New York, pierced by the cries of the peacocks in the garden of St. John the Divine, watched over from the roof of the cathedral by Gabriel forever blowing his horn and by Archangel Michael in bronze victory over Lucifer, she had thought herself confident of the great change she was choosing—a willing romantic exile to the Midwest. *Oh-oh! oh-no!* the peacocks had called over and over, as if in the throes of uneasy rapture, but Nina had laughed away their cries.

He could be gentle. He stroked her hair, her cheek, her bare shoulder, traced her lips with his forefinger. Her hand fanned out on his chest, into the dark forest covering the bone-vaulted cave. They lay inches apart on the same pillow, looking at each other, looking and looking. It was like the science of love: to look until all that could be known was known. The rest would have to be taken on faith.

Night after night she walked south through the neighborhood of old houses and apartment buildings on the bluff and then north along the lower lakefront, or that route in reverse; in either case Lake Michigan always stretched as far as the eastern horizon. The last rays of the sun from the opposite sky might be slipping shell-pink in and out of the cups of its waves, or the full moon rising over it; every night, every hour the effects were different. Beneath shifting skies its huge, watery stage fluctuated constantly, even under plates of January ice. It was so enormous, if you knew nothing else, you might think it a sea. In the absence of other ideas, you might think marriage just this: a man somewhere else; a woman, who might be taken for stoic, walking alone at night beside a very large body of water, in a small body of desire and uncertainty. Before marriage, she had thought she knew what she was doing.

When she returned to the apartment she bathed and then read, stories of people in this century and in others, all over the world. These people, all exiles in one way or another, did their work, used energy, cooked food, loved and abused each other, gave and stole, healed and worsened; they lived in high places and low, by water or not, sheltered together or alone. Nina felt herself expanding to take them all in. Before Phillip, she had not yet considered that it was simply her own heart she would be asked to marry.

Still. Had they not agreed to live together?

On his evenings in the apartment, sometimes too tired to read or even talk, Phillip would nap on the sofa while she read in the armchair nearby. Alive beneath the weightless construct of her reading, the blood of desire might pool then into a longing to be entered by him there, anywhere, book tossed aside, legs flung open, bodies sliding together like mercury into the indiscriminate gravity of the primal. But then, looking more closely at his eye hollows and ashen cheeks and lips, she would feel something else, like a solicitous tenderness, and would practice floating above her heavy, seductive, quicksilver blood while she continued reading. Finally he would rouse himself and groan and sit, elbows on knees, hands dangling, curly-haired head hanging, and look up sideways, not so much in discovery of her as to make clear the legitimacy of his exhaustion, the import of what he held behind his face from the theaters of surgery and consequential corridors and rooms of genuine suffering, all of which went on without her and belonged to the self-sufficient and specific gravity of his expertise. His distinction in this way wordlessly established, she and he would get ready for bed, perhaps still without speaking much, make physical love or not, and another day would be over. Nina might lie awake for a long time then in the ghostly light filtering in from the street, the ambient city night, where so many others lived, had chosen to live, together and alone.

At the end of the block, just where their street joined the drive curving down the bluff to the lakeshore, perched a handsome gray house that from her first weeks in the neighborhood had seemed to beckon Nina personally, mysteriously, the way some places do. Probably built in the late 1880s, it had clapboards on the first level, shingles above, leaded windows, and a wonderful entrance porch with a steeply pitched carved bargeboard and timber trusswork and two inviting wooden benches. A beech tree spread over half of the small yard.

Then one dusk last fall she'd glimpsed a tall elderly woman in old clothes still out in the yard, raking, raking, then using her rake as a supporting staff as she picked up something from the heap of leaves, bending with surprising fluency, unbending, like a dancer. Nina had stopped and stared across the street into the golden half-light. It was as if she were seeing a pantomime concerning herself. In some way she didn't understand, she was to become that woman. The fluency, earned, would be the currency to take her the whole course. Finally, shivering, prickled by familiarity, she'd made herself walk on down the hill to the lake.

Over the winter she hadn't seen the woman at all, though lights burned in a few of the rooms, the snow got shoveled, a basket of greens and bare red dogwood branches, like sprays of exposed veins, appeared beside the door in December. The story Nina made was of a widow, an artist of some sort, all right, a dancer, who in dancing had also bent before the altar of family life, whose children had swung from the beech and been read to on the porch benches, whose husband had been driven, proud, and often absent. She had nearly separated herself from him—or perhaps she had for a time, but then, recalled to the mystery of wedded lives, chosen to come back. Meanwhile, the house, a quiet witness to all trials of love, would have continued to stand in its neutral boards and beams and mullions for equilibrium, equanimity.

One windy night in April, a Realtor's sign, newly planted near the beech tree where the tall woman's children had played, jolted Nina into a different restlessness. At the museum the next day, where she was being paid to entice many people into an institution, her mind kept flying back to the single house—the beech tree, the porch with its benches, the imagined foyer and wainscoted living room with its wall sconces and odors of damp fireplace ash. The large, many-paned, between-story window in the front elevation must light the landing of a staircase, where the long cushion on the window seat would by now have frayed to reddish silk. Underneath the broad turning of these stairs a ziggurat of packing boxes already signaled that the woman was at last leaving behind the house of marriage: Nina would have her go back to New York and live near a grandson, call him Gabriel, Gabe, in whose harmonious company the last act of her life would play out. A tender story of late rewards. Perhaps it really would take that long, until the light in a grandson's eyes, before the woman would be truly recognized. Meanwhile, like a disciple, an apprentice in supple heartwork, young Nina would dedicate herself to the house of family.

From the museum she left a message for Phillip at the hospital, which he didn't return until she was about to shower before bed. Wrapped in a towel fisted between her breasts, her hair pinned up, she told him about the house that was quite suddenly for sale.

Where?

She had to repeat herself, as if he'd heard nothing.

He said he couldn't picture it.

She understood then that he must have been driving through the neighborhood with his mind dwelling not here but somewhere else, perhaps on the patients he served, perhaps grilling himself on whether each part of his treatment had been correct. His greatest fear, he'd told her once, was making a grave mistake, which of course was as futile as fearing his own death: sooner or later, in one way or another, he said, it would happen.

She was only a bride, yet it had been as if he'd lugged home a coffin, slid it down beside the marriage bed, and said here, never forget my dear we sleep in the arms of death. A dream repeated: Philip walking ahead of her in a corridor and she calling out and running toward him, trying to run, trying to call, and then he at last turning about-face, but in the mask of a frightening stranger.

A house wasn't a good idea, he said now, not with their future so open. Who could say where they'd be in a few years?

Of course, of course. Shaking with chill, she clutched the towel as they murmured their good nights.

It was just as well. She was still in many ways a girl, with nearly everything to learn about being a woman. Why should she think she had a destiny inside those gray clapboards? Nevertheless, the next night she stood transfixed before the house like an orphan. Her parents, long divorced, had tried in their various serial living arrangements to make room for their child, but Nina felt she knew far less about sheltered family life than about suitcases and modes of travel and makeshift comforts.

The spring weather turned warm, then once again damp and cold. By now the male peacocks in the cathedral garden would be fanning out their mating plumage; in the absence of females, they would even display indiscriminately for the pigeons. Nina wasn't there; she was here, still in bride-shock over the way humans had so far organized their world. From the shoreline rocks on her nighttime walks she watched unfamiliar water birds that must be in migration northward. The common gulls and green-headed mallards she recognized, but not some of the others, with black hoods and sharp, elegant, white-banded wings, or yellow eyes, or bright white circles like coins of snow behind their eyes. Largest of all was a snowy swan, no mate in sight, like a single bird-boat transmigrating from beyond. All swam together in the cold water, eating the cold food and resting on cold rocks.

He slept. She hadn't heard him come home. He slept beside her as if claimed by sleep. She studied his face. Perhaps, she thought, the only cure for the questions of marriage was more marriage and yet more. What she could do now was to take care of the atmosphere in which he slept. Yes, and she could take care of every part of the shocking world that came to her—it wouldn't matter what or where. This she could do. Lightly, she kissed his temple, over the pulsing blood.

He woke, but with a kind of blankness, as if surprised by her presence. She waited before the mirror of his face to be identified. Then he reached for her. The blankness, the mindlessness, had only lasted a moment. She was happy. She was also miserable.

That night she returned from work in a shower of dancing, widely spaced snow crystals, side-lit at brilliant intervals from the west. Her head ached; she didn't want to live with tonight's head. Outside the car the individual flakes of snow danced like sub-atomic constituents, appearing and disappearing inside an endless whole. Not changing out of her good coat and short skirt and boots, she drank a glass of water and ate a banana and some graham crackers and checked the answering machine to see that there were no messages. Then she got back into her car and began to drive. She wanted to take her head someplace else and leave it there.

She passed the gray house where the fluent old woman had been so happy and so miserable. A few lights burned at the back of the downstairs, as if she were just now making herself a little dinner. Scrambled eggs. No, soup. She was tired from all the packing, so much of it futile—some of the boxes surely never to be opened again. She was tired from all the years of effort. Now she knew how little was essential, really, in fugitive life.

Nina accelerated down the bluff road. In the story so far of this night she was on her way to orphaning herself from the arms of Phillip. She would have to do it; she couldn't survive being tossed like this from one extreme to another. She would choose to be detached and pure, alone. In this story she wore this same short skirt, like the skirt of a girl, sleek boots, a long wool coat. Through the lake-effect snow crystals she sped along the shore, too fast.

In its own time, a white-gold disk of moon was now rising along the lavender band at the horizon, instantly answered below by a watery highway of active beaten silver. The dark blue of the sky had deepened, and the heavier blue of the lake was going along with it companionably toward night, as if Nature already knew everything that was to be known about mating the elements, the water and its sky always chromatically perfect, the two great fields always balanced in their rightful places by the powerful single line of the horizon. Nina raced as if to outrun a reflection of herself, but the beaten silver highway of moonlight always followed, like the spoke of a wheel.

Then she turned away from the lake and the lake-effect snow crystals and the moon, now bobbing in the deep space of her rearview mirror, as otherworldly as the single swan; she veered toward the center of the city, an intricacy of interchanges and vehicles and buildings, and other birds, so many birds flying into the orange and pink western light. Even here a semblance of order held, a union of natural and man-made, the universe still trying to stay married and put up with its myriad wayward children and their civilizations. But nothing lasted, did it: patience could wear out; Nature could decide to go back to water and sky, water and sky, nothing else, so much easier. In her short skirt and tall boots Nina felt reckless, still driving fast.

She passed the tallest buildings, the baseball stadium, the

cemetery for the veterans of all the wars. It was darker. Everyone on the road feigned a separate destination. She should have been arrested, wayward bride, but she was not. Cutting across lanes, she swerved toward the exit leading to the hospital, not the hospital where she volunteered but the huge complex where Phillip served. In that maze he could be anywhere. Nevertheless, she swung the car into a lower-level slot of the garage and wrapped her coat around her and looped her purse over her shoulder and headed as if with purpose in the direction of the warren of basement hallways she had followed once with Phillip, who had appeared to know where he was going.

One segment of passage led to another. Her footfalls resounded in the hard-surfaced tunnel, her boots, hard heels of futile vanity. She had no idea how to find him; he could be at work in any room, any corridor. She was out of place. Her headache belonged here, but she, the shocked bride, did not. This was not the time to go in search of a cure for marriage.

Then the man, not a dream, tall body, thick as a pipe column, backed against the concrete block wall, clothes open: she almost knocked against him as she pivoted the corner, close, close to the exposed sex he worked and worked as he moaned, his anonymous breath heaving over her, moaning, and then two words, *fucking whore*. Quickly beyond him she still heard him, even with the thudding of heart, pounding of heels, even when she banged through one door and then another into the hospital proper where it was impossible to hear him; she heard him and saw him in continuous replay, the breath, the words, the nondescript dark coat, the shirttails, the pink cudgel that was so affixed and stubborn the man could only think to use it one way, one way, one way.

She flung herself down into a chair in the main waiting room and pressed her fingertips to her temples and waited, staring at her boots. She was going to sit right here and wait for this human world to fall apart and reorganize itself entirely. Pressing her temples with her thumbs, she raked her other fingers outward again and again from the center line of her forehead. She felt like pulling her hair to the limit of its roots. In a minute she was going to take off her head and carry it over to the admissions counter.

The segment she had seen, that man, that man in the grip of himself, replayed without pause because in this pounding, messed-up head of hers there could be no relief for him: sentenced to wield his pigheaded cudgel until doomsday in the concrete block corridor. Getting nowhere.

Feet passed, this way, that way. Finally Nina calmed down a little and looked up. There were many others in the way station, passing through or waiting to pass. Around the clock the extreme business of life and death continued to go on and on. Everyone who came here came here from need. They were all in the body of need, particles in the body of need. Sick with need. They all needed to turn in their human heads to that placid black woman over there in admissions. Then it came to Nina that what they suffered from collectively was like an autoimmune disease, a kind of mistake in thinking, with their detached minds not recognizing each other and therefore distorting, abusing, devouring each other. For an instant she saw the mistake, exactly, as if the clock had opened up its face, but then she could see nothing but tired separate people in chairs, at counters, beneath the circle of numbers.

A child cried. People shifted their positions. What was she really waiting for in this room of waiting? She could have Phillip paged; he would come to her, perhaps in white, perhaps in surgical green; she would have to rise with her blooming crown of headache and explain herself, explain incisively, surgically, the delicate transformation necessary on the great body of the world so that they would all recognize each other once more. She needed him; they needed to work together.

The child continued crying, not pacified by the flawed actions of her distracted parents. A man in a black turban held his bent head between brown hands. Beside him a beautiful unsmiling woman sat with downcast eyes, her own hands knotted in the folds of her skirt. Nina covered her knees with the tails of her long coat. Time circled; the room waited. She was remembering something Phillip had told her, in bed: doctors were trained in this exhausting way, he said, because you could never know what you had to know until you went around and around the clock with your patients. In the night, he said, people said things they would never say in the day. In the night fear was naked as they tried to surf their pain and not become engulfed. Everything was elemental. Tears came to her eyes now as she remembered Phillip talking to her quietly in his tired voice, their heads close on the same pillow, her wifely hand stroking his back—winglike scapula, muscle across muscle, long vertebrate runnel. Then he'd stopped talking about pain and fear, told her it felt good, whatever she was doing, with her hand on his back.

Now wife Nina got up from the waiting room chair and returned to her car by way of the skywalk and drove toward home slowly. The whole episode was like a dream, as if she had never raced in distraction to the hospital on the other side of the city. The lake had opened its waters, taken her action into the deep, and sealed its surface once more with moonlight and cadenced movement. It had swallowed the man with his cudgel. Her headache, too, began like a miracle to resolve, as if the man had been made up of the same mind stuff that had produced her headache, so that as her cells relaxed so did the potency of his image dissolve. She did not eat when she returned, she did not read. Turning on almost no lights, she stood under a hot shower like a tired child; this child: no one had ever before been this child she was.

She lay in the quiet beside Phillip's empty pillow. Sleep was the necessary thing now. Could she sleep for him, too? Could she take care of the shocking world tonight in sleep? Waiting for the sea to swallow her, she lay very still with her hands on her belly, empty, hollowed out. She didn't understand how in this beginning, with him, there could be so much grief; she didn't understand how the beginning could feel so much like the end of the world. She knew almost nothing about being a woman, and yet it was as if the girl had already been married forever, and in this beginning with him, in this grief, in this loaded happiness she held a skein of everything to come, which yet had to be uncoiled day by day, the whole story lived again.

There was a reception at the museum for an exhibition of prints and drawings. Nina had to be there, of course. Phillip said he could not. She wore a long black wool skirt and her boots and her gray silk blouse. A necklace of small beads. Lipstick. Mascara. She knew more people than she had known she knew; she met others. It was easy to talk to them in the presence of the energy of the prints and drawings. The energy of art was real. Behind the images breathed the makers; that was the wonder. Nina breathed; she used speech, with the purpose of taking care of whatever came to her. Yes, that was coming clear as her essential purpose. She enjoyed standing in her body, well tuned from so much solitary walking, with people and art composed around her.

Then she saw him across the gallery, here, even though he had said he couldn't come. He was not a stranger; he was Phillip, her Phillip. He was looking at her. He might have been looking at her for a long time. She smiled and began to make her way to him, through the well-dressed, well-meaning people. Behind his head was a lithograph in tones of charcoal and gray, of an overgrown path leading to stone steps set into a bank of vegetation, a smoky gray sky at the top of the stairs beyond the trees; she had stood before the print earlier, wishing she could follow the overgrown path and climb the steps and enter the grainy absorbent field of sky. Phillip was not smiling. He looked exhausted and appealing. He was the only person in the gallery still wearing an overcoat.

When she reached him, he said nothing. She touched the lapel of his coat. He clamped an arm around her back and pulled her tightly in against his side and began to steer her toward the exit, through this gallery, then another, then out into the belly of the great hall under the vaulted, ribbed skylights, beyond which was the night, this particular night. He wanted her to leave, now, with him: Could she do that? Now? Yes, now. They could talk at home. He would walk her to her car. He came with her to get her coat. She felt him watching everything she did, as if tracking her actions had become his only end.

In the passageway to the garage he brought her again into an alliance with his side, left no space between them. Then, against a white-painted wall in the hollow, venting sounds of the passage, he turned her and kissed her, with a force of personal meaning, as if his kiss issued from a tunnel of experience she had not shared. He had been somewhere and now was coming back to her. His hands inside her coat defined her ribs, slid down her hips, grappled and bunched the material of her skirt.

By now she would have abandoned herself, here, no matter where, hooked a leg high around him and made herself available, here against the white wall—anything to understand who she was, in this position, who this man was, why she had been so sure, back in New York in the neighborhood of the cathedral, that she had known what she was doing. Then he brought his hands to her neck, the sides of her face. But very gently now. She didn't know what was happening. All her questions waited on her tongue. In the middle of a kiss he stopped and backed away and looked at her.

At her car he watched as she pulled out; in her rearview mirror she saw him still standing in the same place, in his coat, his shoulders slightly slumped. He had been somewhere; something had happened to him.

He hung up his overcoat and went straight down the hallway toward the bedroom. She turned off lights and followed. He had taken off his shoes and was lying in his clothes on top of the bed- spread, staring at the ceiling. She lay face-up beside him, and then they were like two silent dolls whose owner has left the room.

He reached for her hand. She thought he might continue then what had begun in the passageway, his hands all over her, his lips. She wanted the pressure of his whole body; she wanted to be fixed in knowledge of how the world worked; she wanted to be pushed all the way into knowledge of what worked behind the world.

But he lay still. Then she rolled on her side, close to him, and placed a hand on his chest. She waited; she was with him; they were together. Under her hand she could feel the gentle spreading of his lungs.

At last he began to talk. There had been a death, his patient, a woman, older, with definite orders not to resuscitate. A heart had stopped, and it was not to be restarted. Nina saw the tall woman, the dancer no longer dancing, saw how the hand of gravity had reached up through the table and pulled down the current in her, saw how the monitors then read only flatness, like a flat stage.

There'd been no struggle, Phillip said, no heaves of the chest or rattles in the throat, no convulsions, no staccato breaths, just the end. He'd felt incredibly helpless. No chance for heroics. It was almost as if she'd gone through the operation in order to die.

The daughter who had been with her had not wanted an autopsy. There'd been a grandson, too, in the waiting room.

Gabriel, thought Nina. *Gabe.*

They'd wanted to sit with her, so Phillip had had her moved to a private area. He'd put off having her taken to the morgue; he'd made sure they were not disturbed.

She got her yard raked; she had her last basket of greens by the door; then she packed up a whole life, which now was left for someone else to open.

Why had he thought he'd have due warning for his first death? Not this way, he said, not like this.

Nina watched the profile of his lips. She was waiting for his next words, but they didn't come, as if the entire story had already been vented. A mirror held over his mouth now would record only breath. The invisible words had stopped. She closed her eyes and waited, her hand on his chest, even though she knew her answers wouldn't come through his lips.

He slept. She heard the difference. He had been taken into sleep. Quietly she pulled up the comforter from the end of the bed and covered them both. By now the people in the museum would be separating themselves from the larger group, returning to their cars, their individual homes. She didn't know what came next; she had never been this woman before; she would have to live to know her. It was going to take everything she had.

Beginning

SHE thinks: it's a miracle that allows her children to be so close to her here, high up in the evening blue. Lily, Peter, Margaret, Larry, too, her husband, dead but not separate. The miracle is that she's free to imagine them, cherish them, wherever she is. She sees the loved ones of her children, how they inhabit her heart, and she sees Robbie, her grandchild, as if he is already grown into his life purpose, the man he will become packed into the infant, facing her, yes, watching her, watching her every choice.

What if these tissues of cloud are really tides of love? There could be nothing but love, streaming all around, and this mind equal to eternal communion. It's all right, the cloud of death will come for her as well, pass around her, envelop her, like aerial vapor, beyond which, look, are those the first stars? In this mind, washed by experience, grateful, more at peace than she has been in years, Laura is surprised all over again that she is doing what she is now doing—complicating her life, adding more people, flying off to see a new friend, to see about living once more in the present with a man, this time named Duncan.

The traveler beside her sucks on his teeth and takes up his story again. While he was eating, he did only that, feeding himself with hunched determination. Now the airline dinner is done and gone, highest altitude attained; it is that space of time in every flight most unloosed from one place or the next. He has been drinking, but he doesn't sound drunk, only soused with grief. Yes, it is none other than his daughter, he continues telling Laura, who is out to break his heart with her own hard heart.

Laura listens. Yet another stranger has commenced to divulge his freight of secrets. It's part of the story of her life now, how voices come right in as though she were a landing field, cleared, put here to receive them. She has always felt permeable to ambient emotion, intuitive about others, but never before have so many people seemed to find her approachable. Could it be the death? She has emerged from it different, she knows that, scoured, open-eyed, less stuck on particular outcomes, more at home in the wayfaring sphere of the moment. Maybe others sense how light she is traveling, how likely she might be to have room to listen.

Does the lady have grandchildren? Yes, she answers, one, a baby boy. Well, he says, his daughter has given birth to two girls he hasn't even been invited to see. Can you beat that? His own blood.

"Have you asked?" asks Laura.

"It's up to her, after what she said to me, that's what I say."

"Time could change things," says Laura from widow's experience.

"Time's nobody's friend, lady. You can't argue about that. Time's a bitch." His square head reminds her of someone she can't place. She has lived long enough that everyone has begun to look ghostly like someone else, a world of cousins. "And I'll tell you something else . . ." But here he stalls. He gestures with a thick mottled hand, which then falls back to his lap in a kind of helplessness. Laura waits. She has been listening as she so often does now, with little sense of foreignness, as if every voice were pitched to touch a twin from a cast already lodged in her. There's consolation here, inside solidarity, and reward, too, for often someone else's mundane words reveal what her own heart has been working to tell her.

Something like that would be useful tonight: a piercing message about what she is doing with herself, heading where she is heading, at her age, when more of silence and solitude might be the better measure. Prayer. Isn't she now at the age when prayer is the main thing? She has tried asking her heart for direction, but so far has gotten no clear answers. Her children, whom she has not yet told about Duncan, would probably be glad to see her emerging after three years from her widow's chaste routine of work and quiet living, but her children are young and charged with the mission to be young. They can't know of her simplified desires and her urgent questions about the proper use of her self.

Her seatmate seems to have lost his tongue. Glancing over, she sees that beneath his broad low brow, knobbed and furrowed as a bulldog's, his eyes have fallen shut. So much for the hope of breakthrough messages through this particular man. Around the airplane the sky accepts a deeper blue. Long out of sight is New York, still far back somewhere behind and below, locked in its grid of power. This is open space. In it there are mutable clouds, stars, light-years—no one knows how many more days.

The man's head falls forward, then jerks back. A sound escapes him, a growling sigh. He really is asleep. Well then. Laura is released to herself. She, too, is tired, and there are still, so true, miles and miles to go. She looks out once more to the darkening sky on which are superimposed the first floating reflections of the human forms inside the airplane.

Life does remain to her, life in a body. It is the *area* in which her body moves now that feels so different. In the thirty-six years she and Larry stayed married, they were often peaceably in step as they moved together inside their shared, shaped life as if by means of a secret harmony that became at moments clearer, when they would guess their gestures with each other counted for more than they could measure in the larger dance. They had loved then to imagine in the caretaking of their love, the creating of their harmony, that they were helping to care for love in all the world, the ransoming power of love.

But now that she is once more a woman on her own, she must somehow figure out firsthand her new place in this enormous shape-shifting field of the dance. In some ways her children are her guides: fluent in joy, more than most of her own contemporaries, they seem to her like fish in water, fearlessly letting oceans of life stream through them, as if filtered by intelligent gills.

Duncan has said they will drive straight to the beach house, an hour and a half north of the Milwaukee airport. They will have three days. During her last visit, a day stop she had arranged between business flights, they walked along the lake in his Madison neighborhood and then ate an early supper in his town house, and it was here she saw displayed the photographs of his life before—his long marriage to Marianne, their son and daughter as children and now adults, the vacations in snow and sun, the houses, the dogs and cats and extended relatives, all with names she could dedicate herself to learn. It is easy for her to picture herself with all her good intentions flying into his life, or perhaps only back and forth between her life and his, days and nights organized once more for a multitude of two, which could yet expand time and again to draw in his family and hers. There would be large meals of celebration set out on one buffet or another, timely presents, telephone calls; more birthdays, graduations, weddings, funerals. She can hear herself listening, laughing, consoling, embracing. It is not that she cannot imagine herself bringing, to a new context, everything she has learned so far of the ways to keep on choosing what feels like the heart of life.

A weight lands on her shoulder. The man has crumpled sideways, and now, with a complacent sigh, he homes his head in toward her neck. Is he that unconscious? Well, all right, no harm, she knows how to be a pillow, and what could be the use in the long run of begrudging comfort? The alcoholic breathing of her fellow traveler grows more regular. A lax, homely beauty takes over the thick hands in his lap, spotlighted by the tiny bulb above. With the sleeper on her shoulder, Laura can't do much with her own hands.

Years ago Larry told an interviewer that when it came to his physical well-being he by and large put himself in the capable hands of his wife, who knew how to sort the healthy from the not, like the essential from the harmful fats. So far it had saved a great deal of time, he said, and most likely his life. He just did his thing, his music, and she more or less kept the rest of the show going, the whole shebang. She had the imagination, he said, to see how best to arrange everything. Of course, his pretty story had been only partly true, as all self-dramatizations are—a morsel to throw to the journalist, a fatty bit. It hadn't gotten to the sinew of what had held them together, strong threads of talk and touch and understanding, always, miraculously always, renewable, even in the hardest times—when for her it was a kind of awe at feeling in hands larger than their own that had kept her true. Who was he, this often exacting and difficult husband, and why should his hold stay sweet; what was the purpose of their marriage? That had been the durable mystery, and was still.

Laura supposes she and the sleeping man must appear married: the exhausted husband, the obliging wife. I'm really beat, he might have said to her while they were waiting to board the plane, one body talking in the here and now to another, an intimate witness of its physical journey. Watching the night beyond the reflected bound image of herself and the man, her temporary husband, Laura remembers how drilled into place she used to feel holding the weight of her babies, but accepting of the condition because the axis on which she was drilled connected her down to the center of the earth, held her to a profound task, while yet allowing every day on the surface to turn into something a little different, another scene in the spiraling show.

The airplane shudders and dips. The sleeper sighs. Then all continues as before—the toiling craft, the sleeping man—how sad, she thinks, that he and his daughter should have hardened their hearts against each other—yet all not quite as before. Something starts up in Laura, not so much a physical discomfort—although she does try to ease her posture beneath that heavy head—rather a darker twitching, as if an implanted creature has caught hold of an untidy tail of her memories of marriage and motherhood and is lashing about *the whole shebang*. She is thinking about fatigue and fear, the shortness of time and the strangeness of empathy, how it's possible to dread your individual life is no longer your own, that your momentum, your energy, is being used, used up, and all your gestures are being taken and completed by others.

And then she sees, like a flight pattern on a forgotten map, a straight line connecting this moment to another day of travel, years and years ago, when the old man, her father—but before he was old and ill and petulant, her father at fifty beside Laura in the backseat of the hot Buick in the California desert, her brother at seventeen up front driving, their wilted mother in the passenger seat as always—her father, groggy from his stint at the wheel, scooted toward her on the seat and without a word pushed his head down into the curve of her shoulder for a nap. *What else is a daughter for?* That was the presumption. Fifteen years old and as prickly as she would ever be again, Laura shrugged him off, not wanting an ounce or an instant of his unawareness, and then felt bad, guilty, but it was too late. The exhausted man just dragged back over to the other side of the car, bunched up something to cushion his head against the window, and was lost. Later she could never bring herself to the point of apology. Maybe she was already glowering in the long foreshadow of all that the rest her father's life would demand of her after the early death of her mother. He had taken old age personally, as of course everyone must; but in his self-absorption, as he thrashed against the loss of his health and grasped so unthinkingly at what there was of vitality in her own strenuous forties and early fifties, she had feared for a time she might be taken down with him. She had feared—all the time knowing fear itself was the actual interloper—that she would be used and used until there was nothing left, that the little country she called herself would lose indispensable ground to a foreign potentate whose claim on her was nevertheless grounded in her being.

Larry's death three years ago was the opposite. No time for the shock of old age. No time for them to find out together if time was foe or friend. Her hands had been of no help to him when he was struck from behind on a London street. An ocean away, she had stopped short in the hallway of the foundation offices, certain someone had called her name, but the passageway had been empty; again in her office she heard a breath of air that sounded like *Laura*. Even now, when the telephone rings, or when she enters certain places, auditoriums and theaters particularly, she feels at times that he still exists, palpably, that he has not yet landed. She sees him flung upward, a tall human doll dressed in a tuxedo, only momentarily limp, dear to her beyond reason, tossed

out of reach, always upward, into a kind of breathless caesura
from which he will eventually come down, place the call, appear
in the crowd, and once more single her out for embrace.

You must forgive him, a friend had told Laura not long ago.
Forgive? Forgive *him*? But it was an accident. Yes, him. And life
itself, dear Laura, for containing pain.

But how on earth, when you weren't even aware of the need,
do you really forgive—she casts her eyes on the foreshortened face
of the dogged sleeper, the furrows and folds and bony bulges—
and in what company?

Arriving in the dark, through a stand of evergreens and then low
sand dunes with tufts of coarse grass flaring momentarily in the
headlights, they come to a stop before an unobstructed view of
Lake Michigan. The full moon, escaped from its orbit, hovers
between beach and horizon like a gigantic incandescent balloon
over the face of the water. It is a large and beautiful view, but
Laura is so tired she can hardly take it in.

"This is it."

"I'm transported."

"Good." He is almost whispering. "That's the way it should
be." With both awkwardness and courtesy, like a gesture of asking, he leans across the gearshift to kiss her, without urgency,
soft-lipped in a scrub of beard.

He is Duncan. He is not anyone else. During the car ride she
has been working to connect the months of playful e-mails and
intimate long-distance telephone calls with the actual man. Reality is abrupt. Tonight it's almost too much. A headache paces
around in the backstage of her awareness, pressing familiar warning signals. This is her third meeting with Duncan; how new
they are, she thinks, kids, aging novices. His semicircle of white

beard, joining his hair, reminds her in the moonlight of old-fashioned bindings for toothache, or earache, or wounds from long-ago wars.

"I love it here. I want you to see everything."

"Yes, I want to."

She steps from the car into an early September wind, the night emptied of all but the two of them. In the sudden absence of travel she reels and steadies herself. The lake makes a lingering, slapping sound against the beach like *erase* or *caress*. Laura buttons her blazer and tucks in her fluttering neck scarf. "Load me up," she says, going back to the open trunk and holding out her arms. All these things, these thousand things, she already knows how to do with a man. He hands her a canvas bag of groceries and takes the suitcases himself.

The house sits low and unobtrusive in the dunes. She follows him to its back, lake side where there is a wooden deck bleached bone white in the moonlight, a few broad steps above the sand. Duncan sets down the bags and fiddles with the lock—the moisture, he apologizes. She wishes he wouldn't apologize. She doesn't need perfection—she knows about this changing world of human beings and their objects—but hearing how much he wants every little thing to go smoothly, she does her part by standing by with attention, as she so often did with Larry and his efforts and ambitions; this time she imagines all the metal ins and outs of the lock and key matching up with a click. Male and female. She's glad no one is watching to comment on the trite symbolism. She's glad, for this particular social experiment, to be out of sight of everyone she knows.

It's chilly out here, the wind right off the lake, the kind of wind, he told her in the car, that brings in warmer surface water and makes swimming more possible. The moon, that glowing dirigible, looms as if lured by the desire of the shore. For a moment Laura stares transfixed at the mirroring ink below the moon where one long white crest after another pushes to lose its form in a running collapse up the slant of sand. Evolutionary bits of life riding the water have an opposite task, she thinks: when we land, holding a form is what we've got to be about, for a time, again. If we find ourselves here, still here, there are things we have to do. But, O God, how many births there can be, even in one life, and each like this stunned, beached pause in which we wait all over again to be recalled to our purpose.

"Aha! We're in!" Duncan disappears inside the house, and then lights reveal, like a stage set, a neat, well-equipped kitchen. "I'm afraid it needs airing," he says, coming out for the groceries and then holding open the screen door. Laura enters the dead-air smells of someone else's soaps and waxes, wood cabinets, wood smoke.

"How pretty," she manages to say. Surprised how new the house is, how unexpectedly feminine, she realizes Marianne did not have many years to enjoy the spaces she had planned. Nevertheless, Laura can feel her presence in all the choices made—pale birch cabinets, muted blue-green countertops, curtains patterned with birds. She can almost see the tray of medicines that must have accompanied Marianne everywhere in her last year, pills of different colors already counted out for certain—no, uncertain—hours of the day.

"We had the property a long time before we were able to build," says Duncan. In his eyes Laura can see how it must have been to anticipate, to build at last, and then to lose half the picture, the woman. They stand as if stalled in the center of the kitchen, looking at each other in this bright laboratory for cooking. "Yes, well, this way then," he says at last.

In his hesitation Laura hears, as she has not before, echoes of several of the boyfriends of her youth, the gawkish but brilliant ones with their plaid cotton shirts and slide rules and stiff dance steps, the ones she trusted—and she supposes teased—and employed to discover, safely, her own hidden female powers.

She follows him through one end of the beige and blue, many-pillowed living room and into the bedroom wing. Switching on lights as he goes, telling her random, knowledgeable details about the process of designing and constructing the house, he yet seems to be feeling his way. More even than his house in town, this is real home territory, Laura thinks, the deepest retreat. Here, in the holy place of rest, he is now faced with a different woman for three round-the-clock days, with the days following so unforeseeable that perhaps not even he, the scientist, has been able to work up a hypothesis. He is a serious man; his questions are most likely not unlike hers, which is to say honest questions, trying to take everything already known into account, yet leaving room for the unknown. How do scientists receive their answers, she wonders, when they come down to discovering the heart?

He flicks another switch just inside the doorway of a smallish bedroom done up in a chatter of flowered prints—the walls, the bedcover and curtains, the flounced chair by the window.

"This room, then, I thought, for you?"

"Thank you, this is wonderful." As she sets her purse and tote bag on the bed, she realizes all she wants at this moment is to be alone. Overt sociability seems as gratuitous as the chirrupy fabrics. It is the hour for silence. The incipient headache continues to flash its warnings.

"Ah, well, it's small. We decided to keep the bedrooms small."

"It's just right, it's perfect."

How pitiless, how grateful Laura used to be for the awkwardness of those brilliant boys of her youth, against whom she honed herself into a creature ready to be made into a woman, but the man for that final stroke was not to be any of those boys; no, rather someone who did not hesitate, or laugh in nervousness, or smell like a youth.

Duncan is not one for nervous laughs. He sets down her bags, strides over to open a window panel, and then draws the curtains together, unnecessarily, it seems to her, across an expanse of glass she is sure gives out onto nothing but beach and open water. Then she realizes that of course here he is not unknown; he is the professor, the sixtyish widower who lost that lovely woman Marianne, what a shame; and neighbors out walking the beach in the moonlight might wonder to themselves how he is doing and whether they shouldn't just edge up a little closer to the house and exchange a few friendly—and of course curious—words with him if they find him sitting out on the deck. Laura thinks how she treasures those times when anonymity melts away her own masks of personality and allows her to walk about in restorative, self-forgetting rapport with the life of city streets.

"It's so late, and even later for you, easterner—I suppose you're tired," he says, his arms hanging at his sides.

What a good man he is—she thinks he is. She likes his height, the size of him, the shape of his head, the dry kindly landscape around his eyes.

"Yes, you're reading my mind."

He has a large, straight, broad-based nose and good teeth, what appear to be good teeth. But she is ashamed of herself for cataloging features. It was actually his voice that attracted her first, six months ago in the conference hall—a beautiful deep voice, modulated with humor and intelligence, no apparent arrogance, even as he gave his institute's stellar progress report on the research that had already drawn so many of the foundation's dollars. Listening, she felt as if something had just happened to her, a shift in the constellation of forces that made up her life.

"Me, I'm always worn out after a flight. What can I get for you—anything to eat or drink—fruit, tea . . . ?" He is looking at her in perhaps the way he scrutinizes the structure of a newly isolated protein, and standing quite close. His field jacket smells as if it has been stored in a huge chamber of fresh air. "By the way, the well water here is safe. I test it every season—I find it delicious myself."

Laura put off those brilliant boys of her youth by making herself into a pal; she waited, neither sure of herself nor unsure, for what she might not then have known to call gracefulness. But she likes the feeling of remembering those boys, of still being in some ways who she was then, sixteen, seventeen, a gift, even to herself, especially to herself, waiting to be known and given.

"I don't need anything else tonight—you're making me wonderfully comfortable." She slips out of her blazer, folds it lengthwise, and lays it on the end of the bed.

"In the morning you'll see everything."

"Yes."

"We'll walk on the beach after breakfast."

"All right."

After Duncan's speech he and she talked together in the conference hall and again the next day in the foundation offices and then at the group dinner that night and again the day after when they met alone in Central Park for a long lunch and a walk. He called her office from LaGuardia while waiting for his plane home to say he just wanted to hear her once more. It was his voice, his breath, his unseen mouth forming words, that held her through the months of telephone conversations when they retrieved and opened for each other chapter after chapter of their lives, which for a long time no one else in either of their worlds had asked to hear. Message by message, they have been turning themselves into friends.

"Well. You'll have a good sleep, I hope. Bathroom's just across the hall. Sleep until you wake up—there's absolutely no agenda." He pauses. "I mean that, Laura."

"I know. That's good. I guess we're capable of making it up as we go along."

Over the decades Laura has learned that several of those boys from long ago went on to careers of considerable distinction, but she doesn't know how they have lived through the years behind private doors. It's impossible to know, unless you're there.

Duncan doesn't move. He's waiting, perhaps, for her to excuse him, or claim him, or just to help him classify this strange species of experience. A light hand flat upon his stiff canvas sleeve, a small step, and she is lifting her face to kiss him, feeling herself to be, wanting herself to be just now no more than like the evening air, touching his lips. She has already given herself over to the idea of solitude and sleep; before long, she hopes, she will be sailing beyond her headache, out over the lake, herself like the sky boat, the silver dream from the childhood lullaby.

But for a time she does not sail beyond her wakeful singular mind. She was born alone, she thinks, and she must die alone. Her children, in truth, in one version of truth, are far away, elsewhere, inside their own lives. They do not know where she is; no one has been told where she is. In the morning she will call her home and office numbers for messages; yes, of course she will stay connected, but she must also answer for herself.

As if jostled by the stillness of her body, images of the day play themselves on and on into the night. Once more she is lifting off, landing, the first lap of the flight, second, crossing half the continent, watching cities of myriad dependent lights recede or approach, making her way through concourses clogged with other travelers, knowing no one's name until in the third airport there is Duncan, in his basic jacket, right in front of her, surprising her with his solidity; but there can be no stopping yet because beneath them the highways string out more and more of the same overriding story about passage; and though she tries to see him as himself, in the dark behind her eyes, one man keeps turning into the other, like never-ending music taking shape phrase by phrase from what played before, returning over and over to the primary themes. Finally the country roads are slower and feign alighted lives, discrete, illumined, which the travelers continue to pass by, leave behind, all the way to the last long driveway that once more carries them through pines and dunes, tufts of sand-loving grass appearing and disappearing in the headlights, ahead a vast paleness of open sky and a shine of active water, made lighter by that gigantic mirroring ball above the stage. A sight to behold, her grandmother would have said in her definitive voice, the grandmother who was sixty and had just lost her husband when Laura was first old enough to ask her age.

Just now the sound of a train enters the darkness of the room, the bedroom where Marianne's decorations are almost invisible, the sound of a train passing somewhere out in the night, inland of course, though Laura can't remember having crossed any tracks. There is no rattle or clack of cars, only the *woo, wooaa* falling away and leaving in its wake another memory, of the trains that threaded through college afternoons long ago, the hour of winter dusk when she had not yet brushed her hair for dinner but was still at her desk by the window, at least that was the hour when she was most aware of the trains passing through the intensity of her education with their rushing, lingering wails that somehow coalesced into a single stream all the pages she had covered, of reading and writing, simplified everything into a heart-opening, ongoing incomplete completeness that brought tears to her eyes, not of happiness, not of sorrow, but of something else, larger.

Laura was nineteen at that time, then twenty, then of course twenty-one, and so on, like everyone else. She had been eight when she first asked her grandmother's age, her great age, which seemed to the child the very end of a life, sixty, never to change again through a succession of uniform days except to cease, as her grandfather just had. In fact, her grandmother had lived, unmarried, thirty-two more variable years.

In the morning Laura sees what was not visible the night before, sunlit hues of water, sky, sand, vegetation, but all muted into context, as if by today's agreement a chromatic middle range. The lake that at night was black ink silvered by sliding mercurial moonlight is today a horizon-bound pot of azure and turquoise and purple, yet even those streaks of color or the occasional maple tree on shore fired up early by fall do not rise beyond the tempered composition. She and Duncan walk north along the wet sand between tracings of just-receded waves and a higher collar of wave-tumbled stones and debris and tiny gray shells, empty and open like wings, which Duncan says are from zebra mussels. They walk in mild light. They have been given muted sun; they have been given warmth. The wind is reduced to a gentle breeze, traveled by gulls, crows, and butterflies—look how many monarchs—on their long journey south, riding the thermal currents.

Laura ties the sleeves of her windbreaker around her waist. Duncan is already down to his short-sleeved gray T-shirt. It is the first time she has seen him without a sweater or jacket; his body looks as if it can do all the work it needs to do, without calling attention to itself. Both he and she appear to have their health, for now. They walk north with the morning sun against the right sides of their bodies; they walk not touching each other, only the sun and the breeze touching their bodies. Once her vision has adjusted to the semitones at her feet, particular stones begin to attract Laura like magnets; soon her full jacket pockets bump against her bare legs.

"I know they always look better when they're wet, but I can't resist."

"That's all right. You can sort them out on the deck and make your final choices later."

At breakfast, which was an omelet and dark raisin bread and Mountain Lion peaches, Duncan told her how after Marianne's death he had had to acquaint himself with all the pots and pans, their sizes and lids and various uses, how slowly he had moved in the kitchen at first, stunned. And Laura told him how stunned she'd been one day by the mere sight of the calendar on her kitchen wall: it had been the twenty-third of February when she'd buried Larry, and since then, one, two, three months had passed, all with a box called the twenty-third, while underneath the page of May were more pages, more numbers, open time. And he said, yes, that about said it all. Silent then, the two of them at the table by the kitchen window had seemed for a moment to occupy the whole room.

But now on the beach her body feels small; her life feels small. She's still a little tired and headachy. Ahead of them the sky is contiguous with land only far up the shore; overhead it is endlessly high and pale, almost white in its pale blueness. Something about that sky, she tells him, makes her think of winter. Then she remembers having been wakened very early, and briefly, this morning by the swift, horizontal honks of migrating geese, singular and numerous, high above in their wildness and purpose. Duncan begins telling her of the degrees by which the ice adheres chaotically to the shore, how it breaks and refreezes and breaks again and is never trustworthy. People die through trusting the ice, he says; some foolish ones treat it as a playing field, and it is not. Laura imagines how this ice might take on a color like the sky today, bluish white, a temporary inland arctic, and how the underside of this ice might look, translucent and beautiful and deadly, if one were to fall through and be swept beneath it in the undertow. She was born in Connecticut and has never been further north than Vancouver, than Copenhagen. Now she is not even that far north, but in a zone that might seem easy to those traveling from the harshest regions of ice. She has no ambition, as some do, to venture into those polar regions. There are other ways, she tells herself, to locate the poles. What, for example, could be more exacting than learning to walk in your own daily balance between sky and land?

"Duncan, would you ever go to the Arctic if you got the chance?"

"Funny you should ask. A geologist friend of mine takes teaching expeditions north almost every summer, and he's been after me the last few years—well, ever since Marianne died—to go along for the ride, but so far I haven't. I'm sure you've noticed that as soon as you lose a spouse, other people get all these ideas of what they think would be good for you—as if you can no longer make decisions for yourself." Duncan seizes upon a flat stone at his feet and skips it out over the water—one, two, three, four, five. He watches to the finish, like a golfer following his ball, and then looks satisfied with the number. "How about you—would you ever go to the Arctic?"

"I'd be very surprised to find myself doing something like that."

His eyes upon her are penetrating, though perhaps amused. The breeze riffles his white hair. Today he seems more at home with having her here; the change must have happened sometime in the night, when he was in his room and she in hers.

"I suppose you surprise yourself now and then?"

"Oh, never!" She laughs. "I'm entirely predictable."

He scrutinizes her again. "Sure you are. Me, too. Up to a point." He finds another stone and this time hands it to her.

It feels like a lifetime since she skipped stones. Turning sideways to the water, she does what she watched Duncan do, bend forward, flick the wrist; the stone arcs, plops, sinks. Saying nothing, he finds another disk for her, then another and another, until they are both laughing, both refusing to give up, and the water over which she is squinting becomes brighter, more lively, like a beckoning dance of light and dark, and she hunkers down into hot determination. At last one of the stones enters the correct low flight path and hops out across the surface of the water. Three times. Duncan looks as pleased as if he had done it himself.

"Pure chance," she says.

"Nah, you've got a future."

"As a stone skipper."

He looks at her again, that kindly scrutiny, then says, "One thing I've noticed is that you really seem to like your work a lot."

"Oh, I do! I love my job." She wipes her palms on her sash of knotted windbreaker as they resume walking. "I've figured out that helping to give money away makes me feel socially radical. It satisfies a youthful desire."

"Yes? Go on."

"Well, I guess it's that the grant money usually flows in the direction of excellence, not so much toward aggression and greed. That's got to have some sort of subversive effect, don't you think?" Laura feels her heavy pockets knocking against her legs. "It's not quite logical, of course, because there's some unsavory history behind this money, as you probably know. But. Still." She shrugs. "What can I say? I like doing my job. I seem to have a gift for seeing things given away."

He gazes out over the water. "Yes, I think you do."

She studies his profile. "Did you always want to go into science, Duncan?"

"Almost always. I think I was hooked the day I first looked into a microscope. When I was eight."

"Eight. Oh, I can just see you."

"I suppose you see a little nerd."

She laughs. "I see an interesting kid."

"Well how about you—what were your ideas about yourself at that age?"

"Eight. Well, for a while I thought all the time about flying."

"Flying?"

"In the body—you know, the way one does in dreams."

"Do I know this? I guess I do. I don't remember very many dreams."

"No? Hmm. I bet you will someday. But anyway, levitation aside, there was usually a man smack-dab in the middle of my pictures about myself—those were olden times, remember. At first I thought I might marry Abraham Lincoln."

She expects him to laugh outright, but for a second he says nothing. "And? Did you?"

"Duncan." She says his name in amiable reproof and then cannot go on. The dead have swallowed her voice. Looking up at him, her friend, she has to face the sun. Her eyes are watering. Even in sunglasses she needs to shield them. Gulls cry in the emptiness overhead.

He takes her hand, saying nothing.

As they continue up the shoreline, a flock of the gulls just ahead of them, roosting on the sand like similar stones all bulged toward the wind, starts up into the air one after the other. He and she walk through the sandy stretch that had been so attractive to the gulls and then around a curve in the shore. Here the dunes become higher, the vegetation on them denser, and along the grassy ridge there are several houses, backed by pines, oaks, and a few maples tinged with red and gold. Steep flights of wooden stairs connect the houses to the water level. No one appears to be at home up above. On the beach, among strewn driftwood, are the charred remains of several campfires. Laura continues to interrupt their progress by picking up irresistible stones. There is nowhere she would rather be than here with Duncan, yet the long view beyond today shows her only an openness, of water, sky, a small string of other people's houses. The smallness of herself is like one stone.

They approach a mass of driftwood heaped up around a bleached fallen tree, as if for a great fire, but as they get closer Laura sees a triangular opening into a spiky tent. "Look, a hideout." She pulls him toward it. A wooden sign with childish lettering instructs them to stay out. Side by side, they lean over the sand threshold and peer in. There are several crate seats and a gathering of various beach objects, also a piece of mirror, bound by a length of dirty twine to one of the branches. Laura wants very much to enter and crouch inside the thicket of filtered light. She imagines the children nested there, secretive, excited, finding out about themselves inside the guise of making a house in the world. She can hear them breathing.

"Wow, does this ever take me back," he says.

"I know." She needs to whisper. Something has come to her entire, a feeling that is also like a clear picture of a slender boy, crouched down to poke in the sand: it could be Duncan over fifty years ago, or Larry decades before he and she joined together in their adult promises, or her son, Peter, not so very long ago: it is any boy in the chrysalis of youth, yet also an uncannily particular boy, and she is seeing him entire, loving him. "What did you used to do in places like this?" Shaken, she is still whispering.

"Oh, you name it—collect things, study them. Secure the fort. Play Show."

"Ah. Is Show what I think it is?"

"Of course."

The breathing is the man beside her; she can smell his skin, heated by the sun. For a moment of pure sensation she closes her eyes. Then, gently relinquishing his hand, she straightens up and turns out toward the wind. Far across the lake a freighter has entered the picture from the left, its progress at the watery horizon hardly measurable. Laura takes a deep breath of the air that is arriving from its long passage over the water. There's a kind of increased pressure on her, from her questions, from the linear purposefulness of the boat, from the air itself—who can say?

"Well," says Duncan, also standing upright, turning. "I guess that's it. Funny how one wants to linger."

"I know, I feel the same way. What's in that boat out there, Duncan?"

"Iron ore, probably, or timber. Could be salt or coal."

She notes how the words add, one by one, to the weight of this visible world: ore, timber, salt, coal. Once again she sees the child, squatting to poke dreamily in the sand. There's only one ongoing task, she thinks; all the others are part of the one: to be in love with life and the source of life. No matter what.

A few steps farther on they come upon the monument of another of the children's games, this one like a miniature Stonehenge of rocks and planted sticks and feathers, precise and ceremonial. Uninitiated adult giants, they stand in their own shadows looking down at the children's magic circle. "Touch that one at your own risk," says Duncan.

"Exactly. These are fairly intense children, I'd say. Do you think they're anywhere around?"

"The school year's just started—they're probably back into Saturday soccer or whatever."

"Yes, I suppose even children like these must play soccer." The small bodies crouch in the sand, their bony, sand-dusted knees up to their ears as they reach out to position each stone, each stick, each feather, everything at the same time pleasing to them and also mysterious, already full of the unknown life ahead. Her grandmother, Laura remembers, disapproved of boys and girls playing together; her opinion was that the sexes should stay separate until marriage, and then also, apparently, in proper widowhood.

"Duncan, do you think you and I would've been friends if we'd known each other as children?"

He scratches his beard and once more looks amused. "Oh, I think we could have had ourselves some fun. But your sights, you know, were rather high. Could I have handled the whole job—I mean secession, emancipation, the Civil War?"

"Oh! Well, my Abraham Lincoln phase passed soon enough."

"That's a relief. There was a chance for the rest of us, after all."

"There was always room. Weren't you ever like that about girls, sort of daydreamy and idealistic?"

"I don't think so."

"I bet you were."

"Nah, I'm a what's-in-front-of-your-eyes guy. It's been enough."

"Right. As long as you've also had your beloved microscopes." She lets her shoulder bump companionably against his, whereupon he takes sudden firm hold of her, his arm clamped across her back, steering her in an about-face.

"Laura," he says. "You."

He begins drawing her southward, away from the row of houses on the dune ridge and tiny Stonehenge and the driftwood hideout and the burned-out remains of fires, on toward the curve in the shore and the homestretch. He does not loosen his hold. The sun is now on their left, higher over the water, hotter. She walks in a body that all its life has kept letting itself be warmed, surrendering to the needs of its human cells. The freighter on the horizon is progressing in the same direction they are, but in its own frame. In the air all around them there are even more monarchs, like living origami, orange and orange and black and black, fluttering as if stirred up and down by random breezes, but in truth on a breathtaking transcontinental flight, together.

The telephone begins ringing as Laura and Duncan are knocking the sand out of their shoes beside the deck. It sounds to her as if it has also been ringing in their absence, in the empty house. Duncan lets out a brief groan, then leaps the steps. Laura would have done the same, thinking of all her children at once. But they do not know she is here, and at any rate she can feel they are all right, she just can. Someone, though, seems to be in trouble. She finishes with her shoes and then takes a few minutes to empty both pockets of stones and constellate them on the deck—thirteen, it turns out, several with tiny embedded fossils. Then, barefoot, she follows Duncan into the house.

"Just try to tell me exactly where you are right now," he is saying.

She passes around him, running her fingertips across his back, the damp gray T-shirt stretched tight as he bends over the receiver. It's strange, they have not made love, and yet she feels as if they have, as if they know each other now as relaxed lovers, and the way she is padding barefoot around him is part of the indolence of sex.

In the bathroom, urinating, she feels the downwardness of life, of its fleshly, earthbound quarter.

The bedroom in which she slept bears only traces of her presence. Her suitcase is closed. There on the bedside table are her lotions and little travel clock. It would take five minutes for her to be ready to leave. She lays her windbreaker on the taut floral bedspread and withdraws.

In the living room everything is in place, all the many pillows, the glass coffee table and its objects, the brass fireplace tools. Only the home-scale telescope on its tripod in front of the wall of windows looks as if it might be moved around. Bending and positioning an eye to its viewer, then seeing not a boat, not a horizon, just blackness, Laura realizes the lens is capped; removing it herself, though, doesn't seem like the right thing. She will wait for Duncan. She goes over to the couch and sits in the middle, her bare feet crossed at the ankles on the beige carpet. Marianne liked everything to be chosen and placed. She liked comfort and order. She also loved Duncan.

Laura's head falls back into the couch. She is trying not to let Marianne's decorations get in the way of what she needs to be thinking about, deciding. Duncan's voice is indistinct; he is listening much more than he is talking. When Larry used to be on the telephone, she could often tell from a few of his words or sometimes even the tone of his voice who was on the other end. *Just try to tell me exactly where you are* could as well be spoken to someone in Duncan's lab, about the stages of a tricky procedure, as it could be to one of his children. His tone does sound concerned.

How deep and soft this couch is, so much softer than her body, which is still tuned for life, this female body, which remembers itself, doesn't it, its total experience, everything from the beginning, dust, cell? It's like a capsule of time. But now the soul:

what the soul knows must be like memory without dimension, without time, beyond thought, beyond imagination. And what the mind knows, the small mind, the busy, thinking mind, is, well, only what it does, so far.

Try to tell me exactly where you are. All right, here is where she is, presented with all now before her eyes, moment by moment not to be discounted. Look: the lake, and a bush with willowlike, minnowlike leaves bending soundlessly in currents of air beyond the glass, and the bland furniture on this side of the glass, and the intriguing telescope, and look how everything is being held together by some great faithful agreement, which does include her, just as she is, bare feet crossed, on both ankles a tracery of red veins visible under the skin, as if deeper underground rivers were surfacing into deltas of spidery trickles. Only there, in her aging, is there definite material for augury; otherwise—and here Laura takes up one of the couch pillows and clutches it in her lap like an impossible pregnancy. In this room no windows are open; it is very still, except for the voice from the kitchen, and very tidy, and intact. Grave.

Tossing the pillow aside, she springs up and retraces her steps through the kitchen, this time not touching Duncan, who has taken the receiver to the table and is writing rapidly on a yellow tablet as he listens, saying nothing. He glances up at Laura but doesn't smile; he is in a mode she has not seen before.

Outside once more she gulps in the fresh air off the lake and then heads barefoot down the stairs and across the width of beach. The freighter has gone on its way, beyond the theater here, but never fallen off the map. On the sand the fluted lines left by the waves are like readings on some sort of dissolving graph. She turns south and walks a short way, avoiding the little wings of mussel shell, and not picking up any more rocks. Just ahead a breakwater divides the beach and juts out into the water, four stacked layers of concrete bars, like disorderly piano keys, jumbled by conditions yet still held together by vertical iron rods. Illiterate gulls perch beyond the KEEP OFF sign all the way to the watery end of the breakwater.

At her feet is a large dead fish, being pecked at by one crow, one gull. She goes on beyond its stench and then sits, without disturbing the gulls, on a large log of bleached driftwood near the breakwater. After a few minutes she, too, belongs there. On the ground near her feet, in the print of a very small foot, not hers— it must be a child's—she notices one of the monarch butterflies, alighted or dead, she can't tell; its left wing is askew, its whole body quivered by the breeze against its wings. Alive or dead?

Laura studies it, thinking about her own life, her questions, how it is through these thoughts that she is seeing the butterfly, and how she does not know if she could come to see the butterfly with nothing in between.

The monarch, it appears, is not dead: an earthbound insect has just marched into the arena, and as it begins to harry the butterfly's legs, the monarch shakes off the tiny flat-backed thing and starts to struggle up out of the footprint. As a damaged flying creature it is now down where the rules are different, where everything takes longer, is heavier, is buffeted rather than borne by the wind. Then Laura sees another downed monarch, lying on its side in a slight indentation of sand, its legs waving feebly; she leans forward and tries with the tip of a gull feather to set it upright, but the monarch falls over again and again from the weight of its wings. It appears to be alive, but something's wrong with the legs, no way to gain purchase for takeoff.

Her eyes now light upon a small arching branch of driftwood bearing dozens of ladybugs on its upper bridge with many more harbored beneath, so many, a teeming orange and black colony, while nearby a single small green apple, one bite missing, swarms with yet more of the industrious beetles, each with just a slightly different pattern of dark spots.

All this while Laura is also keeping track of the monarch who is trying to climb out of the small footprint. The labor goes on and on. The damage is great: a whole wing unusable. But at last the mesa is attained, the harrying insect left below; the butterfly pauses as if surveying what remains to her: for now terrain and more terrain.

Laura rests her chin on her knees and watches her feet on the sand. The toes are spread. The feet are warm and calm. Sometimes Larry used to take hold of one of her feet when they lounged together on opposite ends of the couch, hold and stroke it, as they read or talked, on drowsy Sundays, both of them relaxed, open to each other. Yes, it was like that, often, often enough.

She eases down from her log and stretches out on her side on the baked sand, cradling her head in her curved arm and closing her eyes.

And then, all right—she takes a breath as if from deep within herself—and then there were also those opposite times with Larry when she would not want to see the sight of him, or listen to the sound of him, his voice or his music, or be touched by him, when she would imagine herself, in her exhaustion, her faintness of heart, delivered, from him.

O God, as she finds herself now.

Inside the cocoon of her eyes the sunlight balls up into pure, original orange. Even if you were to curl up, sleep for a year and wake transformed, she thinks, you could never not be in relation to all that you have done and said and thought, everything.

The little mind tries, it does try so hard; but it is only partially trustworthy, isn't it? Because it can be so promiscuous and confused and worn out, so heartbreakingly ignorant about which thoughts to entertain, and about how to be still. What else can you do but forgive the mind? Forgive the heart when the messages seem too faint to hear. Forgive yourself. Forgive everyone. Begin here, in the orange truth.

And forgive life, for commanding form, for claiming you and using you entirely—because it's a given, isn't it? You are accomplishing nothing that is not actually life, using you.

Stretched out like this, she remembers how as a young mother she would sometimes be so tired she would lie down on the floor near her children at play, and if the small bodies gravitated toward her, she might stay as still as a mountain range and let them have the use of her as they crawled over her body, searching for places to sprawl or nestle, for at least if she could sense them all around her she would know they were safe, and she could perhaps close her eyes and quarry some restfulness, even while answering their questions, carrying on whole conversations without ever leaving this room of renewal, orange today.

A voice has been saying *Laura*.

Yes?

Laura.

He wants her awake.

I couldn't see you at first.

She feels him sitting down behind her on the log.

I wasn't trying to hide.

Laura. Her cheek is touched; he wants her awake. *I wish I didn't have to lose sight of you.* His voice is like an elegy. Something has happened.

She opens her eyes to the close graininess of sand in a narrow strip, then a band of water, then all the rest, three-quarters of the world, sky.

"You've got some nice color," he says, still in that voice of loss. "You were pale when I picked you up at the airport. I said to myself that nobody should be pale at the end of the summer."

She rolls her head and looks up at him. The sun is nearly overhead. She rests an arm across her forehead like a visor.

He runs his finger up along its underside. "Laura." Then his hand drops away. His eyes have aged in the last hour, the area around his eyes; he looks as if he has just come back from a long, exhausting trip in a parched climate.

"Something's happened, hasn't it?" She, too, feels as if she has been far away, on her own mission.

"I've been talking with the airlines."

"What are you saying?"

"That was Eddie on the phone."

"Eddie? I'm trying to remember who Eddie is—the lab?"

"No—my godson."

"Oh, yes—the one who was sick?"

"I wish I could say *was*. I've kept hoping. All this year he's been fairly stable, but now he really needs help. He talked almost nonstop; I could hardly make any sense of it."

Duncan comes down from his perch and lies behind her, matching his front to her back, like a familiar lover. His arm folds over her. They are both looking out, toward the water. He and she already know about marriage, she thinks; both of them have crossed over the territory of a marriage. The territory they have not yet crossed laps in toward them like the waves, always arriving, one wave after another, made of water fallen from the sky.

"I have to go to him, Laura. This afternoon. I just talked to his doctor. Eddie's out in L.A. I don't know how he got there. He's supposed to be in Evanston. He says he hasn't slept in over a week. It's a miracle he had the presence of mind to try me here. Last time things got bad we had to bring in the police to find him. He was that disoriented. I just hope he's really where he says he is."

"He's your brother's boy? The brother who crashed in the small plane?"

"Yes. Along with his wife. But Eddie was sick before he lost his parents—it started in college. He's a genius, I think, was, is, I don't know. He's a wonderful kid. He had a full scholarship, then. He just, I don't know, got sabotaged."

Laura listens as Duncan's voice washes over her, the story of Eddie and his manic depression stabbing intemperately above and below the line of the horizon, evident brilliance submerged time and again. She thinks how last night and today, while she and Duncan were placing one foot carefully in front of the other, Eddie was out there, forgetting his balance; Eddie was part of what was going on.

"I'm the one he's got now," says Duncan. "Well, he's got a brother, he's got doctors, but I'm the one he called today. Laura, I have to go find him."

"Yes, all right."

"I have to find him as soon as I can."

"I could help you, Duncan. Let me go with you." The words just come out.

He says nothing. She can feel his breathing chest, his breath on her neck, his beard. She can feel him thinking. She is watching the water, coming in and going out. Everything is held right here, she thinks, even winter, commanding and austere, is packed into this moment.

Then Duncan is rolling her toward him. He is covering her with himself, their bare legs mixing together in the sand. He is kissing her with surety. Endless sky is behind his head.

He lifts his face and gazes down at her. "Thank you for what you said."

But then he looks out to the lake. He is thinking. Everything he has heard from Eddie is in his profile.

She touches his cheek and he turns back to her.

"Even the idea of having you with me out there makes me feel better. Let me think."

"I wouldn't want to do something like that alone," she says.

"The thing is, I don't know how long I'll be gone. So many things could happen. What about your work?"

"My work." She searches his face. "My work."

His eyes on her do not waver. "Laura." Then he is kissing her again, slowly, gently, repeatedly, kisses like a developing sequence of thoughts. She closes her eyes, and now she and he are both melded inside the same complicated orange.

Then his voice begins again, but this time changed, as if lofted on an unseen current: "Hey, do you know what? We never got to swim. And I really wanted to go swimming with you."

It takes Laura only a second to see what comes next. She is already shimmying out of her shorts, then wriggling up from his embrace and stripping off the rest, everything, still saying nothing as she holds out her hand to pull him up. He sheds garments as he runs beside her toward the water.

Now she's laughing, can't help it, he, too. "So, tell me, does this qualify as a game of Show?"

"You bet. This is a good one. More than I ever knew how to hope for in the old days."

Neither of them hesitates at the verge; there isn't time; they wade quickly through the cold shallows and then plunge forward, outward into shocking, bracing, primal liquid, dark and darker in its depths. They swim as far out as the breakwater is long. Laura turns onto her back, gasping. Gulls hang overhead. How could she have known her stay here would be over so soon? Does the real always come as a surprise? Duncan strokes closer, slides an arm under her. "Listen, when you learn to do this magic flying of yours," he says, in bursts of breath, "do you think you can take me with you?"

"You're talking tandem?"

"However. Do you think you can do that?"

"If it's possible, I will. I promise."

On the beach they zigzag streaming and naked to gather their strewn clothes. Everything must be done quickly now; Laura feels the pressure of Eddie's need; she sees him, crouched, somewhere. A young man, still just a boy.

"Duncan," she says when they are in the kitchen, both clutching little bundles of garments like shivering inmates being sent out into the world at large, "did Eddie ever come to this place?"

"Yes, he's been here. Even before the house was built, we all used to come out to the land for picnics."

"When he was little."

"Yes, all the children were still kids, but he was the youngest. Why do you ask?"

"Because. I'll tell you sometime. Not right now."

She showers quickly and dresses in traveling clothes and packs her cosmetics and clock and windbreaker and the shirt and shorts she wore on the beach. She puts her beach shoes in a plastic bag and packs those. She slides her book into her tote bag. She is almost ready; she only has to go out to the deck to retrieve the stones.

Duncan comes and stands, dressed in a clean shirt and khakis, in the doorway of her room. "Laura, I'm so glad for your offer, it's wonderful, it's what I want for myself, but what I'm really thinking . . ."

"I understand."

He comes toward her.

"I've been thinking myself that it might be too much for Eddie if I were with you—a stranger, a strange woman."

"Ah, but not strange to me, I'm happy to say."

She lays the flat of her palms on either side of his face. "You're going to find him, I feel it. Duncan, you're going to find that boy. And someday I want to meet him."

"I hope you will. It would be very good for him to be with you."

His hands are on her waist. He is close, completely substantial. This is right. Yes, this, for her, this is the way. The choice is always the same—isn't it?—over and over, the same choice; only the faces appear to change. Now she knows how she will be torn from him, as they both go their separate ways into the sky, how she will want to be this close to him again and again, to practice with him, to practice what she knows, to keep learning the substance of love.

His flight takes off before hers. That, too, seems right. A child has emerged as the center of the picture, a child who is all the children, generation after generation, who will take up her sentences and the unfinished labor of her hands. Laura is reminded that she and Duncan are at the age of giving, giving everything, like a continual prayer. Eddie has come, a messenger, and taken his rightful place.

Eddie, she thinks, Eddie, *stay with us*.

In the aisle of her plane a man offers to hoist her bag to the overhead bin.

"All right," says Laura. "Thank you very much."

"Whew! That one's a lot heavier than it looks—what d'you have in there, rocks?"

"Yes," says Laura.

"That's okay," says the man. "I was just joking."

Laura is light. Has she ever felt so light with the weight of this life, the blessed weight? She slides into her seat next to a young woman with earphones, cassette player, multiple earrings, red hair in multiple beaded braids, nose ring, embroidered shirt. Laura smiles at her, folds her hands, and waits for takeoff. She feels as if she has lived a complete life in twenty-four hours, another one. There are tears in her eyes.

The sun has not yet set. Now the plane seems to rise above it. The solar system is after all just the solar system. Beyond it swims the night of space, like a dark sea of time, pulsing, continuously generative. Worlds come and go. What is this love, she wonders, when the bodies are not here?

Now is the hour to rest her head. On its own tomorrow will come, like a wave, a breath: the morning and then the night.

Mother of Chartres

❦

I could hide behind the drapes. In this environment my miniskirt and cropped sweater might as well be shrunken rags. *She should have known better.* Right. Well, at least I'm here. Listening at the moment as my chunky cousin Lolly, in tasteful clothes of course, blabs away—wait a minute—*engaged*? Lolly's *my* age. She can't get married. Is that my strangled voice saying *hooray*? Oh, I'm so happy you're happy, says Lolly.

Out of the corner of my eye I keep tracking Dad as he works the room of relatives and Grandpa and Trudie's elderly friends. He flew here for his father's birthday, and of all six children I got to come, on the frugal bus, because my college is so close to Minneapolis. Near the drinks table Dad greets yet another woman with a kiss. On the cheek this time. Lolly says her fiancé's name is Raymond. I've never known anyone our age named Raymond. Another woman, another kiss. Lips. I've watched Dad kiss women all my life, so I don't know why tonight it should make even my knees feel forlorn. Dispossessed.

At least I'm wearing tights. I wish my sisters were here to help represent our Chicago twig of the family. Even Russell would do. Mom, of course, but she put down her foot over the airfare. This Raymond of Lolly's could be older, I guess, a whole lot older, not a weird idea when you consider how Lolly is a sort of clone of her mother, clothes and all. Usually this outfit of mine, a favorite for special occasions at school, makes me feel wonderful. It's perfect for dancing.

I lose sight of Dad as Lolly and I turn toward the buffet, she prattling on about Raymond, who, it turns out, really is an amazing thirty years old. I give myself a tiny star for intuition. Then she says *guess what*, she has huge news: she and her mother have talked it all over and they want *me* to be the maid of honor! Because we are so close, just like sisters, she goes on, and we shared so very much traveling in France last year. Oh, isn't this exciting! I reach over and steady her laden plate back to horizontal. Actually, this is unreal. I'm having a hard time here. How is it possible that my fat, unadventurous cousin could be making off with the whole idea of marriage? All our lives, but most especially when we were in France, I've been relieved to think of her as lagging way behind me.

We traveled together because Grandpa gives all the grandchildren trips when we turn twenty, and Lolly and I of course turned the same year. I adored France, but Lolly was so worried about who knows what she wouldn't go down side streets or into intriguing doorways or courtyards with me; she was afraid to be out late at night; she wouldn't even take the early-morning train out to Chartres cathedral, not exactly your most dangerous place on the planet, but as it turned out, that was okay because I don't know if what happened to me there *would* have happened if I'd had Lolly trudging down the ambulatory behind me.

"And you, Maggie dear, how *are* you?" Lolly really sounds spookily like her mother, Rosemary, poised either to pity me or to save me from what her family calls the godlessness of ours.

I tell her firmly that I'm fine.

I've been telling people all night that I'm fine and that my absent mother and all my siblings are also fine. My brilliant, gregarious father they can see for themselves.

And I can see for myself that as usual, along with all the kissing, he's been drinking. Dad speaks five languages, kissing is like the sixth, and another one must be the secret language he talks to himself when he's pouring another drink, or surveying his children, or measuring his academic achievements. Only since I've been away at college have I guessed how his life, given his talents and worldly experiences, might not have gone as expected.

Sometimes Mom calls him Peter the Great or just Himself. My busy intuition tells me that airfare for herself and my brother and sisters is only part of why she didn't come to help Grandpa celebrate his eighty-fifth birthday, just months after his marriage to Trudie. I think she's also protesting in her own way the showy vigor of the men in my father's family. Even Lolly's pudgy dad, Nathan, my father's only sibling, puts on a strenuous display, not cerebral or romantic like Dad and Grandpa, but the born-again sort. Dad says we have Rosemary to blame for that.

I wish I could escape and go somewhere quiet to eat—maybe upstairs in Trudie's classy modern house to Grandpa's study, where I could even dial the home number and listen to Mom's down-to-earth voice while I chew—but here comes Aunt Rosemary herself, beaming mother of the bride-to-be. As she gushes about the wedding, all I can picture is the horror of being zipped into a Rosemary-approved maid-of-honor dress. She says she's sorry my "poor" mother can't be here. And how are all my sisters and little Russell?

"Fine, they're fine." I'm feeling very frustrated. I'd like to point out to Aunt Rosemary that my mother, whose name, in case she has forgotten, is Caroline, doesn't need to be called *poor*—well, maybe on occasion—and also that we five sisters have names of our own and shouldn't be shunted off into one generic female subgroup.

But as usual I'm careful about what I say. Maybe I'm saving up my words the way I'm saving up my biggest kissing: that is, for the most excellent, exactly right time. I don't know. I chew and listen. At last, as the bride and her tickled-pink mother turn back to the buffet for seconds, I'm free to clump away in my big shoes and small skirt. Marriage. What an incredible drag it would be for me right now. I love college; I love my studies; I love my friends. Next June I'm supposed to graduate, and what I'm honestly thinking is I could use more than one year to be the age I am. But then, there's the question of catching up.

In the sleek stainless steel and marble kitchen, my father and Uncle Nathan are sitting on stools at the island counter, eating and arguing—or rather, Nathan is eating and my father is talking and gesticulating and drinking. I lean against the doorjamb and eat a few more bites.

Where's birthday boy Grandpa, the father of these bickering sons? I haven't seen him for a while. It strikes me that Grandpa, who's a retired surgeon, probably feels right at home in this gleaming machine of a kitchen. I like this house, but then I'm the artistic type. While my father bragged, my mother was very bothered when only a year after Grandma Agnes died Grandpa remarried and moved from the large stucco Prairie Style house in St. Paul that we visited all through my childhood to this glass and concrete and steel vertical box designed by Trudie's late husband. It's set into a steep hillside overlooking the modern art museum and downtown Minneapolis, and what my mother seemed most bothered about—even though Grandpa has wonderful posture and still walks several miles a day—was that he would surely break a hip on the many stairs or the icy hill. When my father pointed out the little elevator, hidden behind a door that looks just like another closet, her answer was that just when you need a contraption like that the most, there will surely be a power outage.

Mom of course attended Grandpa and Trudie's wedding last April, no getting out of that. At the dinner Grandpa stood up and announced that since Agnes's death and his rather late acceptance of his own mortality, he found himself saying a great many heartfelt things he might formerly have kept to himself, and what he wanted to say tonight was that he could now admit love was the best medicine in the world—in fact, the only medicine guaranteed to give you trouble if you *don't* take it. My father shouted *Hear! Hear!* He leaned over and dramatically presented his pursed lips to my mother, whose attention was as usual divided by her many other preoccupations, six of which were we, her children, ranged around the table in various degrees of behavior.

I look down at my plate of diminishing party food. *Margaret, are you grieving?* Dad used to say, mimicking my faces, and it wasn't until college I learned he was actually quoting from a poem. Grieving? I don't know. But I guess I was a sober child. I had to be. What exactly do people mean when they say *family values?*

Uncle Nathan raises his voice. "Brother, will you stop talking for a minute and listen to me? If you could just let our Lord into your heart you wouldn't need that glass of wine. Believe me, I've seen it work."

My father makes a dismissive sound I know well. "I thought he *was* the wine."

"Be careful," says Nathan.

"You be careful, Nate. Religion has been known to get the world into massive trouble. I prefer to think for myself, thank you."

Nathan is getting hot under the collar. "Don't you think it's high time you stopped worshipping your own blessed IQ? You're going to be left empty-handed one of these days. High and dry."

"Oh, for crying out loud!" My father barks out a laugh. Get a grip, Nate."

They go on like that, while I press myself into the woodwork. This is a very disorienting night. But if I tried to escape, I'd just have to show up somewhere else, wouldn't I? It occurs to me that every one of us suffers from delusion.

Is my father an alcoholic? I don't know. At night he drinks and studies and then in the morning gets up on time and walks over to teach at the university. He organizes conferences; he travels to give lectures. He plays tennis several times a week. He drinks and drives and does not have accidents, whereas my mother doesn't drink at all and has a reputation in the family for minor but expensive mishaps, almost as if she's having the accidents *for* Dad, if that's possible. It's weird, but at home we don't talk at all about Dad's drinking; it just goes on.

On the other side of the kitchen island, opposite the arguing brothers, a caterer transfers more chicken breasts onto a silver tray. In mid-sentence Dad snatches up a pinch of spinach stuffing, and as he's licking his fingers he catches sight of me lurking in the doorway.

"Ah! There's my date!" He beckons me to enter his extended half circle of arm. Nathan takes advantage of the intermission to wolf down a few bites. My father bobs up from his stool to kiss me on the cheek and then inspects my plate. "Good girl, Mags, looks like you've been working on all the basic food groups." He pats my behind, and I let myself lean into him, a little. It's not very often I get to be the only child with my father.

"Isn't she something?" Dad says to Nathan. "This girl's going places."

Where! I want to demand. Tell me! But my lips stay pressed together. Hasn't my father already been all the places I might ever think of going? He tips back his head and drains his glass. The wine looks so deeply red I can almost taste it myself.

"Join us, Mags." He still clamps me immobile against him, rocking me a little. "Help me rescue this poor brother from his muddle of piety."

"How are you, anyway, Margaret?" asks Nathan. He looks tired of all the interruptions that have separated him from his food. Jesus Christ asks a lot.

"I'm fine, Uncle Nathan, thank you." Before his marriage, I've been told, Nathan used to be a good tennis player, much thinner and not saved, and I guess my father must miss the brother he used to know.

"Oh, goodness, are you two brothers still at each other?" Trudie enters in her clicking party shoes. She's so much shorter and even at age seventy-three fancier than Grandma Agnes that I'm still getting used to looking at her.

"I've never heard such a two," she goes on. "Can't you tussle with each other some other time? Now Maggie, dear heart, you're just the person I need! I've lost your grandfather, and some of the guests must leave before long. Will you go find him, darling, and tell him it's time to blow out his candles?"

"Yes, wherever is our aged Romeo?" My father keeps rocking me against his side. "Romeo, Romeo, wherefore art—"

"Oh, shut up," says Uncle Nathan. "Let her go."

I set down my plate of food, and my father says, "Good girl, Maggie," and gives me a final send-off pat. He sounds pleased, maybe because he got his brother so close to outright, godless swearing.

In the front hallway a startled-looking woman comes out of the powder room across from the two identical doors of the coat closet and elevator.

"Hello! What a pretty girl! You must be one of Nathan's?" Her pink lipstick glistens like nail polish, and she talks in a fake, breathy voice.

"No, I'm one of Peter's."

"Oh yes. Now let's see, he's the insurance man from Des Moines?"

"No, he's the professor, from Chicago."

"Oh, of course. So you must be the daughter who is to be married?"

"Married? No! I'll never marry!" I hear myself blurt, thinking that my parents have already done that one thoroughly, long before Lolly.

"Oh, my dear, never say never!" She's almost lisping. "When I was your age, I also thought there was no one for me, *no one on earth* was what I used to go about bemoaning." She sighs. "And you are such a very pretty girl." She touches my hair and with another fluttery sigh totters off down the hall, a painfully preserved woman on brittle heels. I'm appalled at my pleasure in her compliment. It would be better to hear it from my harried, honest mother.

Grandpa, obviously, is not in the bathroom. Now I have the wild thought that he might be hiding, as in our games in the old house, the house of Grandma Agnes, and if I fling open the right door, there he'll be, gleefully manipulating the elevator or plastering himself up against the coats, panting, his face zesty, overjoyed to be found. He always had a surprising enthusiasm for games of that sort. He'd laugh in almost the same goofy way we kids were laughing and then start directing us and making up new rules, until Grandma Agnes would finally intervene. *Jack, now Jack, why don't you leave some of the excitement for the children?*

I do peek behind doors. No Grandpa. I head upstairs on my quest, pausing on the landing with the glass-brick wall to listen to the party below and the silence above. It's strange that the meticulously planned house of Trudie's architect husband is now being used for the celebration of another man's birthday. Do the dead know about us? I'm missing Grandma Agnes; I want to hear her call from the kitchen, *Now Jack*; I want her to measure me on the same kitchen door marked by the growth of my father and all the others—in the old house we can't visit anymore. Maybe she could be the one to tell me where I'm meant to go.

The illumination in Grandpa's study comes only from one small lamp and the window of early-evening lights from the city. He's not in here. I stand on a rich field of oriental carpet and run my hand along the edge of the big mahogany desk and the top of the leather chair, the only objects I remember for sure as his. When Grandma Agnes tries to visit him now, does she wing her way to the old house, or has she discovered this one? I'd like to just sit here awhile in the half-light.

The bedroom is dim, too, but there, stretched out on one of the twin beds, is someone in a dark suit. Grandpa, of course—who else would it be? Even so, my heart jumps. On the table between the beds is a large quartz crystal with interior glints.

"I'm not sleeping. Who's there?"

"It's me, Grandpa. Maggie."

"Of course. Come closer. Turn on another light, will you?"

I turn on a dresser lamp.

"Come here, Margaret. I can't see you."

"Are you tired, Grandpa?"

"Hmm. Maybe a little." He cocks one open eye over at me. The bones of his face look more prominent than usual, his cheeks sucked inward. His thick white hair is rumpled.

"Trudie says it's time to do your cake. Some people have to leave soon."

"Ah, of course, there's still the cake to go. It was a well-planned party, wouldn't you say, Margaret? Very nicely carried out from start to finish?"

"It's not over yet, Grandpa."

"No, that's right. Let me get a good look at you. Is school agreeable?"

"Yes, it is." I realize how exhilarating it is to speak when you're saying the simple truth.

"That's good. Enjoyment is the key. Now, how are the others? Your mother? How is the beautiful Caroline? Come closer, I can't see you very well." He motions for me to sit beside him. "Turn on this light, will you? My eyes aren't behaving."

"Everyone's okay, I guess." I've just computed that between my mother and father there are actually more years than between Grandpa and Trudie. I turn on the lamp and sit near his knees. "Karen likes Colorado all right so far, and she can hardly wait for the skiing to start."

Grandpa nodded. "I remember. And Susie? This is her junior year? Is she still playing the clarinet?"

"She plays in everything. Orchestra, concert band, jazz ensemble." I'm amazed Grandpa remembers so much.

"And Mary, is she still the image of your mother?"

"I guess so. The thing now is she wants to go to parochial school."

"Well, that should keep your father on edge for a while. What does your mother say about it?"

"Not too much." Which does seem like a mystery, given that when I was little Mom used to go to Mass a lot. Then she stopped. But she kept on having children, the most dangerous part of the religion for women, and I think it would help me if I could understand why.

"Now who comes next?" goes on Grandpa. "It's Carol, isn't it?"

It feels good to be sitting beside Grandpa, talking about the people who are part of me. I tell him Carol wants a kitten so much she's promised to make her bed for a whole year to earn one.

"A kitten? That's easy. She should have it without the year of probation. Life's short." Grandpa's speaking as if he's already been thinking about these very things by himself, lying alone in the dark room, keeping us all in his mind even when we aren't with him.

"Mom says there are enough warm bodies in the house already."

"Hmmm." Grandpa wets his lips with his tongue and studies the ceiling.

I remember one other time I was alone like this with him, in a thunderstorm long ago. Maybe it won't ever happen again. My glance falls on the jagged, glinting quartz, which looks as if it could be blown up to make the terrain for a fantasy adventure movie.

"That isn't your crystal, is it?"

Grandpa laughs. "You're a smart girl. Well, I'll tell you, I took Trudie as I found her, voodoo and all. Besides, I'm at the age where a little extra oomph from here or there doesn't hurt. I'm not arguing. I've given up arguing."

"Your sons haven't."

Grandpa arches one eyebrow at me. "You don't miss much of anything, do you, Margaret?"

Thrilled, I gaze back without speaking. I'm on the verge of telling him all about France, what the trip he gave me gave to me, even about that day in Chartres—though how could I ever say it.

Grandpa reaches for my hand. "You know, you're starting to look a little like Agnes when I first met her. Did I ever tell you how that story goes? Never mind, it bears repeating. She's dancing with this other fellow, you see, down there in St. Louie where I'm only visiting. Her steady beau, I'm told. The beautiful Agnes. Well, I can't help myself—I just cut right in between them. She is that entrancing. I don't know my life has already changed forever, but at least I have sense enough to seize the day."

Grandpa pauses again to wet his lips. "Her father isn't sure about me at all, don't you know, but Agnes, thank goodness, has a mind of her own. And then we marry and all the years go by and I never tell her how—"

"There you are!" Coming into the bedroom, Trudie looks even smaller because I'd just been picturing stately Agnes. "Jack, darling, you haven't had too much of a good thing, have you?"

Grandpa holds out his other hand to her. "Not at all. It's a splendid party, my dear. Margaret and I are just having a nice chat."

Trudie strokes his hand. "There's a lovely cake down there. As soon as I see the whites of your eyes, I'll fire up the candles."

"I'll be right along. Margaret did do her job; she delivered your message. It is I who has been detaining her." He winks at me conspiratorially.

Trudie says, looking at me, "Well, I can see how pleasant that would be. But do come along now, Jack." Carefully she places his hand, his surgeon's hand, back on the bedspread.

"You have my solemn word, my dear."

But when she leaves the room, he doesn't rise.

His eyes flash back to me. "What do you think, Margaret, tell me the truth, haven't I gotten too old for birthdays?"

As I stare at his face on the pillow, everything seems lustrous and peaceful, as if Grandpa and I aren't different ages and there's all the time in the world. "Grandpa, do you remember once when we were visiting and you were babysitting and there was a storm?"

"Just me babysitting? That's a switch. So what happened? Was it an electrical storm?"

I nod. "It woke me up and I went and found you reading."

"And?"

"You just started talking. I sat on your lap. You explained the science of storms to me, all about why the lightning comes before the thunder and so on."

"I did? Well, cheers for me. I must have been a pretty decent grandfather now and then. Did it work? Were you any less afraid?"

"I guess so. In the morning we found branches down all over the yard."

"Oh, yes, those extreme storms. I always worried that one of the big old trees would crash down on the house."

I nod, remembering the trees we played under. I don't want to move. I just want to stay here talking with Grandpa until I don't need to anymore.

"Well, give me a pull up, Margaret. The moment has arrived."

He fixes his suit and hair and asks me to brush the lint off his back, and then in the hallway he says, "Allow me to transport you," and presses the button for the elevator. He hands me into the cage as if I were a lady in long silky skirts; then he steps jauntily in. He winks at me. "Isn't this fun? Just between you and me, I really married Trudie for her elevator."

"I won't tell."

As we descend he says, "We haven't talked about the boy. How is Russell?"

"Incredibly active, Grandpa. He rides his bike like a horse, you know? Always trying to rear up?"

"Oh, I know that boy very well, I've known that boy before. History repeats. You help your mother look after the younger ones then, Margaret?"

"Sometimes."

"But of course you're in college now, I know that. You're well on your way, aren't you? By the by, that's a nice outfit you've got on tonight. Very refreshing."

I'm in *love* with my grandfather.

As the cake is being presented, I hang back a little. The whole room of people is in my view, all the various heads of hair and different faces around Grandpa, all clustered together in the light like a single crop. Even my absent sisters and my brother seem to be here, as if Caroline and Peter had not six separate children but a unitary, all-feeling child, me, who feels now like crying. But I don't cry. I study Lolly, who is complacently licking frosting off her fork.

"Maggie doesn't have any yet!" It's my father's voice, coming toward me. "Here you are, Mags, I've got a piece with your name on it."

I look down at the piece he has chosen for me, but except for a fragment of yellow rose the slab is plain and white. My father has already orbited away, and no one seems to notice as I step backward slowly into the hallway and then pivot toward the stairs.

Up in Grandpa's study I sink into the leather chair, dial the home number, and get the answering machine, Dad's canned, cultured voice. Still I don't cry; I feel what I feel; I eat birthday cake, which is an essential food group all by itself. Every few minutes I press redial. Before me the window of city lights in the dark blue night looks like a frame full of what's called civilization. I'm sitting with it, eating a small, baked piece of it.

In the town of Chartres, the climb from the train station in the heavy mist was like wading back into the centuries when the cathedral was being built. It was easy to imagine all the builders and artisans in wool and linen, and the Black Death, body after body piled in carts, smoke and fear in the streets—all the things

I'd read about. At the top of the hill, archaeologists worked in a dig opposite one of the huge doors. I watched them for quite a while. A few looked about my age.

One of my sisters must be on the phone. I nudge the empty plate aside and rest my head in my arms on Grandpa's desk. The wood smells well cared for. My mouth tastes of sweet.

Grandpa's money gave me a summer in Europe, gave it to his sons, too, though my father prolonged his trip into a decade of study abroad. When I first got over there and saw so many people kissing customarily, I thought with a pang that this was the long-established, ceremonial place my father had left behind when he retraced his path to the New World and got entangled with the younger sister of his best friend and made a family, a big family. Us.

Inside that huge interior space of Chartres, the first second struck me like a sound—I mean, it was like space making its own single sound, which then broke up into many sensations. Echoing footsteps of other people, chilliness, color pulsing high above, all around me a stone forest, a labyrinth designed into the floor at my feet, and of course layers and layers of time, with me inside of it. I began to tread down the ambulatory. Then, between a carved screen and an immense column, I was like struck in the chest. Tears started up. I sort of lost my legs and slumped to the stone floor against the base of the cold tree, with that vaulted shape overhead so beautiful, but as rigid, I thought, as a carcass. For the life of me, I couldn't stop crying—mysterious, soundless heaves and gulps. Thankfully, no one leaned down to question me because I was beyond answering. It was as if I'd walked into something eerie and forceful, having to do absolutely with me. At last I was able to stand up and make my way around the inside curve of the ambulatory behind the chancel. I sank into one of the little wooden chairs in front of a dark Madonna. What made this mother so dark? The crying eased off, and I started settling down. I'd only had two semesters of French then, but a French word, *le sourire*, began to sound over and over in my mind as I returned her gaze.

Someone answers: Russell. The boy.

"Hi, Russ, it's me. What're you doing?"

"Nothing." He's breathing into the phone as if he just got off his bike.

"Did you ride Bronco this afternoon?"

"Nuh, it was raining."

"Oh, that's too bad. Can I talk to Mom, Russ? What's she doing?"

"I don't know, nothing." And then he screams *Mom*!

He's still there, breathing. I can almost smell his warm, little-boy smell. "Well, Russie, maybe Dad'll get home from the airport before you go to sleep."

"Yeah," he says in a husky voice, as if he isn't really counting on it.

"Who is it?" I can hear the alarm in Mom's voice in the background. "Is that your father? Hello, Peter? Is that you?"

And I have to tell her it's just me, her firstborn. One of the girls.

"Where are you calling from, Maggie? Oh, your father isn't going to miss his plane, is he?" I picture her stationary below the high arcing path of the flight Dad isn't even on yet.

"We're at Grandpa's, everything's okay." Then I say in a rush, "Mom, are you all right?"

"What kind of a question is that? Are *you* all right, Maggie?" I can hear Russell close to her, asking for something.

"I'm okay. What are you doing?"

"Supper dishes at the moment." Then she says, "Russell, what *is* it? No, you've had enough for now."

I'm twisting the coils of telephone cord around my hand, almost painfully.

"Maggie? Are you still there? Is it a nice party? What did Trudie serve?"

"Stuffed chicken breasts and salad and some rice thing." Then I remember Lolly. "Mom, guess who's getting married!"

"You?"

"You're kidding."

"Am I? Well, go on, tell me."

I keep coiling and tightening the cord. Somehow the oomph has already gone out of the story. "Ask Dad to tell you."

"Well, I will then if that's how you feel. Russell! That's enough fuss—do you hear me? Maggie, will you please make sure your father gets a cab in plenty of time for his flight? I'm counting on you."

"All right." I want to hang up, and I also want to keep the line open for whenever I still might need it.

"It's probably Lolly who's getting married," my mother goes on. "Rosemary wrote that she has a steady young man. Does it upset you?' "

"No. Yes."

"You know, Maggie, this could be a very good idea for someone like Lolly. Russell! I'm telling you for the last time!"

"Mom? I think I better go."

"All right, sweetie, I'm sorry it's so busy here. Have a safe bus ride back to school—take care of yourself."

"Okay. You, too, Mom." I can hardly get the words out. I feel primed for major waterworks.

She laughs. "Well, thank you—aren't you a thoughtful daughter!"

But I don't cry after all; I stare out into the network of lights. *Margaret, are you grieving?* Yes, no. Maybe this is one of the ways I smile, in the dark, mouth quiet, eyes brimming. I see that history repeats and does not repeat. I see my father coming down out of the skies toward the lights of Chicago. I see the strands that pull him back home, time and again: Caroline, the thick rope of our mother, the kind that in all weathers will hold even a nervous, brilliant man secure, and then the six of us children, just filaments still, but look how we are strong enough to help draw our father down out of the skies.

Could *this*, I wonder, be the secret reason for her children, her many children—to remind him over and over to keep on returning to her and her interesting creation? I hear my own breathing—out, a sigh. How can I even guess why she goes through it?

River Hills

AFTER the shock, after her fury at the lies, hers to herself as much as his to her, when she'd flung obscenities erupting from an unknown self, after all the disorder of having to discover a new place to live, even so, she'd found herself coming around again to gladness—day by day over a season of living alone here in this town where she was anonymous except to a few. People from her past might think she would continue being miserable over what had happened. Not so. This afternoon, for instance, her good feeling brimmed into the November light of the old bank lobby as she helped customers and kept everything in order in her teller's station. It was like the return of an intimate companion, her girlish high spirits, but modulated now by all she had come through and of course by this new trusty-citizen job, which her friend Audrey, in a parallel partition, said went a long way toward helping them both to stay out of trouble.

Mona agreed. She had an energetic imagination, and she could see that too much trouble, if taken too much to heart—that is, considered to be permanent—might turn you into another of those filthy, betrayed, and dismayed women with weather-blasted faces who poke in trash cans and harass people on the streets and in general just throw themselves to the winds. She had no intention of throwing herself to any more winds. All she wanted now was to live simply, going back and forth to work and learning about the town and nursing her dream of one day growing up enough to open her own quirky little shop—funky scrounged objects like brooches and purses and vintage sweaters and buttons, as well as a scattering of her own offbeat creations, maybe even some items sewn to order. But what she wanted most was to find out what it meant that after a childhood of being put down and criticized and a rushed inappropriate marriage, she'd landed here, alone at twenty-three in an unknown river town, working of all places in a financial institution, and feeling—well, all right, as if an essential well-being couldn't be shocked out of her.

All afternoon the feeling stayed, like a buzz of love for everything in particular, as daylight changed over the brown-and-pink terrazzo floor of the lobby and up along the faux marble columns on their real marble bases and in the arched windows trimmed with what might or might not be real mahogany and on the gold leaf of the eggs and darts in the cove molding high above, up there with the opaque lenses of the surveillance cameras. Working accurately and pleasantly inside the decorous, diffuse murmur of the bank, most of the anger and swearing well behind her, wearing the blouse she'd just sewn—dark blue silk with a ripple of bias-cut scarf—she'd felt watched in her bosom happiness.

In the ladies' room at the end of the workday, Audrey called out to her, "Mona, if I ever got engaged, would you do my dresses?"

"From scratch you mean?" Mona listened to them both peeing, female animals now in parallel stalls. She'd never had a sister, just a moody, hypercritical brother, Roger—who'd nevertheless been very helpful when she'd left Jerome, giving her a temporary place to sleep and never demanding that she stiffen her lip, as their fed-up mother put it, and go back and *act* like a wife—but after all a brother could only be a brother, and a sister would be, well, a sister.

"Yes, bride and bridesmaids, the whole works."

Mona called back, "If I did it once, I suppose I could do it again."

But she wasn't so sure she could. Last spring when she'd found out about Jerome, she'd shredded the dress she'd been so enchanted less than a year before to fashion for herself from a bolt-end piece of silk satin, overlaid with a thrift-store lace table-cloth, over-embroidered with her own enhancements—all that fancywork gone in three minutes of rage. Incredible. And then, after savaging the dress, she'd hacked off her hair and might have done much worse if she hadn't dragged herself across state lines like ruined goods and landed in Roger's apartment near the university, where for days on end, picking at take-out food and swearing only when spoken to, she'd practiced being a corpse on his couch under his smelly comforter, the whole business having taken almost all the fun out of being a girl.

At the washbasins she spoke into the mirror. "Are you saying you're getting closer to it, Audrey?"

"Don't hold your breath." Audrey, leaning in close to the mirror to apply eyeliner, mascara, the whole arsenal, flashed Mona a look.

"Don't worry. You can die holding your breath."

Mona creamed on lipstick and went to get her coat. In the hallway hung an oil painting of one of the past presidents of the bank, a man named Graves, according to the little brass plate, Henry Graves—a straight man, as far as Mona could make out, and she did consider herself less fatefully clueless than before. Graves was a good name for him: his face was dignified and calm, his eyes large and rather dewy, she thought, for a banker, his lips full and not in a hurry to pronounce on anything, though capable of sound utilitarian advice; he was the kind of father she could imagine listening to. Maximize, my dear, he would say, simply learn to maximize the good consequences; be bold; do not look back.

Yes! That's what I'm trying to do, she would say to him. And as if in proof she would offer her refusal to be cheated out of the rest of her life.

Audrey emerged, made-up for the night. "I wish you'd change your mind and come with us, Mona. You might win, you know."

"Oh no, thanks, I'd just end up sorry."

"How do you even know?"

"Just a feeling. It's not for me, not now." She liked Audrey and the others, Betsey and Janet, but she didn't ever want to go to the casino with them. The movies, yes, and beforehand they'd eat at Chinese Garden or even the hotel or that place near the old ice harbor with the stamped-metal wall covering, and a few times over the summer and early fall they'd driven in Audrey's car to picnic in the park above the locks and dams at the north end of town. But the casino, no: she didn't even want all those scenarios with deluded players to be in her head. Delusion was what she didn't need any more of.

"Well, bye-bye then. Be good."

"Absolutely," said Mona. She put on her new wool-lined rain-coat—"mussel" the color had been labeled—in front of the painted gaze of Henry Graves. She wished she could see his hands, but they were behind the frame, as Henry Graves himself was beyond this life. How soon it all passes away, he'd say to her—the money and the suits of clothes and the terrazzo floors—but nothing about his manner would cause her to be agitated about the brevity of what she herself had barely yet tasted. His composure, a kind of acceptance, was in itself, she saw, part of his enjoyment in the passing scene. In her employee review Henry

Graves would be interested in all sorts of things beyond her teller's duties, and she would begin her story not with her beginnings—her pained, disappointed mother and her irritable, domineering, now dead father, or with the whole mess of her aborted marriage—but rather with the solo trip on the train, how her fury had been sucked out into the horizon beyond the traveling window, how she'd begun to understand the thievery of unfit thoughts that could darken and distort each frame as it occurred, and then how on the return she'd stepped down as if prompted to stretch on a station platform at the base of a bluff and looked across the river at a small city in the hills under a noontime sun in brisk spring, how she'd run back into the train for her bags and jacket and then stood on the platform watching the train pull the tail segments of itself out of the tunnel in the bluff and continue on east without her. For an interval everything had stopped; then once again, in the wind, on the platform, newly begun. Here. During her story Henry Graves would nod. I noticed you right away, he said, as if he himself had been on the platform. You can go places.

The feeling of surveillance didn't stop when she left behind the bank cameras and the portrait of Henry Graves and set out to retrace the downtown blocks of four- and five-storied businesses and shops, of post office and square, on toward the little cable car shelter at the base of the bluff. The watcher was like her real life, keeping track of her, knowing what she still did not, perhaps borrowing this face, that face on the street to display one more piece of her education. She buttoned her raincoat against the chill. At five-thirty it was already dusky now, tonight a flaring of sunset in the sky at the top of the bluff, that fire, too, watching her, beneath its secretive lid of blue-gray cloud.

Every workday she rode the little cable car down and then up the bluff, between the red sandstone bank building in the lower town and her shabby, comfortable rooms in the nineteenth-century clapboard house above. Every day she walked about carrying her few parcels and stopping here or there to see more of the town—the Carnegie library and its plain addition, the many churches, the eating places, the post office with its Depression-era murals of farmers and miners and Indians, the old square of maples and lindens and benches and grass—an old graveyard, said a marker, bronze on granite, from a long-ago epidemic of cholera. Once, stepping into a red-stone funeral home and for a moment sharing the parlor with only the waxlike deceased, she'd thought about the face of her own father on the satin coffin pillow last January, in whose presence she'd been too astonished by his absolute absence of anger to cry; but now she did, alone with the stranger in his bank of flowers, telling him that she was only asking to learn how to live. Advice from the corpse had not been forthcoming; he'd said everything with flowers, with the doneness of his life. What a shame, she'd thought through her tears, to send that superior blue suit down with him to the grave.

Tonight, beyond the business district and into the last few blocks before the bluff, she paused in front of a row of redbrick and stone houses from the early town. Many generations of people had lived in these houses, experiencing their lives, had passed through these doors, over and over. Imagine: so many hearts carried around in different bodies, different clothes. At that moment a glint from the sunset sky at the top of the bluff, like an identical pulse, caught her up, and for a moment she and the sky and the row of old experienced houses made up a surprising paradise, like a town of untouchable gold hidden all this time inside the other.

One of the two small cable cars waited empty at the bottom.

Mona climbed in and pulled the bell cord for the operator in the station house at the top, the man with the withered arm who ever since her first trip down in the spring had seemed to be keeping track of her. The six seats, three on each side, rose like wooden stairs; she sat on a middle one and held to its edge, expecting the start-up jolt. Just then a guy in a many-colored knit hat, hoisting high a bike, a bag of ballistic material strapped across his back, leapt aboard.

Mona slanted her knees aside as he slid the bicycle up the stepped aisle. "Sorry," he said, breathing as if he'd sprinted the last block.

"No problem." She glanced at him. His eyes were green. She looked away, toward the station on the bluff.

Up the steep grade they took off; the second car, descending at the same old-fashioned rate they mounted, would pass theirs at the midpoint where the tracks bulged like a zipper pulling apart. She was conscious of the side of her face above the upturned collar of her coat. She was conscious of what showed and of what did not—inside the coat her body, which had been used and misused, but only with one man, and inside everything the bright current of more than blood. She could hear the young man breathing. Thickets of wild rose and forsythia on either side of the track had bloomed months ago; now goldenrod, asters, and the tall heads of sumac still held traces of degraded, frostbitten color. A book of local history she'd gotten from the library pictured former vineyards and orchards in orderly rows on this and other hills, switchback paths, a Stone Age burial mound on one of the crests, on the flood plain below a few of the steeples that still spiked up among the downtown buildings, and always, then and now, and eons before the buried bones of anyone, the river beyond.

"Two more weeks and they'll close down on us."

"Pardon?" said Mona, turning.

"The funicular. Thanksgiving, and that's it."

"Oh. I didn't know. How do people manage then?" Thanks-giving: Mona realized she hadn't thought about being alone for holidays, eating alone. But for now she had the word *funicular* to savor.

"Me, I bike the long way around, get the car out only when I have to. And you?"

"What's winter like here?"

"Sort of pretty, but the hills can get slippery. You're new?"

"Yes, since spring." His eyes were outstanding, so many crin-kled greens.

Now came the second car, clattering and creaking next to theirs, and both she and he, as if similarly spellbound, watched it descend the grade they had just climbed. Mona wasn't going to get all excited about happening to ride with a brilliant-eyed guy wearing a messenger bag. She reminded herself how susceptible she'd been to Jerome, his dark eyes, his thick hair and muscular body, even the distressed glamour, the irresistible patina, of his leather jacket—all tangible evidence, she'd imagined, that he was the one who'd materialized to catapult her over another stifling year of living at home and slogging off to the ugly buildings of the community college. *Damn foolishness*, her brainy brother Roger had said before the wedding, during, and after, but as he'd been saying more or less the same thing to her all her life, she'd interpreted it as just more of his peculiar form of brotherly love. No, she wasn't going to get excited about sitting with her knees pressed against the sleek bicycle of the most interesting guy she'd seen since she'd gotten to town. *Simmer down*, her father used to command if he came home from the warehouse and found her in one of her giggly, rackety, or enthralled moods; he'd wanted a lid on the household, his lid. He'd been glad to get her married off, she could tell. And now, well—he was dead.

With a bump the car stopped at the top by the cable turnstile.

"Excuse me, I'll get this out of the way." He lofted the bike to the platform by the operator's house. She gathered up her purse and the bag with her bank shoes and stepped out. The sun had not yet set, quite. "Have a good one," he said, as if already in flight, in the leap not yet taken onto the seat of his bike, but then, looking at her once more, he paused. "So you've been riding up and down every day?"

"Yes, all summer."

"Funny I haven't seen you."

"Maybe you have."

"No, but now I'll remember to look." He adjusted the bag. "Well."

"Good night," she said, keeping the lid on herself.

"All right, so long. Take care."

All this, she knew, had been observed by the stringy operator with his poor, clenched arm and perched hat from whom all summer she'd bought tickets and with whom she'd exchanged greetings, each time glancing beyond his scrutiny of her into the brown interior of the housing for gear box and switches and tools and dilapidated chair and magazines and flickering TV. Was she from here, he'd wanted to know at the beginning. What did he mean, she asked. Oh, he thought he used to see her at the high school basketball games, sitting with the girls on the bleachers— he still went to them, why not, they were free. No, she hadn't grown up here, she'd told him, but knew as she spoke, as if for the first time accepting the idea of freedom, that there was no place now she couldn't encounter who she was to be. Tonight, in a plaid wool jacket and the same small, odd hat, an oily gray, like a remnant of an indeterminate war, he was leaning on one arm, his good arm, on the ledge of the open ticket window. He could be thirty, or fifty; he still went to high school games and noticed the girls. How did he keep warm now, in his little house? There must be some sort of heater, powered by the electricity that also ran the motor for the cars. What would he do, come Thanksgiving?

"Good night," she said to him, and he said *good night then*, still watching. At the beginning of the summer he'd offered her a street map of the town, more detailed than any handed out by the Visitors' Bureau, with every little twist and turn that accommodated the hills, some of the streets, he said, having started out as paths for long-gone cows.

Mona had four uphill blocks now to her rooms. The young man and his bicycle had disappeared. If she saw him again tomorrow, or the next, all right, that might mean something.

Ahead was a vacant street, edged on one side by a limestone wall shoring up the terrace above, a cascade of drying vines, fallen leaves clustered where they had blown and stuck, everywhere the rustle and tartness of fall. Mona plodded upward, as had the humble cows. She had a lot of life yet to make her way through. From one of the old houses came the scent of burning fragrant wood, a real fireplace fire, not the electric logs of Mrs. Willet, her landlady. Mona hadn't given thought to Thanksgiving, and there was no doubt a heap more of unthought-of future that would be dumped on her this winter as some of the freshness of the adventure meant to take her away from disappointment passed into harder weather. Climbing, she focused on her walking shoes and the fallen leaves and the bits of stone that had sheared off the walls. That guy with the bicycle must live up here somewhere—eat and sleep and work on his bike and his computer, or whatever it was he carried in that high-tech bag.

Growing up, she'd wanted—what—to be connected, not to another person, or to an idea, or to anything she could name; she'd catch a brief sense of it in the mirror, a crucial thrill, like sitting in the same circle of experience with what thrilled you, aroused by the same energy, which was always going back and forth, back and forth in a kind of endless transaction, a never-ending encounter.

Some of these cement walks were cracked and tilted. It was a part of town where many of the large houses had been turned into multiple units, porches sagged, paint was long overdue, and a coach house here and there had nearly caved in under the strain of insufficient funds. Mrs. Willet blamed the deferred maintenance of her own house on the appalling financial difficulties of being left a widow.

Mona had offered that her mother, too, was a widow, a new one.

Oh, my dear, when was the passing? Mrs. Willet pounced upon it.

January, Mona said matter-of-factly, resolved that she would answer any questions about the whole past shocking year in a plain, truthful voice, as economically as possible. But as Mrs. Willet reverted swiftly to her own all-consuming case, Mona had been required to put forth only the bare facts of death and divorce—and, most important, proof that she could pay the rent.

Every night Mrs. Willet watched her television below the room where Mona had set up her sewing machine, near the window. It comforted Mona to know hers was one small, lighted room nestled with so many others into the interesting hills. Had Henry Graves once lived up here—maybe with the same fascination as she for the folding into one another of the peopled bluffs? Tonight after dinner she would try to finish the gray-and-brown tweed jacket, the sleeves of the pale green lining joined to its bodice pieces and then the whole silky interior slip-stitched in place.

Now a dog came directly toward her down the walk, a black-and-white mongrel with an alert, fringed contour of determination who sniffed her shoes, her knees, and her bags and then continued on his mission. She turned to watch him trotting downward through the domain of seasons, so purposeful and precise in the crisp air, as if already alerted to the oncoming vehemence of winter. Every creature, she thought, had to live inside the sovereignty of time, to go through one thing after another. That's the way it was. But time had also made the hills, it kept too much from happening at once, and it did give an afflicted past the chance to be the past.

When she turned back to face the last half block of her climb, her heart jumped as she saw a figure seated on the front steps of Mrs. Willet's house, in the dusk and the chill, a guy with tousled hair, something utterly familiar about the tilt of his body, the way his elbows rested on his knees, his hands hanging between his legs. In a few more steps she was certain but still too far away to call out the name of her brother, who now looked sideways and saw her and pushed himself up from the steps and came out through the gate toward her, a silhouette made of shadows yet also the substance of her only sibling.

"Roger? My God. What're you doing here?" He looked good. He also looked, somehow, tragic.

"I don't know."

"What do you mean—you always know what you're doing." Now she was close enough to put her arms around him, and she was glad he was here to touch. The wool of his pea jacket felt chilled. "Have you been out here long?"

"I don't know, awhile. Your landlady wouldn't let me in."

"She didn't know who you are."

"I tried to tell her who I am."

"Why didn't you wait in your car?"

"I don't know, I was sick of it."

Mona looked toward the house and saw a curtain drop back into place.

"Come on, let's get inside. You also could have called me at work, you know." She was terribly happy to see him; she was also—what—cautioned? "Just tell me how you are."

"I had the flu or something," said Roger on the way upstairs. "I'm okay."

"This is amazing—I mean, you've never done anything like this—how'd you know I'd even come home tonight?"

"Took a chance. Anyway, you did it to me. Showed up out of the blue."

"All right, we're even." She turned on lights in the little kitchen. She had three rooms. This was happening. "Take off your coat. You can put your duffel over there for now. Are you hungry?"

"I suppose I can eat. Do you have a beer or anything?"

"What do you want with alcohol if you've had the flu? No, I don't have a beer or anything."

"How come?"

"I stopped going there. Roger, tell me, what are you really doing here? Never mind—that can wait. Please, take off your coat." She filled the kettle and set it on the stove. The unfinished tweed jacket hung in the living room; she had six eggs left; either she or Roger would have to sleep on the couch. But, how amazing, here was her brother. She remembered how he'd ripped the comforter off her one morning when she'd been hiding out in his apartment and told her he couldn't keep running a heartbreak hotel; she was fouling up his studies, obstructing his social life. *Social life?* Since when? she'd asked. There was actually a girl? Suppose so, he'd answered, but the point was that Mona had to do something to change her perspective, and it was that very day she got packed off on the train to look at the America whose history Roger was so intent on penetrating, clicking his way through text after text into—he'd tried to explain to her one night—a universal archive deeper and, yes, freer than the prevailing and pernicious supplies of untruth. Still furious at everything, Mona had allowed herself a long, audible fart under the already obnoxious comforter and drawled that he sounded impressively inspired, or something bratty like that. But the truth was that the gift of the trip, maybe of America, of Earth, had changed her life.

"What're you smiling at?" he said, still standing in his coat, still hanging onto his duffel, his thick hair still in the shape of the wind. "Has anyone ever told you how foolish it looks to smile too much?"

That's just the sort of thing he used to do when they were growing up: make her self-conscious about her happy moods, even make fun of her teeth.

"Maybe I'm glad to see you."

"Well, that's something anyway." He grimaced and looked around the kitchen. "Wow, talk about Midwest noir."

"What? Mrs. Willet and her furnishings are as innocuous as they come."

"That's exactly what I'm talking about."

"Roger, you're here with me, your little sister, not in some graduate seminar."

"This is me—take it or leave it."

"All right then, whatever. Will you eat an omelet? Don't answer—it's all I've got. How's Mom—have you talked with her lately?"

"Sort of. Not really."

"How are the migraines, do you know?"

"No. We've been talking money. She's ungovernable."

"And you're the governor?"

"Someone has to do it."

Mona went over to him, took the duffel from his hand and set it in the corner, and then began unbuttoning his coat. "Why don't you go look around, make yourself at home? I'll bring tea."

"I had the flu."

"I know. Go on. Move."

She took a deep breath and slid the frying pan out of the clattery stove drawer. With a jolt she felt again her mother's terrible humiliation over the mess her headstrong daughter had made of marriage, the crying shame. For a little while before the wedding, in her mother's burst of giddy pep over her own mother-of-the-bride dress and the idea of having a handsome son-in-law, Mona had enjoyed the novelty of maternal favor—what girl wouldn't eat up the attention? Then, so soon, she became once more Mona the troublemaker, the provoker of headaches.

Brother and sister ate with their plates on their knees sitting side by side on Mrs. Willet's beige couch, the teapot and mugs and salt and pepper on a tray balanced on the cushion between them. There were mushrooms and garlic and scallions and broccoli bits and goat cheese inside the folds of egg, cilantro on top, a dollop of chutney. She had made toast and spread it with sesame butter.

"This is really weird food—but not half bad," he said. "When did you learn how to cook?"

"I cooked at home a lot—you must remember. Mom would be lying down with another headache and I'd be cooking."

"Maybe I forgot."

"But I didn't make stuff like this. We ate wrong—are you aware of that?"

"If I were picky, I'd have starved long ago." He pointed across the room with his fork. "Where'd you get that sewing machine?"

He'd noticed: how touching. "Bought it," she said, "with the money from the wedding stuff."

"You should have gotten a computer instead."

"I don't need a computer."

"That's stupid—everyone needs a computer. So what are you trying to sew?"

"A jacket."

"You should be doing other things."

"Roger. Sewing is something I know how to do—I'm *good* at it."

"Why do you waste your time worrying about clothes?"

"I don't worry about clothes, I enjoy them." She thought about how pleasure in clothes was one of the few things she had shared with their mother, who had taken her shopping, who had taught her—impatiently, nervously, her hands sometimes trembling, yet still had taught her—to plan, to cut, to sew.

"Clothes are part of what's wrong with the world."

"Come on, if people wear clothes, they might as well be nice ones."

"What's it for, Mona? Tell me."

"Why are we talking about this?"

"Clothes got Mom absolutely nowhere—you, either."

"You can be so awful to me."

"Reality is good."

"This isn't the only reality—it's just the way you think." She noticed that in spite of his strong opinions, he had managed to clean his plate. "You think I'm frivolous." She took his plate and stacked it on her own. "Well, that's not the way I look at things." Then, close to lapsing into foul words, she carried the tray into the kitchen. If all boys were this fragile, this bossy, why on earth were they allowed to run the world? Which, if you were looking for what was wrong with the whole setup, was more to the point than people's costumes. She rinsed the plates and scrubbed the omelet pan and the cutting board like mad, and when she returned to the living room Roger's head was tipped back, his mouth open, eyes closed. Look at him. No matter how much he tormented her, she could never see herself as anything other than in relation to him—a brother, how mysterious.

Mona stole to her sewing table and switched on the floor lamp and the hooded bulb over the needle of the machine. It was quiet, nothing even from Mrs. Willet's television; maybe the widow with her appalling lack of funds was at this very moment standing on a ladder with her ear to the ceiling. Be careful, everybody. All the pieces were now ready for the assembly of the jacket, just these lining sleeves to pin and stitch, which perhaps she could do without waking him. It was the sort of jacket Henry Graves, anyway, would admire. Why wasn't sewing as good a place as any to put your mind? Sometimes she even imagined that the stitches might work a double order, making something new and at the same time mysteriously unmaking or disallowing catastrophe. She set to work, and in a few moments, in the stillness of the house, in the stilling of his criticism, once again recognized her gladness still softly pumping.

Now and then she glanced over at her brother's abandoned sprawl. What a miracle if this good feeling could jump from her to him, from her hands, say, just that short way across the room, filling him, stilling even his need for criticism. She must never forget it was he who had given her the trip west, those days of soulful landscape in the window of the train when she'd done nothing but doze and look, doze and look, letting herself merge into the plains, the immense sky, the never-ending language of clouds; then one evening, as the plains were rising into foothills, she'd felt as if she were catching herself midair, as if the backlit distant mountains were an abyss and not a soaring range, and she got off that train and waited for another, heading back the way she'd come, and vowed to work on what she hoped was not spoiled: herself. It was as if, on that train, between one moment and the next, she'd been nudged into a new condition. A day later, again as if prodded, she'd come upon this town and then within one magical week the job and the furnished rooms. No matter what Roger said to her, she must never forget it was in part because of him that she was here.

She rested her hands a moment and observed the way he was put together, his body and his face. Neither of them much resembled their parents. Years ago, when she'd been fourteen maybe and he then sixteen, during a phase when he'd become even grouchier than usual, he'd entered her room one night in his underwear and stood beside her desk and asked her to consider what he called a bracing possibility: suppose they both had entirely different parents, a fact concealed from the two of them all this time.

What could be so great about being an adopted child or a changeling?

Ah, there you go, he'd said, changelings would be an even better idea, very Shakespearean; it would explain everything.

Explain what?

But he couldn't say.

When the pinning was done, she positioned the matched pieces of lining material under the needle and pressed the foot pedal—good, even with the whirring and clicking he stayed asleep. Too bad he'd had the flu; maybe the virus was still irritating his system. She wondered if Roger even remembered having talked about being adopted. It was common, wasn't it, for kids to go through a time of thinking their real parents were elsewhere or some other monumental secret was being kept from them? But for Mona's part, if she'd ever felt like a changeling, it had probably been during her own exuberant, frowned-upon moods, when she'd wanted to shake one truth above all out of her parents: Why weren't they happy or even just pleased once in a while? All the forms taken by their discontent, now that she thought back, seemed like crimes against humanity—anyway, nothing to be proud of.

The scissors slipped and clanged to the floor. One second she was just thinking about the past and snipping threads and then—what had happened?

Now he was awake, but saying nothing. Under his abstracted eyes, she picked up the fallen scissors and resumed sewing, but warily. At last he got up and tramped off to the bathroom. When he came out, he didn't return to the couch but stood looming in the middle of the small room. She paused again in her work. "Yes?" she said at last. "You look like you're about to speechify."

"I was going to complain about that beer."

"You could always go out and get one if it's that important."

"You know a word I hate?"

"No, I don't."

"Merchandise."

Mona thought about her dreams of a shop, the windows, the bits and pieces of harmless—she hoped harmless—adornment.

"Merchandise? Roger, why on earth would you hate a neutral word like merchandise? It's innocent."

"I don't know."

"You've said *I don't know* an awful lot since you got here."

"Good. That must mean I'm wiping the slate."

"Did you have a high fever with that flu?"

"You think I've gone off?" He smiled crookedly.

"I don't know what to think—I'm waiting for you to speak out."

"What do you mean?"

"You came here for some reason."

"Mona, why did you ever marry that jerk?"

"Is that what all this is about? Well, all right, why didn't you, for one, tell me he was a jerk?"

"I did."

"I don't think you did."

"I did, I said it was silly, you were too young, I said he's a jerk."

"All right, but you didn't say what kind." Then she stared at him, something worming up. "Did you *know*?"

"Not exactly."

"But you didn't exactly stop me."

"No! I've never been able to stop anyone in this family from doing anything!" Mona thought that at last Mrs. Willet might get her desired earful. Then, in a quieter voice, he said, "Maybe I wanted you to find out and come to your senses once and for all."

"Oh God . . . Roger."

"Do you realize how weird our family is? Mona?"

Mona folded her work and turned out the sewing lights. She slid the scissors away from the edge of the table. Then she faced him. "Roger. Let's talk about you. Did you come here to confess this to me?"

"Who's confessing anything?"

"All right, all right!" She sprang up and without a word went to the hallway and got her purse and both their coats. She threw his at him, hard.

"Where're we going?"

"Out for a beer."

By now it was too cold and windy to suggest the cable car. The town, sparked with lights here on the hills and down there on the plain, was the same as other nights and also not. It was an unrepeatable night of time. She had no idea where to take her brother; then she remembered a place with a bar of dark wood out near the locks and dams where she and Audrey and Betsey and Janet had eaten a good fish sandwich one night. Roger could get his beer and also enjoy deriding the mounted catfish and painted riverboat scenes, and he could order French fries, one of his weaknesses. His car even smelled of fries. She directed him down the hill and after some wrong turns got them on the right streets to the North End. It was nine o'clock. In another two weeks it would be Thanksgiving. She thought about the guy on the cable car, his breathing, his eyes, and the hard metal sculpture of the bicycle.

In the parking lot Roger turned off the motor, but his hands stayed on the wheel. A mercury vapor lamp above the car cast his face in a greenish sheen, and Mona supposed she looked the same. At home the tweed jacket would be as she left it, like a mold about to be filled by her, in which she could move into the world, speak as herself.

"Mona, have you been tested?"

"What? You came all this way to ask me that?"

"I don't know, partly."

"So what else? Say everything."

"I don't know what."

"I think you do." She waited. She waited a long time. A freight train wailed at one of the street crossings not far behind them, on this side of the river. People passed in front of the car, even a family with little kids kept out at this hour. She felt pity for those children under the ghoulish nightlights, pity for their long childhoods, their dependency—and for all the lies they might endure.

Then she said, "Please, let's have it out."

"Damn it, Mona! Don't you know there is no *have*, there is no *out*?"

"Would you stop, just stop trying to prove how smart you are? I already know that—I've had to know it all my life." She flung open the door on her side. "Let's go in—we're both a sickly green out here. The plain answer to your question is yes, results negative."

Roger banged his palms on the steering wheel. "Okay, that's something anyway."

Inside they were put in a booth with a small red-shaded lamp flanked by ketchup and sugar and salt and pepper. Roger picked up the ketchup bottle and set it in front of his place. "Now we're cooking." He even grinned, but crookedly again, self-consciously, like a parody.

If they were in a movie, she thought, they'd be extras, faces panned by the camera on its way to the next part in the showy main plot, leaving them alone in a booth to figure out their own.

"So what did you mean about Mom? She's still so mad at me it's hard to call her—and she never calls me. She never writes."

"She's a disaster," he said. "I don't think she even cares about us. It's like she's setting herself up to give us a huge amount of trouble some day. Mark my words. I try to talk to her about practical things, and all she can go on about is how I should be glad she gets up every day and dresses well and keeps a refrigerator that doesn't look like museum when you open the door. She's taken none of my advice about the money, none. She's impossible." His voice had risen.

"Maybe she doesn't want your advice. You do know an awful lot, Roger, but you don't know everything."

"I know some damn broker is in the middle of churning everything."

"Is that a bad thing?"

He groaned and leaned forward, covering his face with his hands. He had nice hands, Mona thought. Nimble. In his apartment last spring she'd been fascinated to watch them tapping and racing over his computer keys late into the night, in and in, link to link, on a trail of ghostly geography.

Finally he said, "Okay, I don't know everything—like why you of all people thought you had to get married."

"You're on that again? Suppose I wanted some freedom."

"Beep—wrong answer."

"Suppose I thought marriage was what people do—especially people who want to get away from home."

"Mona, what age do you think you're living in?"

"Good question—I've been asking Henry Graves the same thing."

"Henry who? God, you can't be dating again!"

Mona said nothing. Talking with Roger was like trying to find your way around town without a map, only the sense that in some way you'd never understand you had to keep traveling with this person.

Roger did order fries—that much was predictable. His beer arrived, and fortified by the first gulp he said, "You know, Mona, there are places in the world where girls have to do what their brothers tell them to."

"Pardon me?"

"I'm not kidding."

"Roger, do you know you're not making sense?"

"Of course I am."

"No, you're not. You don't want me married, but you don't want me to be free to live my own life, either."

"Admit you need advice."

"Maybe so, but I'm not always required to take it from you."

"You should."

"Let's talk about you. What about that possible girlfriend?"

"Impossible. Anyway, I don't think I'll ever get married. I'm never going to turn into Dad."

Mona leaned back with her coke. "Where are you going with this?"

His fries came, and after he'd bloodied them with ketchup, he said, "You're a baby."

"Will you please just say what you have to say straight out?"

"Who's Henry Graves?"

"A banker."

"Banks are creepy—I always hated to go with Dad. Banks make me feel as if I should be richer or something."

"They're part of the world."

"They're part of the problem. Money only gets you what money can buy. I don't want this world the way it is. I'm sick of it. I want to lose this world—do you know what I mean?"

Mona thought about her shop—the pretty merchandise. "How's your work going?"

"It feels like it's going nowhere. I'm sick of it. My stomach is a mess."

"I thought you loved your work."

"Everything's the same, everything's flat. Equivalent. Do you know what I mean? I'm sick of history, there's too much to go on, nothing changes, the absurdity is nauseating."

"Why don't you change your perspective—like you told me to? Now *that* was great advice, Roger. I mean, really, that trip—I hope I've thanked you enough. Maybe you could just get away from things yourself."

"I am away." Roger stared at her, his face a degree more relaxed, as if he wanted to be saying something else entirely. But then he squashed another pinch of fries into the ketchup and filled his mouth. "There is no *away*."

Grow up, she wanted to tell her older brother, but instead she said, "Why are you eating fries if your stomach is a mess?"

"Why aren't you getting more education, Mona? You shouldn't be dating anybody yet."

"I'm not. Henry Graves is dead—it's a personal joke—sorry."

"Not funny. A dead man. God, Mona, you're not normal."

Mona looked around the bar. You could monitor a place like this all night and even with surveillance cameras and hidden mikes never be able to figure out what people were saying to each other.

"So do you think you're better than Dad was?"

"Yes. Shit, I don't know."

Mona looked away again. There were voices all around them, country music she hadn't been paying much attention to—something about a road, a lonesome road; of course. She felt like crying.

The best times with Dad had been when he'd taken her down to the warehouse with him, and she'd gotten to be his daughter, in dress-up clothes, made so much of by the other men that for a while, like a reprieve, he'd find little wrong with her himself.

To think of their father, flat out and cold, never again to feel his attention swinging her way—to be crying inside in the middle of a kitschy bar—so was this called grief?

"I'm so mad at him I could piss," said Roger.

"You're mad at him for dying?"

"I almost killed him once."

He stared at her, hard, like a dare.

"Go on."

"What do you remember about the fire?"

"What fire?"

"The warehouse! Mona, wake up."

"That was a long time ago."

"It was yesterday."

"You weren't there, were you?"

"I'd give anything to get it out of me." Roger had stopped consuming the fries, even the beer. "He dragged me out of bed to go down and see it. The smell stays here." He clutched at his throat. Then he started talking, and it was as if she'd already heard his words, even when she hadn't; as if even when she hadn't, she'd been thinking about her brother, year after year. In the bar he conjured for her the enormous charred box, gaping windows, water from the fire hoses already freezing like crazy, filthy frosting on what had overnight become a profitable ruin.

"He wanted me to vouch for him. He wanted me to stand beside him. He wanted us to look like a normal father and son who had to leave their beds because the family business was burning sky high."

"I never knew all that."

"You never knew anything, that's a big part of the problem. What's the matter now—why are you crying?"

"Why do you always blame me? You know what? If you want me to have patience with you, you're going to have to stop abusing me."

"This isn't abuse."

"Of course it is!"

"You don't even know what abuse is."

"Well, all right, let me ask you, do you consider yourself better than me?"

"What does that have to do with anything?"

In their own booth, they were alone; no one else cared. She fumbled for a tissue and got done as fast as she could with the crying business, no help from him either.

"What do you really know about Dad?" he asked.

"Bad heart, short temper. Bossy." It was hard for her to look straight on at her brother. "He was pretty good at business, wasn't he?"

"Well, I'm here to tell you he was an arsonist and a cheat." Roger sucked in beer. His face was set. "And I'm the one who knows it."

"You mean he started it himself?"

"Bingo. Brilliant."

Even as she grabbed at the scrap of ironic praise, she was disgusted with her need, with her vulnerability to his opinion. Her vulnerability. Period. She drank from her sweet Coke, but it wasn't what she wanted. She looked away, toward the room of night people. Were Audrey and Betsey and Janet still at the casino at this hour? She imagined them giggling, shaking dice, still believing they staying were out of trouble. What on earth was everyone hoping for?

"How can you be sure?"

"Because I can't breathe," he said. "Because I can still smell it. Because he's not dead, he sucks my breath, he always took too much of the power."

"Let's get out of here," said Mona. She slid to the edge of the booth. Now that he was into the words she hadn't known she was asking for, he was geared to go on, and on and on, stupid tragic history without end.

"I thought you wanted to have it out." He stared at her.

It was like those nights in his apartment when with unblinking eyes burning in the light of the monitor, he slammed open the portals to site after site in what must have been a quest to rescue himself from the flat-out awfulness. On his deep couch she had turned away, slept; she had pretended not to be thinking too much about her brother. "Roger, please." She felt sick from the Coke. Her eyes were scratchy with fatigue. *Give it up*, someone called—or was it *live it up*?

"I've got to get outside—give me the keys—I'll wait in the car." She stood, but he did not.

He tossed down more beer, and she turned away without the keys.

Hey, over here, sweetheart, a man called out. There was laughter.

"Reality too much for you?" He had caught up and grabbed her arm as she crossed the room. "Little Mona doesn't want the true story?"

"Roger, please."

"*Roger, please*," he hissed in her ear, but she kept on walking.

HELP WANTED, NIGHTS read a sign in the front window.

It was easier to breathe outside. The same light cast its greenish sheen over the car, but there was something else. "Look, frost." Mona scraped her fingernails over the windshield. Her nausea passed, and in the cold she felt solid in her bones, fierce. They stood on opposite sides of the car with the silvered metal field of the roof between them. "Want to see the locks and dams?" She was thinking of the cataracts from open sluice gates, of the wide river, of the scouring wind, the one wind and the water. Why did people seem to go out of their way to make peaceful living so difficult?

"You're a baby," said Roger as he drove.

She spoke nothing but the directions to the river.

A flag still flapped on the pole by the maintenance building. Inshore were two domestic buildings with lights burning. She got out of the car.

"Where are you going?" said Roger.

People just didn't trust happiness, she thought. She could hear him striding after her to the chain-link fence. The locks themselves, the nearest one closed by chevron-shaped gates and filled to the upper level of the river, were flooded with light from the control towers, but here near the metal fence it was shadowy. Down the line some boys slumped against the fence were laughing under the wind, doing whatever it was they were doing, raising muffled hell. Far out over the water a lone figure walked along a kind of catwalk on the rim of the dam, between two of the towers. Mona felt sorry for the river, for the massive impediment of the dam, yet the water shone.

Roger stood next to her, his fingers laced in the fence links, his whole body rattling the mesh toward him, away, toward him and away. "I'm big," he said. "You're small."

"How did you almost kill him?" Her breath made a cloud and then became part of the night.

"There was a big hole where a window had been. He was standing right in it. He had forgotten all about me. He was done needing me. No one was looking—I could have pushed him, it would have looked like a fall. He ruined me. He ruined all of us."

"No."

"Yes."

"Not me. Not you, either, unless you think it."

"You can't think some things away. Mona, listen to me."

She looked up at him, and at that instant, as if in helpless gravitation, his face inclined toward her, his lips bulging into— what—a kiss, descending? Quickly she looked away and stood very straight in the wind, in the fierce hard structure of her bones, gazing toward the river that kept going, kept going. "Go ahead, I'm listening."

Again he rattled the fence with the force of his body.

"Admit you're not all right here by yourself."

"Why don't you admit *you're* not all right?"

"Yeah, well, I may be sort of crazy but I'm lovable."

"Could you please stop rattling the fence?"

"Listen to me, Mona. You and I should at least live in the same place."

"Last spring you told me to get out."

"Well, that was then. I've been thinking. You obviously need someone to look out for you."

Mona heard the boys laughing down the line. She used to laugh like that with her girlfriends, goofily, when they were trying to spirit late-afternoon food up to her room without waking her mother or rousing Roger from his studies. Here, she appeared to be the only girl around, unless in one of the keepers' houses lived a woman now glancing from a window toward the man pacing along the rim of the dam. People just wanted to love life, Mona thought, to keep some sort of faith, but they didn't know the secrets.

"I don't know why Jerome did what he did," she heard herself say, each word slipping out into the embrace of the night. "Why do you think he did what he did when he had *me?*"

"Admit your mistakes, Mona. Admit you're not all right here."

"You don't see me, Roger. You don't really see me."

"Yes, I do, I've seen you my whole life, and my idea makes a lot of sense, when you think about it. We could even share an apartment, split expenses. Money's going to be a problem for all of us, you know. Leave this backwater—it's a dead end here—we could look out for each other."

"No. Not now." She heard the sound of the water, how it was made first of space, an unimaginable spaciousness. Then she said, "But thank you, Roger—thank you for thinking about me."

"You're afraid," said Roger.

"Call it anything you like."

She turned around and gazed back at the town spread across the flatlands and up into the ancient hills beneath the vast sky of wind and hidden light. "This is where I'm living," she said. "I'm fine. This is how I'm going to live for now."

"You're missing the boat here."

"Roger, when do you think we'll ever learn how to talk to each other?"

He shook the fence. "I'd like to know what you think we're doing now."

Time's Body

❧

WAS a smoother ride too much to ask? Todd stiffened his legs against the urge to leap over the chasm and seize the crank from the hulking grave digger.

"Daddy?" The whispered voice was Sylvie's, her gloved hand sliding into his. He enclosed it but kept his eye on the casket as it staggered downward, the gears of the metal winch frame creaking and groaning with the weight on the cables, the weight of oak and the weight of Melanie. But not so heavy as it might appear from the poorly calibrated mechanism and the oaf working it: who knew better than Todd how breathtakingly slight the weight of his wife was by now, like a girl before puberty, before everything afterward. Near the end, when he'd lift her from bed, she seemed like the young Melanie available before only in pictures and the stories of others, but even so her eyes had known him, eyes full of the heart of the woman she had become. If she were here—and was she not, in some new way, *here?*—she might just laugh at that troglodyte cranking the crank; she might say, Oh sweetie, you're only angry at him because I happen to be dead.

"Daddy?" Could his daughter be trying to rescue both of them from this appalling descent? He nodded that he was listening but stayed put. He pressed his lips together. No one else, not even a beloved child, could decide for you what you had to stay and see through. His eyes smarted; his neck ached. He'd been awake most of the night, at first in the desolate bed and then during the small hours in Melanie's chair by the window, the Mississippi below invisible until first light revealed wide brownish water between the bare trees of the bluff. Hoarfrost, like an efflorescence of calcium, had coated branches, still-dormant grasses, and perennial flowers between the bluff edge and house, the flagstones of the empty terrace—a day of chalk in which to bury his wife of thirty-four years, decades during which she, the implant, had improbably, even readily taken root in the hometown to which long ago he had thought he was bringing her only temporarily. Now, at the end of the morning, a March prairie wind shaped to the earth delivered biting grains of snow, even under the undertaker's canopy.

Todd gasped as the spray of lilies and roses on the casket quivered and slid precipitously to one side, finally cause enough that the grave digger stopped for an adjustment. High time. But wait, shouldn't the flowers have been lifted off before the lowering, laid to one side, and later placed as a cover for the bald mound of earth? He clenched his jaw. This really was just the sort of foiled solemnity Melanie might have found hilarious, back at home after someone else's interment, as she tossed off her solemn clothes in the warmth of the bedroom, out of the wind and the biting snow. How he ached to dive skin-on-skin into bed with her, relive this welter of impressions, sort things out. Whomever would he talk to now? Who would answer and encourage him to improve his attitude? In his bright orange jacket, the grave digger looked like an ice fisherman or hunter hauled in from the wilds for cemetery duty. Todd had glimpsed him earlier, lounging against a backhoe some distance from the site, partially hidden by an oak tree.

There was a thud at the bottom of the hole, and the whole apparatus shuddered. Had Sylvie, too, shuddered beside him? Melanie couldn't possibly be amused by this absurd theater. On the other hand, who knew what she might be finding out while he remained stupefied here? *You must be devastated*, someone had said to him earlier, and benumbed he'd repeated, *devastated*, the word opening up into a vastness of forever-dispersing parts. He'd had to shake himself. Such things people uttered! The language! He frowned downward onto the still-pristine oak roof—so small, what a damn small house for a body that at sublime moments had been his whole universe. Around it in the sliced sides of the grave, topsoil down to clay, severed tree roots poked out here and there, just far enough on which to hang the hat clutched to his chest.

Now it was a clanking matter of cables being disengaged. The digger would want to roll up the artificial turf, the acid green on which Todd and his middle child stood, and get back to the business of moving earth. Everyone had business. It was astonishing how the world lurched from one moment to the next, hard at it— and for what, for what? Maybe he'd evaded the whole question by telling himself years ago that the real purpose in all his efforts was dedication to Melanie and the maintenance of all she was making, here, where he himself had never intended to stay. And he had never imagined he'd come so soon to a day like this—he shook his head—such a sorry day. Beside him Sylvie still held to his hand; at last he turned and trusted his eyes to take in his second daughter, pale even in her pregnancy, her gray-blue eyes limpid and soulful, exactly like her mother's, long tendrils of brown hair also like Melanie's escaping from the black stole. What the wind hurled at them stung like a fine dust of shattered glass. Nothing could ever be the same.

Time ground on and on as usual, like a habit. He felt ancient and chilled, unsure of his feet. And poor Sylvie, pregnant, who should be taken inside, out of this weather—where in God's name was the husband? Not entirely easy since the get-go with the entrance of men into his daughters' lives, he'd been suffering since Melanie took sick a terrible, stirred-up confusion about the relentlessness of intimate history, its pitiless repetitions. Everything he'd been living now seemed to be question. Men, he was afraid, ruined women, they engendered unspeakable dangers; women, to be honest, used up men. And he didn't know what the hell could be done about it. The whole setup was disastrous, tragic—and irresistible.

Over Sylvie's head with its unraveling tentacles of hair, he noticed many of the mourners huddled beyond the rows of folding chairs; he must go now to thank them, the readers in particular, who had managed to summon voice to speak at the grave. A few dark figures were already making their way up the snow-blown slope toward the cemetery drive and the line of parked cars. The little boys in bright-colored parkas, his grandsons, appeared to be heading off in the direction of the backhoe. Who was watching out for that three-year-old in particular? Todd had no idea how long he'd been steeling himself at the precipice. Someone gripped his other elbow—ah, Hauser the undertaker—no doubt to steer him away from the coarse performance of his digger and on to the next thing. *Thing*: strange, how the word dinged in the mind, like a clock. People did live like that, just one thing after another. Astonishing. Hauser wanted to know, was he waiting to throw a handful of earth? Some still did; it could be done. Todd shook his head no. He would throw himself. It was an impossible requirement, to leave Melanie down there, alone.

They were still clamped to his arms, his daughter and the undertaker. Amazing how everyone wanted to touch him lately:

of course his girls, Anna and Sylvie and their husbands, his son Jonathan and winsome new wife Kim, and his and Melanie's close friends, but also townspeople, many from Melanie's work at the historical society, their hands on his hands, his arms, his shoulders, his face, making free with him as if his physical body had become communal property—*so sorry for your loss, poor man, are you sleeping, will you stay in the house, do let us know if we can help*—even one of the towboat pilots from his company, who during the wake at the funeral home had reached a surprisingly gentle, stubby arm up around his boss's shoulders—*well now sweet lady she's closed her eyes on the scenes of this world.* And even the hospice nurse had caught up his hand, his discredited hand, which Melanie with a twist of her head, her breathing harsh, had shaken off as if he should have known better when he'd tried to stroke her forehead. At least he'd been spared the embarrassment of being rejected by his wife in front of his children: at that moment they'd all been out of the sunroom, gone to eat a bite of something perhaps, whereas Melanie had been lying in the rented hospital bed day after day without food or more water than needed to moisten her mouth. *It's all right*, the nurse had crooned to him in his tumult of disgrace, *she's working on her death, keep talking to her.* And so he had, without again touching his living wife, or interfering in her headlong, hurtling passage, the ruthless heaves of her chest, her gasps, whatever it was Melanie had had to do in that final bit of time that could not be done in his arms.

As he was being guided from the pit, he caught sight once more, now some distance off beyond the cluster of mourners, of a woman in a worn hooded jacket who before the ceremony had sidled up to him as if out of nowhere and almost possessively pinched at the sleeve of his good wool coat—*you may not remember but*—and he had not remembered and couldn't even now recall exactly what she'd told him, something about strawberries every year, a truck farm, and something crazy about wanting to take home Melanie's winter coat. Her monotonic voice and presumptuous demand had unsettled him; he'd nodded and excused himself. But Melanie had simply been like that, people, all sorts of people, connecting with her and imagining themselves part of her world. Wanting more than short encounters. He should know: one night out with her and he'd have done anything to be taken in for life. Life. *God gives, and God takes away*, the woman had said, her lips chapped raw, her face blotched and stricken, but in her expression a kind of baleful triumph, he thought, and in the way she fingered his sleeve a judgment, as if she were assessing the cloth or begrudging him its comfort, or even his time with Melanie.

Through the mourners and the scrim of snow he again saw the hooded jacket, then didn't—the haunting woman, flicking in and out, unnerving. Maybe it really was judgment day—his, that is. Oh, did he ever need Melanie here to help him set things right in his mind. Without her it was as if he were losing track of the person he wanted to be. So many had been drawn to Melanie. She'd had this way, this marvelous, patient, charitable way of paying attention to you, which made you want to—well—what? Pay attention? Resolutely, he put on his hat and turned to those who still lingered close by, even in this grainy wind—wind like a last remnant of original prairie—to speak with him and to lay yet more hands on him, as if hoping, through him, to petition the aid of whatever new powers Melanie might have vaulted into by means of death. *Remember us.* To them all he heard himself say, *Thank you, so good of you to come today, much appreciated.* Everything was inadequate; they wanted her, not his paltry words. He should have thrown the remnant of himself in with her when he'd had the chance, down past tree roots and striations of earth to the teetering lilies and roses and the absurd little roof, thrown this body, which all these years he'd buried over and over in Melanie. Nothing again could ever be set right.

"Hey, Dad." A different voice, a changing of his young guard: Jonathan now, his captivating Kim twined along his side, Sylvie sliding away at last into the outstretched arm of her husband—Todd kept blanking on the name: the impregnator—oh, why were the children doing this, enacting everything all over again; why were his little girls with their tender cervixes rushing to procreate? Did the world need these babies? Was no one to be spared? "How are you doing, Dad?" *Losing it.* He noticed Hauser bowing out backward to the details of the grave, one of which, the bill, would without doubt be sent later.

In his unsteadiness he was grateful for the familiar arm now flung around his back. Jonathan's voice sounded deeper and his body so much taller since his marriage last spring that Todd wanted to ask his son what magic cake he'd been eating. Well, he didn't have to ask: he'd eaten it himself once—the great sanguine feast of starting out. But now he knew time was the real eater. Time watched as you ate, as you breathed, as you amassed a body you thought was yours, but the body was time's body, the feast belonged to time. Oh, had it been exultant time in its greed prompting him to rush ahead on campus that fateful day so long ago to surprise Melanie, stopping her in her tracks with a kiss: oh God, what if he'd just let her go on her way, striding with her books, her mind on, well, he had no idea what her mind had been on; he'd run from behind, faster than she was walking, and circled around to spread his arms in front of her, so glad, so glad to see her at noon, the twelve o'clock bells ringing, the day before their first bedded night, so sure she carried his future, his whole body bursting with surety that she would love to be overtaken, stopped in her tracks under the sky full of bells in the college yard, stopped with a kiss meant as the gift of himself—but what,

what if in stopping her he'd hastened her end, throwing her to time before her time: suppose the noon bells had given him the foresight of this very day, her premature burial, could he ever have let her go her own way, without him, on across the diagonal path toward whatever had then been in her mind, thrown ahead of her like a light only she could see?

"Dad. Dad? This way, Dad."

He was losing it. He was about to lose everything not already lost, and sooner than he knew—maybe next his marbles, as had his mother, her way, he'd suspected, of opting out of unbearable woe. His feet were shuffling. Overnight, he'd become an old man; he was alone. Another arm pressed around his back. Kim, the bride—that was sweet. "You're doing great, Dad." He'd forgotten what was to happen next. Food, he supposed—everyone was still in the predicament of needing food. His legs felt suddenly too exhausted to get him to the table. Sleep—where had everyone found beds last night—he didn't even know how they'd arranged themselves—all these children, spouses, grandsons, Melanie's brother Robert, her childhood friend Margot from New York. Shift after shift of Melanie's local friends had been gliding into the house for weeks, attending to the family—even breakfast this morning—the incredible kindness of it. Merciful God, it made you want to cry. You wanted to cry and cry and cry.

"Dad? We've got a place for you here."

He remembered that they'd declined the undertaker's ghoulish limousines and as a consequence were now being separated once again into everyday cars; he let them usher him where they would, into a backseat next to brainy Anna in her dark-rimmed glasses; fine, he'd submit his upheaved emotions, his jumbled marbles to her competence, sensible woman, no-nonsense lawyer, two small boys of her own, a large husband Todd called Coach in the driver's seat, next to him Margot, who had astonishingly cut short a trip abroad with her husband to attend the funeral. The generosity of it! Would his own heart, he wondered, have been big enough, without Melanie's prompting, to do likewise for a friend? Oh, for crying out loud, did each howling minute have nothing better to offer than more and yet more evidence of how multitudinously he was now left to his own devices—his body bereft, his personality naked without her counsel? He had no idea how without Melanie's help he was ever going to learn to live creditably without her.

"Where are the boys?" he managed to ask his oldest child, the baby who had accompanied him and Melanie cross-country all those years ago when they'd come back after his father's abrupt death to see to his mother, settle the estate, and try to make sense of the boat works. "You didn't leave them behind in the grave-yard, did you?" He was amazed to sound more or less like him-self.

"Dad. Good grief." Anna blew her nose. "Actually, they're installed up there with Jonathan. Henry's nuts about Kim, you know—he says he wants to marry her. I've been trying to explain that Jonathan got there first." She touched the dark-coated shoul-der in the seat ahead. "Margot, are all five-year-old boys this pas-sionate?"

"Everyone's passionate," said Margot evenly, in her cultured voice. "We're in a passion play, all of us."

Ah, yes. Stiffly, Todd twisted toward the rear window and saw through the riotous snow dust that they were already too far downhill for a last view of the grave site, and he knew then he could never have stayed long enough to make it feel like enough, there was nothing that could ever make up for leaving her there alone in the snow today, or for kissing her in the first place, for stopping her in her tracks; the people who blathered to him about closure were idiots. But even so, stone after stone, like a

whole town of upright books, was now producing a kind of interference in the pure vehemence of his grief, stones and names: Shi-
ras, Massey, Chalmers, Brasher, Willett, Caldwell, Burdock. And
then his vision blurred, his eyes so blasted tired, all lives running
together into the same town of stones, his own, too, without
Melanie his chief archive, but who cared now, who cared. Rub-
bing at his sore neck, he blew against his window and made a
nearby veil of breath.

Their car came to the open gate and began to nose through,
one in a small cavalcade of cars, now trailing out of the graveyard.
Anna was talking, then Margot, and did he see someone in a
hooded jacket waiting as if affixed to the outer side of the enclos-
ing wall, and did the figure raise a hand as he wiped away the
vapor, was that a red beard, but there was no pausing, the voices
continued, and then it appeared interesting how the snow seemed
to rise before it fell, as if not only he had surrendered his center of
gravity, wave after wave of snow rising and falling, intensifying,
making free with the laws of earth. The car glided by a florist
shop with a glass greenhouse beside it, then down a long street
with bungalows on one side and on the other stones and more
stones, and came to a stoplight at the bottom of the hill by a gas
station and a convenience store and a neighborhood tavern—the
scenes of this world. It was a fine, furious blizzard, lifting and
falling, with sunshine somehow riding the crystals even though
the sky was completely obscured. Tomorrow could be sixty
degrees; that was early spring for you.

The snow let up as they ate the meal Melanie's friends had
ordered for them at the Old Ice Harbor restaurant, where the
plate-glass window of the private dining room looked out over a
pocket of water intimately familiar to Todd, observed all these

years from his cluster of buildings there on the other side, at the harbor's far curve—the newer office building, the brick warehouses, and what was left of the old boat works. He often came here to the restaurant for business lunches, but today the view of his little inherited enterprise seemed oddly remote, as if it had already passed into yet other hands. In these last weeks he'd appeared at the office so irregularly, sometimes very late at night, that more than once as he let himself in and made his way, footsteps resounding, through the semidark enclosures by the water's edge, he'd felt almost like a wraith of himself, or his father, or his grandfather, haunting his own present time, owning nothing anymore, and yet with an amazed sense of being more than ever simply alive. He was a human being, with a heart in his hollows, and that was it. Some days he could scarcely remember eating, but it wasn't as if he'd been running on empty, no, rather on more than he could account for.

Today, however, he'd surprised himself by devouring, keen in his need, everything placed in front of him: mushroom soup, roasted chicken and carrots, asparagus, lemon pie, a stunning amount of food. Now he felt drowsy and vaguely disappointed in himself, as if with each bite he'd been muddying important waters—what if he'd fasted, if he really had stayed there alone and alert at the grave, hour by hour more ascetic and hoary in the snow? But of course he wouldn't have been in solitude, consider the digger, and it wasn't snowing anymore but turning into a different kind of day. There was even a fitful version of sunlight reaching into the room, creaming just now over the baskets of flowers someone had placed down the length of the table, sweet-smelling tulips, hyacinths, and daffodils—imagine, the kindness of it. Anna was saying, "So, Dad, about this summer." Their chairs had been pushed back every which way from the table, the little boys had long ago been set loose to circumambulate the adults, and the waitress was still good-naturedly ministering to them all, filling glasses and cups, even fetching more pie.

Todd reached out and nabbed the older boy, Henry, at this moment marching by in Grandpa's fedora, then scooped up the tagging three-year-old Alex, hefting both to his lap, letting the hat tumble away; he held to his grandchildren because he was too tired to answer questions about anything else—the business, the house, Melanie's clothes and jewelry, the gaping, oncoming summer—whole months of sunshine that would not contain Melanie and her gardens, Melanie who had once said, *I suppose I could learn to live without flowers but I can't think why I should even try.*

"What we're hoping, Dad, is that you'll come north to the cottage with us for July, and then when the baby is born you could head straight on down to Sylvie's."

"There you go," said Jonathan, scooting himself straighter in his chair as if to rouse himself from his own postprandial stupor. "It's a plan."

"Maybe the man needs to breathe," said Robert, himself a widower.

"Well, he can do that no matter where he is," said Anna firmly. "Better at a time like this to be with family as much as possible."

Todd curled his fingers in under the boys' ribs to get more giggles out of them. By God his daughters sounded organized today, as if supervision for the entire future had overnight been delegated to them. How small, how far off his life appeared, back there where he had lived it. No one left alive really knew him, knew the circumstances surrounding his choices. How could his children ever read his past? They'd always seen their father as uncomplainingly connected to this place, this inherited life. Could they imagine that he'd never planned on staying this long in the town of his birth; never wanted, even growing up as an only child, to manage the works founded by his grandfather or the property on the bluff? Because of course their matrix was so different. He and Melanie had given them such broad freedom to make their own choices, more than he'd ever had, more certainly than most of the crush of people on the planet; as a result, they'd all managed to take off in their desired directions—Anna to law; Sylvie, at least until this pregnancy, to dance; Jonathan, bless his heart, to teaching history in secondary school. But none of them was showing any inclination to take over here.

"I think I'm still running a business," he managed to say over the giggles in his lap. Lear came to mind, the poor old wrong-headed king, giving himself over to making the rounds of his daughters—now there was food for thought. Finally he eased up his tickles, and the children stopped squirming and lolled back in his arms, a great lapful of boy. In a few years, he thought, they wouldn't put up with being manhandled like this. Even now, Henry arched his back and slid down, lithe and incredibly strong, like a small animal specialized for wriggling away. But Alex stayed; he wormed one hand up under Todd's tie and plugged the thumb of the other in his mouth.

"Naptime?" Kim chimed from the next chair. Her legs were prettily crossed, in high leather boots much like the ones Melanie had worn in the old peace rally days. Todd smiled at her. Jonathan did have it good. But oh, poor kids, poor kids. It could choke you up, to think of everything to come. Over Alex's head resting against his chest he again gazed heavy-eyed out the large window. The worst, close to the worst had been Melanie's intensive-care room with its glass wall opposite the nursing station, how it had thrust her on display, as in a ghastly diorama of a terminally ill woman in the last year of the twentieth century. He couldn't get the image of it out of his mind, that, and the moment at the end when she'd shaken him off, her husband, outright refused his hand.

Well. What could you do? He took a deeper breath. In his arms the boy grew heavier as he began to give way to sleep, as easy for this kid apparently as falling off a log, as peeing. Todd had seen him this morning in the bathtub—*piss* and he was done. Jet boy. Astonishing trajectory.

The sun wavered over the water. He'd have to start taking hold again, though how, and with no one to guide him. Well, for starters he could get up and go back to work at normal hours. At first he'd have to conduct himself as if he were living his life; maybe the rest would follow. He'd have Arnie and all the others. He'd have the usual river talk, which with his erratic schedule he'd missed much of lately. This year the ice had opened early— for weeks he'd been seeing snag boats at their chores—and the regulars were probably speculating as usual about the chance of flood, and therefore gate openings, and arguing, also as usual, about all the generations of river engineering. He didn't suppose that in his absence they'd managed to figure out if fiddling with the channel helped or harmed; what to call progress was a tough call, no matter how you looked at it. Even though it gave you your living, you could still sometimes want to cry a river over the poor, man-altered river. It didn't really surprise him that none of his children was showing any interest in taking over here, in this backwater place, this old life. And at the moment he had no idea of the meaning of his involuntary return, the years of his labor, his maintenance of what he'd inherited, and of Melanie and the children, all those faithful years—oh God, he was tired right now, absolutely bone-tired—*out of steam*, as Melanie used to say.

"Daddy, would you do that?" asked Sylvie.

"Do what?" His voice dropped as Alex, eyelids fluttering, shifted in his lap, sighed, and started sucking again.

"Meet someplace with all of us for Memorial Day."

"No cooking," said Anna. "Someplace easy on everyone. Like a resort."

"I'd cook," said Sylvie.

"You'll get over that."

"Anna, I like to cook. Margot, would you and Hugh come?"

"Oh, well, we'll see. You must keep us in your loop. Of course you must."

Everyone was talking in hushed voices now; such was the tactical deference to a sleeping three-year-old.

"And Robert?" Sylvie went on. "Would you join us?"

Todd glanced over at Robert, whose wide-set eyes, so like Melanie's, seemed almost transparently to be assessing what was to be his connection to the remainder of the family of the sister he had lost. It was a calculation, like a shift in the data of astronomy, that Todd realized everyone who had known Melanie would now be making. He would have to ask Robert later, if there were private time, how you got on with it, trimmed the boat for a single rider, faced the open water. "You're all a step ahead of me," said Robert.

"So what do you think, Daddy?"

"Did you eat enough?" he said abruptly to his pregnant daughter. She was too pale; it made him feel damn helpless to see her so pale. Ever since she'd started dancing as a child, both he and Melanie had kept urging her to eat just a bit more. Long gone were the days when she'd sit in his lap and let him rub her tiny back while she gorged on graham crackers. It was good news, he supposed, that she claimed to enjoy cooking. Maybe the impregnator watched over her eating, maybe she sat in *his* lap,

Todd hoped so—ah, Clarke, thank you, that was his name, why did he keep forgetting, think Superman to remember.

"Yes, I'm up to the gills, and you're changing the subject, Daddy. We're talking about Memorial Day. A reunion."

"Memorial Day. Well. Let's look into it." He glanced down at the sleeping boy and then said, "Maybe you could all come back here—I mean, *she's* here." And then he couldn't continue.

Something had occurred. There was a general silence around the table, like a spell. Only Henry continued chattering to himself as he worked out funny-walk variations with the fedora—which Todd wished with all his devastated heart that Grandma Melanie could see. Kim drew her chair closer to Todd and the sleeping boy.

Finally Anna said, "Henry, please be careful, that's Grandpa's good hat."

Henry paused. "How does Grandpa's hat be good?" Margot burst out laughing, and once again the others could speak.

Now with both hands Kim took gentle hold of Alex's feet in their chunky Velcro-strapped shoes and fixed her eyes on him. "Chickadee," she whispered, like a note of lullaby, and plumb it dropped into Todd's heart. *Oh, me too*, he longed to say. The way she cradled the boy's feet, thumbs over the insteps, the way she brooded over his seamless face—it was all too easy to imagine oneself a child again, hers, to imagine this raptness over the shape of one's life. She had everything in her to do it, and God how his heart ached for her. He tried to catch Jonathan's eye, but his son was himself intent on something out the window: ah yes, out where he'd lost his mother. Todd felt admonished by the fatigue and grief in his son's face. Boys, one of Melanie's friends had advised him, were sometimes the most undone by a mother's death. As for him, his own mother had so long outlived her wits that by the end he'd almost forgotten what it had been like to be recognized for who he was, the son of a mother. At least his children wouldn't have to go through that.

"Stinky Grandpa!"

He heard giggling behind him and Anna saying, "Henry, stop right now!" But before Todd could turn his head, the fedora had been jammed down on him, too low over ears and forehead, he could barely see out, his arms were still full of the other boy. There was scattered laughter, and Robert said, "So," as if he had just summed up a long, ticklish meeting of his board of directors. Hands on his knees, elbows out, he appeared ready to push himself up.

"How long can you stay, Robert?" Todd asked his brother-in-law from under the brim of his now-ridiculous hat.

"Three-thirty flight."

"Today?"

"Today, my friend. And I should leave for the airport in pretty short order."

Todd looked around the table. He saw all their faces, gathered here, and then he knew without doubt he would be alone. In his own house he would from now on hear the echo of himself.

But for the time being they were still a group, to be orchestrated. Anna sent her brother off to request boxes for carrying home the flowers, Coach reached down to ease the sleeping boy out of Grandpa's lap, and all at once Henry rushed from the backfield for an adoring tackle of Kim's legs, nearly knocking her off her pretty booted pins.

"Henry! Good grief." Anna hurried to pry away her five-year-old. "We are definitely falling apart here. Coats, action."

Todd said, "I'll drive you to the airport, Robert." He'd taken off his hat and reshaped it, and now set it back on at its familiar angle; to ease his sore neck he made an attempt to stand straighter, and breathe, come on, just keep breathing. A tidal wave of air crashed against his spine, air *she* had once gulped—oh God, this whole business of having a body and being more or less alone with it day after day was so odd, more than anyone ever seemed to acknowledge—to be alone with the poignant drama of it and then abruptly to be required to be without it.

"No, Dad, no, unthinkable. Let someone else drive."

"Hello there, Anna, I believe this is your father talking."

Again Margot laughed, but then without prelude broke into weeping, her head on her arms on the table, her slender shoulders heaving, her voice crying out something primal, unintelligible; then, just as swiftly, she swam upward, shook back her gray-streaked hair, wiped her face. "I'm sorry, I'm so sorry."

"Margot, dear Margot." It was Sylvie now, pressing herself, baby and all, against Margot's back, stroking her hair, bending around to kiss her cheek. And Todd made his way to them, took the hand of Melanie's oldest friend and held it in both of his against his heart, as the hospice nurse had held his, but unlike her he had no words to croon. He was at a loss.

In the car, with tall Robert folded into the seat beside him, he knew Anna had been right: someone else should be driving. His eyes were so tired he could barely open them to the sunlight. He drove slowly.

"This is above and beyond the call of duty," said Robert. "I said I'd rent a car, but Anna wouldn't hear of it."

"Isn't she something? Keep her in mind if you're ever needing anyone to take over your company."

"How about yours?"

"No, she's not interested in coming back here. None of them is." He flapped down the windshield visor.

"What will you do?"

"I'm thinking about it."

"Things are still going all right?"

"Well, I've been able to hold on to the house and the land, what I cared most about, for Melanie's sake. And with the business, Arnie and I sort of keep on piecing things together. Shipping is so-so now—everything's changed so much—lumber, molasses, even coal. I could do chemicals, but I don't think they should be on the river in the first place. We've started renting out some of the cranes. But the new salvage department is the surprise—the old-time lumber, you know. There's a real market for quality."

"Well, that's great. Where do you find it?"

"Schools, churches. Just finished an old gymnasium. We clean up the tongues and grooves and bundle the lots and it's good to go. Finishes up so beautifully. You can't buy new flooring like that anymore."

"There's a lot you can't get anymore." Robert sounded preoccupied.

When they came to a stoplight, Todd glanced over at the profile of his brother-in-law, in which, especially as he aged and softened slightly, one could find the resemblance to Melanie. It seemed a shame to waste these few minutes to the local airport talking about business. He blinked into the light. *Robert, you knew her when she was a girl—what did she start out wanting in her life? Could you say if she was happy here with me?*

"Are you ever sorry the old boat works is gone?" asked Robert.

Todd felt the whole weight of his fatigue. Was there anyone who could tell him the truth about Melanie and himself, anyone he could ask, *Did we do as we had to do?*

But to Robert he could only say, "Even before my dad died it was sort of closing itself down. One steel-hulled excursion boat was in the pipeline, and a towboat. A few years back they'd helped re-create one of the old sternwheelers, but that was a rare deal, once in a lifetime. The time had come, I guess."

"Your dad died a long time ago," said Robert.

"You said it." A hawk circled slowly over the highway ramp and in the banking of his broad, upturned wings made the wind visible, the wind in space. He longed to say, *Oh, Robert, this is the thing: Did I do wrong to marry her—could I possibly be the cause of her death?*

Robert cleared his throat. "There's something I should tell you."

"All right." Todd kept his eyes ahead. Melanie had loved her brother, he knew that, and based on their long history might have confided in him over the years. He felt his jaw tightening. So this was going to have to be his story from now on: whatever came, just taking it, bearing up. Secrets. Catastrophes.

"You can tell the others as you see fit," said Robert. "Today just didn't seem like the right time. But—well, you see, I'm going to remarry."

The car labored upward against the gravity of the hill south of town. "My God, you're really going to go and do that? You're a brave man, Robert." All of which he realized, too late, he shouldn't have said. He shut his mouth and concentrated on driving. Ahead was the airport, set some distance back on the bluff. The native tribes, he'd read, had made camps on the flats below, down where the creeks merged with the river—before airports and engineers, before waves of settlers, before trappers and lead miners, before, before. Over all would have been these same hawks, ancestors, that is, of these hawks. He wondered if he would ever see Robert again on this earth.

"Oh, I don't know if it's bravery," Robert said after a pause. "Actually, maybe the opposite—sorry, I know it must come as a shock, especially now."

Todd steered the car off the highway onto the two-lane airport road, parallel to the runway where the small shuttle plane was just now taxiing toward the building. The control tower above it was fairly new, but near the chain-link fence there remained a quaint windsock on a pole, today socked stiff with the westerly. Someone like Arnie would have said, *Robert, you old rascal you.* He parked the car and cut the motor and then could feel and hear even more strongly the buffeting of the wind. He, too, was capable of howling. Wasn't there a story he used to read the children, something about a howler in the desert? He pulled the key from the ignition, but neither he nor Robert moved: two men near the end of their sixth decades.

"Don't mind me, please—I must be in a sort of general state of shock."

"I know, and I'm sorry," said Robert. "I wouldn't have spoken except that, well, it's life."

"Yes. As you say, life. Well. When is this to be?"

"September."

"September." It sounded like a far place he'd never visit again. Anna had been born in September, way back then, before his father's death, when he was in the last year of his engineering degree and Melanie was—well, making their first baby, working in the library, living her life. Starting to do what he hoped she wanted to do. He leaned back against his headrest. "Best wishes, Robert. That's all I should have said in the first place. Do you want to tell me about your lady friend?"

"No time now. I'll write to you. And don't get out of the car. You look exhausted. Go on home to your family. I should have had my head examined for letting you drive me, but the truth is I like you, Todd—I've always liked being with you. You're one of my inspirations, you know.

"Come on, not me."

"Yes, you." He clapped a hand on Todd's shoulder. "Pop open the trunk for me, will you please, and I order you not get out. Take care of yourself—think about going somewhere for a rest. You need it, after all this. You've been a brick. Mel did know how to find herself one good man."

"I've got a good hat anyway," said Todd. "At least that much was cleared up today." And then, still laughing, his brother-in-law opened the door and stepped into the wind, the car shuddered as the trunk slammed shut, and then Robert came around with his bag and waved and strode into the building. Todd did nothing. The car rocked in the gusts. Robert emerged in a few minutes from the other side of the building and headed out at a tilt, as if holding himself together, toward the plane that was to lift him off into a different life. He did not look back toward the car. *He thinks I'm well on my way, he trusts me.* With what seemed like tremendous effort, Todd turned the ignition key. All these simple things, starting the engine, driving on the same roads, walking into the house, were to be part of his new condition; you could see any man doing any such simple thing and mistake it for easy.

He went the slowest, safest way home, through the downtown, following the river but opposite its flow. At the turnoff to the cemetery he slowed even more, but something about that corner, with its tavern and gas station and ugly convenience store, seemed empty beyond empty. He drove on. Then, at a further stoplight, he did swerve off the avenue up the steep drive toward the sprawling park overlooking the river, scene of so many family and company picnics that as he entered the gates he could almost smell the cooking fires and hear shouts and the squeaks of swings. Every turn of the ascent felt like another segment of a winding labyrinth he knew by heart. It was a beautiful park, nice log and stone buildings set into the slopes among the trees, limestone steps and grottoes, stone fire circles modeled after a latter-day idea of tribal life. He pulled into one of the auto lookouts high over the river, almost directly above the locks and dam, cut the motor, and slumped back, so tired he thought he might pass out.

He sighed, hugely. Over the surface of the river the sun appeared variable. A few gulls careened through the invisible waves of air almost at his eye level, their high cries deadened by the armor of car. Watching the ease of their flight, how smoothly they'd mastered the constantly changing winds, it occurred to him that he had no idea what it meant to live a natural life, or even if that were the general assignment. He took off his hat and tried to work with both hands on his neck, down under his coat and suit collars. He loosened his tie. God, he ached. Needed a total overhaul. Low energy. So different from those nights soon after the diagnosis when, sleepless and desperate for action, he'd left Melanie asleep and paced the property on the bluff in a kind of vigorous hatred of the cancer, a fierce, slashing desire to locate and hack out of the November chill and darkness whatever moment had first telegraphed disorder to her cells. Obliterate the cause. Some nights he'd strode on toward the point, slapping at the tall dead grasses, all the way to the ancient burial site, and in that intermediate place over the water and under the stars he'd tried to concoct a wager, some kind of extreme test for himself, as in the tales he used to read the children, which would allow him and his love to leap across this terrible time to more time, together. But he just couldn't get the hang of that kind of thinking. Cutting through to a miracle seemed as impossible as taking back a kissed kiss.

All he knew was that one thing led to another. If you kept doing whatever appeared to be generated in front of you to do, pretty soon you were living a life, and you just hoped to God it was the right one. After that first night with Melanie, that first dazed, exultant penetration, had there ever been a similar moment of surety when he could have stopped and said, *This is my truth and I'm doing exactly as I must?* Her pregnancies had been astounding to him, all those sensuous nuances day by day, like an enthralled swelling in him, too, and how willing he'd been for a share in the mystery, how glad for the job of patching together whatever it took to support the whole lap of her enterprise. Yes, glad, glad for the job, glad for the direction. He charged anyone to tell him what better way there could have been for organizing himself than aligning with Melanie and her purpose.

On the other hand—oh God, he had no other hand, he felt pulverized, he had nothing, he'd been hopelessly tenderized, he was mush, exhausted beyond recall. He stared out over the river to the other shore. Melanie had been the one who'd wanted to stay here; she'd been the one. But to say she'd taken root wasn't quite accurate; rather, it had been a kind of dispersion, a secret investment of herself, beyond even her work and her good works in the town and her gardens—the whole property gradually turned into gardens—and the children, of course, of course the children. Oh, she'd talk openly enough about her attachment to certain trees, to the river itself, to the tribal fragment buried in the mounds on the point, to the whole *ancestral domain*, and you could almost suspect her of mock reverence; but then he'd catch her dreamily wading in the tall grasses, he'd see her bending in the gardens, deeply in place, even in her labors in a kind of repose, a languor, sunk into life, touched—he should know—yet also somehow essentially untouchable, as if there were an utterly calm and private understanding growing between herself and the nature of all she encountered, as if day by day she were giving herself up to what this landscape merely represented; he'd see her gazing and would want to hold out there exactly what she was investing with her gaze—wind stirring the trees, say, or a barge cutting through the current, or a gull through the air above it, like that gull there, the one keening just now, a cry deadened by the metal and glass of the car—and even when Melanie was alive, alongside her he would watch, helpless to the passing moment, and think: *there in some way goes my wife.*

And he cried out, such a tremendous unearthly descending cry, which must be human, what else, but so strange, everything in this world now so astonishing. And then he heard himself whisper, in a kind of moan, *Oh, sweetheart, where are you?*

There were cars, even a pickup truck, in the driveway and cars blocking the garage doors; mildly irritated, he parked near the old swing set and plodded down the stone steps by the herb garden to the terrace and the kitchen door. The windows were steamy, and he was surprised when he went in to see a trio of Melanie's friends still trying to be useful; one was just sliding a casserole of what looked like yet another local interpretation of comfort food into the oven. After things settled down, he'd need some sort of stringent regime to recover from all the noodles and desserts, something like Anna's childhood version of what the Pilgrims ate on their voyage, nothing for weeks on end but *salt horse and heart attack.* As he entered, the women looked up kindly, brightly, expectantly: this outpouring of goodwill would have to dry up, he thought, or it would take the entire rest of his life to return it all. He'd have no choice but to stay with the social program. One of today's women was a widow, and with Robert's news on his mind, it occurred to him now with a kind of minor horror that the brightness, the expectancy in her gaze might veil a personal fantasy.

"Ladies, so good of you," was all he managed to say. He went straight through the room to the back stairs. From above came the rippling thuds of children running, which meant naptime was over—he should have closed his eyes in the car when he'd had the chance. He made his legs take the stairs one after the other. The house, built before the first war with a spillover of nineteenth-century optimism for progress and large gestures, had been too big for him and Melanie, even with the three children, and for him alone it was absurdly too much—he couldn't keep running a hotel just for family reunions. Maybe what he should do was give it over to a group who needed a home and go camp out on the point, a tent in the summer, a tidy shack in the winter, nice little stove, a bucket for washing, why not. He'd get a dog. Yes, a dog, a big panting, slobbering, sometimes filthy, sometimes bad dog. They'd argued, he and Melanie, about dogs; it was one of the things that had never been resolved.

At the top of the stairs he glanced into the sunroom, Melanie's favorite room, her final room. Oh, look at that: during the day today someone had seen to the removal of the rented hospital bed and reconfigured the furniture to resemble normal family life, though the wicker chairs, the striped couch—nothing seemed placed with Melanie's eye. Everything was a little bit off.

In the vestibule at the far end of the hallway, in the midst of their giggling and tussling, the boys caught sight of him and broke apart to come running. They hurtled themselves against him. "Hey, hey." He slung Alex over his shoulder and threw a guiding arm around Henry. "What's the story here, boys?"

"Poopy story butt," shouted Henry, and he reached up to tug on his little brother's kicking feet.

"You don't say," said Todd. "Did you boys get outside to play yet this afternoon? You sound like you could use some fresh air. Where is everyone?" He heard a few voices, but the house was rather quiet. His heart registered an obscure alarm. *Please, nothing more today.* Still loaded with active children, he entered the living room and there saw everyone seated with uncharacteristic stiffness, in attendance to a woman with a rough mane of red hair, her back to Todd. There were teacups placed here and there, no other drinks, no television, no games or music; the whole adult group seemed constrained by a single straitjacket.

"Daddy!" Sylvie stood, whereupon the woman turned in her chair, and he saw it was the blotched face that had spoken to him from under her hood at the cemetery. Now she gave him a prim-lipped, knowing smile, as if she were privy to something he was not.

He let Alex slide down to the floor, and both boys escaped back into the vestibule from where Todd could hear them whispering like conspirators. Anna stood, then Jonathan. Behind the woman's back, Anna signaled with a slight fluttering motion of fingers to her own temple. Touched in the head. All right. Todd straightened his exhausted body. Let it come, whatever was to be, that was to be the story now, letting it come, you never knew how or when.

"I have told them the coat was promised to me," said the woman, rising, still with that narrow smile. "I was promised."

"Yes, yes, all right. Why don't we go out to the hall closet?" Even in his alarm, he spoke coaxingly as he might to a sick child. He had no idea what was going on.

The woman did follow him, but as if reluctant to abandon her position of control—imagine, a whole family, and on the very day of the funeral.

"Now just which coat was it?" he said over his shoulder. He was trying to behave as if every afternoon an extremely unusual stranger came to demand the clothing of his dead wife.

"Her warm coat. She promised I could have it."

"Well, I believe she had several warm coats." Still wearing his own hat and coat, Todd opened the closet. "Let's see here." He pulled out the down jacket Melanie had worn for her walks, and at the sight of the familiar quilting, the hood, the pockets still stuffed with red mittens, he nearly broke down. "Would it be this one?"

"I can't say. She said her warm coat."

"Well then, do take this one. Please. It's very warm." He saw that the woman's hands were shaking a little, and with a pang he remembered how at times Melanie would be subjected to little jerking tremors all over her body, as if for just that moment the electricity of life was almost, almost too much to bear.

"I will look at the others," said the woman, taking a step toward him.

"I will show them to you." He stood between the woman and closet and pulled out Melanie's black dress coat, her brown alpaca, her raincoat, and hooked their hangers over the edge of the door. There were more, but he was near a breaking point. What did a heart attack feel like? Was it anything like this shattering in the chest, with the breath caught somewhere, nearly unusable?

"I have communicated with her." The woman's voice was low, nearly a whisper, coming closer behind him.

Todd turned from the innards of the closet and looked directly into her face and said, "I very much doubt that," his voice hoarse.

"Oh, yes, I have, surely I have." Her voice was low and flat, and her gaze, though directly on him, yet appeared skewed, hallucinatory.

He heard himself gasp. "What in the hell—"

"Do not! It is not right to talk like that."

He gathered the coats into an armful and thrust them toward the woman.

Instead of accepting them, she said, "You want to know where she is, don't you?"

In spite of himself he felt a leap of cruel and absurd hope. Then all at once he wanted to shake the woman, slap some sense into her. "No one knows where she is."

"You must learn to get over your anger."

"My dear woman, I'm extremely tired, I buried my wife today, and now I'm only trying to give you whatever you say she promised you. Will you take these coats? Please. I beg you."

He saw over her shoulder that his grown children had come to stand in the living-room doorway, Sylvie round-eyed, her dancer's hands like a hammock under her belly, Anna with arms clamped over her chest and a face intensely at work, as if on the verge of pronouncing a lawyerly decision. Behind his sisters, Jonathan began motioning as if to direct an aircraft to the departure runway—it was Melanie all over again, her humor, her spirit.

Just then Henry skidded down the hallway, followed by Alex. They halted long enough to shout in ragged unison, "Poopy stinky bottom butt!" and then in shrieking triumph were off. As if saved by the next generation, Todd said, "Pardon our little wild Indians here," and with his arms full of coats began walking to the door. He opened it. "This way," he said briskly to the woman, and when like an automaton she followed him and the coats out the opening, he breathed to the spring wind, *Thank you.* A robin, maybe the first he'd seen this year, called out from the linden tree near the drive.

"Do you have a car?" he asked the woman, and she pointed to the truck.

He went around to the passenger side and opened the door and gently laid the coats on the seat. His heart felt as if it couldn't break open any more. Then he came around to the driver's door. "Please."

"You also can communicate with her," said the woman, not getting into the car.

Todd shook his head.

"I can help you."

"I'm afraid you've got your own ideas."

"Yes, you are afraid. I will pray that your limitations are removed."

Limitations? Who in the hell—"All right, you do that." Once more he gestured toward the driver's seat.

Finally she climbed up but kept a foot firmly propped against the unclosed door. "There will come a balloon like a great ship," she said. "I have seen it. No one will escape. You must be ready."

If this wasn't the damnedest—

"I tell you I have seen it. Do not be afraid. But you must be prepared."

He took a deep breath and let go of the door. "All right thank you very much I've heard you now you listen to me: I'm going directly into the house, I'm too tired to stand here any longer, and you—you are going home. Right now."

He pivoted then from the truck, from the woman and Melanie's wardrobe of coats, and without another look behind him stepped toward the house, but it was as if he didn't breathe until he heard an engine finally starting up, a faulty muffler, and wheels grinding on the drive. The robin began singing again, still somewhere nearby, singing its heart out. Was that the spring song, the mating song? Melanie had known such things. *Oh listen*, she'd say, *they're about to do it*.

At last, in the open door of the house he turned around, a little light-headed, as if not quite attached to himself, his hand on the doorjamb for support. The sun was now at the level to gild only the upper branches of the trees. He couldn't exactly locate the bird. The air was still chilly, a watery, springlike chill, but no trace left anywhere of this morning's hoarfrost or snow. Melanie's gardens would all be coming up soon. He had no idea how on earth he was going to tend to her creations.

Inside, he hung up his coat and threw his hat on the hall table, where someone had placed one of the lunchtime baskets of flowers. For a moment he felt shocked to be alive, completely alive. There were things going on in the living room—a newscast turned low on the television with his sons-in-law drawn close to the screen, cups being clinked together onto a tray by Margot, the high-pitched interjections of the boys, whom Kim was trying to interest in puzzle pieces on the floor. That wouldn't last too long—those boys needed air. He could smell the food baking, more food. As he went toward them all, he heard Sylvie saying, "Anna, please, this is my baby I'm having, not yours." Jonathan, positioned on the floor like a support behind his new wife, was massaging her neck and shoulders as she attended to the children and the confusion of colorful pieces. *Oh, me too,* Todd thought. He rolled his shoulders into his sore neck.

His family looked up as he approached—no doubt they wanted the story of the coats. All of this was happening, all of it astonishing. He watched himself yank away his necktie and collapse into a chair. "You know what?" he said, gently swinging the length of dense silk. "First thing I want to do is go get out of these clothes, and then I think I'll take the boys outside."

Fortune

AT the entrance to the park along the bluff, gambling it's too early for the dog police, Burke reels in the excited silky body and gets him to stand still long enough to be unleashed. Instantly, the golden retriever zigzags off, ignorant of ordinances, this way, that way, his nose to the predawn grass. The dog is happy; the dog, anyway, loves him. Burke straightens up slowly in the late August heat and sees that Tiffany has charged on ahead with the double stroller. You'd think at this stage of the world, after all this accumulated experience, so many courses in history, coexistence might attract fewer problems. No, she didn't pause while he let Chester free, but with vigorous, bare-legged strides keeps on pushing forward. Hamstrung as he is by the overstretched tendon, Burke has to push himself to follow. Something has gotten into her this morning; she's like a full bottle of complaint, waiting for the select moment to decant.

He tries to step up his pace. He wishes he could reach out and recall her to his side. He wants to tell her that behavior, hers as well as his, comes and goes, like weather, but behind it is intention, and his now, he feels sure, is the clearest and most heartfelt it has been in all his fifty-three years.

"Do you always walk this fast?" he calls out to her beautiful athletic back—long hair still mussed up from bed, rumpled T-shirt straight out of the laundry hamper, short little running shorts, and legs, those amazing legs, that can wrap around you like nobody's business.

"I don't *always* do anything," she retorts. "I'm infinitely complex."

Now at least she's working up to the issue, which with luck might not take too long to get out of her system. It's fortunate he loves the sound of her voice so much; he tells himself that she could go ahead and say anything and he'd still make himself pay heed—because he has decided, yes, he has made a resolution, that in his case it isn't ever going to be too late to be a better family man.

Before him Burke sees a humid potential for peace spreading out over the park, filling all the spaces between trees with first light, merging with the pale sky, diffusing far ahead into a vegetal blur. He wants to ask her if she thinks that problems, which tend by their chaotic, greedy nature to take up almost all of time, might be only a cover-up for this watery, greenish hint of well-being.

In bed half an hour ago, half awake, he did feel a kind of peace. A dawning calm. The day before, out at the lake with his first family, went better than he had hoped, even though he got home late, and this morning he was enjoying the sensations of being newly awake, tumescent, sweaty, and relaxed, listening to the early birds and letting himself think that maybe he was finally learning how to keep his heart open, how to keep on doing it no matter what. Then Tiff threw herself across his chest and worked on him—not an assault exactly, but almost—until his feet were on the floor and he agreed to come with her, right away. She plucked the kids from their beds; now they are barefoot in the stroller, still in their pajamas, clutching their nighttime toys.

Yesterday must be the immediate cause of Tiffany's argument,

how late it had been when he'd finally left Dorothy's birthday
party for Cynthia. But it's not as if he could have done otherwise.
There was a band, fireworks. Eighteen years old, his own daughter: of course he'd had to stay to the end. It goes without saying.
But apparently it is going to have to be talked through. His years
of business success have taught Burke that everyone every day
encounters two kinds of problems: unsolvable and solvable—
which is to say, problems that aren't yours and those that are.
Everyone has the same twenty-four hours: where you find you
can't be effective you don't have to go any more, but problems
that you can work on you damn well better go and work on.

He finally catches up to her. "By the way, Cynthia really liked
the sweater set."

"Did you tell her I was the one who picked it out?"

"I may have—I don't remember." The lie slips out as if spoken
by someone else, some unregenerate dope he is dismayed still to
be palling around with.

"How can you not remember something like that?"

"It was a pretty emotional situation, Tiff. I can't remember
everything I said."

"So you were emotional?"

How did her legs ever get this long? He wishes he could reel
back to the moment of waking up, the peaceful calm. He wants
her to slow down and remember him, his sore tendon, and how he
adores her, how he fell for her. He wants her to believe that his
resolution, his absolute intention now, is to solve problems, not
to cause any more.

"Teddy! Not again!" She snatches up the stuffed bear from the
sidewalk, but this time doesn't give it back.

Teddy bellows deeply, a baby foghorn.

"Listen to him, Burke. He's all yours."

"Of course," says Burke.

No question. The little boy is his, the little girl, and the woman, his; this new family is a force of nature, of his own making, of course, but more sweeping and mysterious than that. It is one of the great things he has been given a chance to do, to *re*do at his age. The whole tense, losing business with Dorothy finally had to be relegated to the category of the unsolvable; it was the only solution.

Teddy keeps bellowing.

Chester ambles back briefly to thrust his nose into Burke's crotch and then lick here and there over available family flesh before taking off again, leaving wet prints on the cement like the shadows of large clover. Interesting study, that dog: his attitude is not what you could ever call discriminating; for him, it's just naturally give, give, give, all the way, never a slaver of love withheld, which in the long run probably makes sense, for a dog.

Tiffany bends over straight-legged and pokes her head down to the stroller. "Teddy! Now listen to me, this time you have to hold *on* to Bear. Can you do that?" Burke notices that Lizzie, for her part, has an admirable hammerlock on her doll, which leaves that hand free for sucking and the other for kneading her rag of a blanket. Is three too old for sucking? He's sorry he can't remember more about Cynthia and her little thumbs. During the years of living in Dorothy's realm he often felt oddly out of place, as if she wanted to protect her daughter even from him, the father. Yesterday Cynthia's grown-up fingernails were painted the same hot shade as her lips, in keeping with the rest of her nubile plumage, while Dorothy was dressed as severely as a mourner, about to witness with her fine-featured, strained face the opening of a last will and testament.

"How do you think poor Bear feels when he gets tossed out every five minutes?" goes on Tiffany as she arranges her baby boy and her little girl.

The backs of Tiffany's knees as she leans into the stroller are open and glistening in the heat, like smooth, lubricious promises. "God, I do love your legs," he hears himself say as he reaches out to trace up one tanned length.

"Burke! Would you please stop trying to divert me?" She whirls up and tosses back her hair, which even like this, unwashed, uncombed, has a stunning river-of-gold life of its own. "Do you remember that we had an explicit agreement about last night?" Her enunciation is perfect, as it always is, as it was in that now historic moment when she waved her arm in the theater of students, called out her question, and he first heard the rich, articulate music of her voice. Tiffany resumes her pushing. He can feel her splendid mind bearing down on his case.

"Tiff, honestly, I thought the afternoon picnic was going to be the whole show—I had no idea everything was going to go on and on like that. But you know Dorothy—"

"Burke! Listen to yourself!"

"What? What did I say?"

"I do not *know* Dorothy."

"All right, point taken, but all I'm trying to say was she was in full form. I couldn't just leave—I'd have been like a tooth missing."

"Couldn't you at least have called in and let us know what was going on? You absolutely promised the kids, Burke. They waited up for you. What was I supposed to tell them, when precious Cynthia hasn't even been allowed to meet them? They have no idea who she is or what all this is about. It's not fair!"

"I could have called," he concedes, "I should have, but my mind must have been on not blowing it with Cynthia, not after getting this far making up with her."

"It's Dorothy you're afraid of, let's get that much straight. Listen, Burke, something's got to change around here. At the very least you could insist that the siblings get to know each other—don't you have some say in this?"

Not enough, thinks Burke. He casts his eyes down the front of his lightly clothed body, similar to the bodies of all fit men young for their age, on down to the costly, colorful sport shoes plying the sidewalk; somewhere along the line in his first marriage he must have had to forfeit his say. He doesn't know what he could have been thinking.

The sidewalk nears the clump of pines at the edge of the soccer field. Burke tries breathing in a huge draft of heated conifer medicine. A great tree climber as a kid, he liked to disappear high up and sway in the wind and think blissfully about everything and nothing, with all of intricate, orderly life continuing on below, ready to embrace him again when he chose to come down. Near the long pond at Gra's was an irresistible low-armed old pine like this one here, beckoning its branches toward him. He used to get the sap all over him in the old days.

"You're evading the real issue, Burke," says Tiffany, increasing her stride. "Do you know how much I wish that daughter of yours could at least talk to me? I am not a monster! Maybe we could even be friends—I could help her with this or that. She's getting a little too old for this damaged princess routine. We're all getting old."

"Not you."

"Burke." She speaks patiently. "It would help a great deal if you were as realistic as you are pragmatic. Life, I remind you, goes on. And on. No one is immune from age."

Of course. Yet Burke feels his mouth slacken. He hears his own breathing in the hot, heavy air. He's trying to adjust to the sudden assignment to see Tiffany as a future senior citizen.

"Cynthia is old enough to vote," goes on Tiffany. "Therefore, she's old enough to make a few other decisions of her own, like meeting her own wee brother and sister. It's got to happen some-time."

"You're right, of course you're right. One of my hopes, actu-ally, is that a lot of things will change now that she's going off to college."

"She'll get away from Dorothy is what you're saying?"

"She'll have more perspective on everything and everyone, including you and me. Maybe she'll start to get serious about some guy herself."

"How do you know she hasn't already?"

"My God, you think she has?" He grabs at the stroller handle to slow her. It's true that he now has a daughter of mating age. Gra herself married at nineteen and by fifty-five was ruling as a matriarchal widow.

"How could I possibly know something like that?" says Tiffany. "She and her mother pretend I'm not even a person."

She picks up speed again, and Burke labors in her wake.

It's this barely restrained power in her he noticed first that day in the university amphitheater where he'd been invited as a case study for the MBA course she was taking. The electricity in the way she shook back her hair and called out her question tuned him to a new frequency of amazement. Everything that ensued was a surprise. At the time he had no intention of trading in one family for another. All right, he was very disheartened by his first marriage, but so were a lot of other people by theirs; he'd been thinking he'd just tough it out by focusing on what he apparently did best, making money, making a very great deal of it, resigning himself to comfort as an organizing principle for his private life. But after meeting Tiffany, he was jolted back into his enterpris-ing nature: if a venture wasn't working, it didn't make practical sense to hold on and hold out just because it made sense in theory.

Letting himself fall even farther behind, Burke crunches

slowly over a scattering of winged maple seeds. Autumn. So soon. The other day an envelope came to the house with a header of advertisement printed on the front: You have an important, time-sensitive option! Yes. That's what happened to him, with Tiffany, and she, too, seemed pressed toward this great transaction of theirs. Everyone has only so much time for the business of life. You make decisions, one after the other—and then you have to keep on living with all of them.

Now he's stepping down on linden seeds, like tiny gray-green ball bearings, some still attached to slender blades. Burke turns his eyes up into the broad-hearted leaves he has loved ever since he learned the name *linden* beneath the whole avenue of their branches at Gra's estate. He has been given so much in his life to start with, and he has tried diligently like a good grandson to increase it. Someday, so they say, for each of us there will be no money, no sensation. All right. Everything will end in other hands. And yet he cannot believe the loss is complete: Why else would he feel that behind all the expensive years a fortune adheres—sticky, and always his?

"Burke? Are you with us?"

"Absolutely."

She has stopped. She's waiting. He has almost caught up to her, is almost close enough to kiss her—to slide his hands up under the back of her T-shirt, to feel the smoothness, the moisture, the heat—when the bear flies out of the stroller again and Tiffany cries, "Teddy! Will you please sit down! What a squirmy-wormy. You'll fall right down and crack your head open and that will be that."

Horrors, thinks Burke. What language she comes up with sometimes, when she's emotional. He limps over himself to retrieve Bear.

"Hey, Ted, fella, how's it going?" He bends down to the

stroller full of his joint creation. He punches Teddy gently in the chest with the bear. Then he turns to his daughter. "Lizzie, sweet-pea baby." He tickles her toes, and Lizzie giggles wetly around her thumb. His heart lurches. God! Here they actually are, these two.

Burke always wanted more than one child, after all those happy memories of the clan at Gra's, but when Cynthia was about two, Dorothy announced that if you had achieved perfection with one child, there was no need—now was there?—to try and repeat it. Best, she said, not to tempt Fate. And best, apparently, to keep the flawed father from having too much influence over the one perfect child.

Well, maybe one day he and Cynthia can become a normal father and daughter. It's in the realm of possibility, and there are even signs. Yesterday, for example, she actually called him *Daddy* once without any irony or sarcasm or whatever—just *Daddy*, as if he were any ordinary dad making an endearing fool of himself as he tried to be entertaining to her friends.

"So tell me who all was there yesterday." Tiffany is in motion again. Burke almost pulls on the tail of her T-shirt to slow her down.

"Tiffany, you don't need to do this to yourself. Please don't go there right now—just—can you just leave it?" He wants to stopper her. He really wants to kiss her. He can smell their unwashed bodies, their pungent morning humanity.

"Don't do this to myself," repeats Tiffany with precision. Then she laughs, a pitch too high. "Tell me, Burke, do you consider me a civilized person?"

"Tiffany."

"Burke."

"You know, Tiff, all this stuff is just old business between Dorothy and me. You don't have to make it yours."

"So I'm supposed to stay in my little box, is that it? D'you know what it's like, Burke? I'll tell you: it's like Dorothy is pretending she and Cynthia are the real royal family and these kids and I are living in some dirty back lane in the shadow of the palace. I mean, they're carrying on, Burke! Surely you must see that. What's done is done. Why can't we just live together?"

"In one house?" He has a moment of genuine and monumental surprise.

"See, you do that—willfully misunderstand me. How am I supposed to talk to you?"

Defending himself, he thinks, probably wouldn't at this moment be profitable. "Just do it, keep on talking—don't give up on me," he says.

"All I was trying to say was why can't we at least get together as a sort of family now and then? I'm worried about our kids. And it's so incredibly awful for me to be excluded from everything."

She looks straight over at him as she continues pushing the stroller. Her large eyes brim; her body slows just a bit.

"Burke, I'm telling you, we've all got to think more about the future. We're being so stupid—I'm including myself—we've got to do better."

At that moment, just behind her head, today's orange-red sun ball blazes through the trees on the bluff, huge and close and hot. Burke gasps. He takes hold of her. "Look, Tiff. Turn around." Every time he sees a sunrise, he still gets excited, like a kid, somewhere between viewing it as a spectacular effect in a neighborhood play and really starting to get an inkling of the immensity of things.

He stands behind her, his hands on her shoulders. "I love you," he hears himself say. For a small sweet instant he docks his chin onto the magnetic crown of her head.

"Burke." Her voice, a note softer now, comes up to him

through the dazzle of sunlight. "However can we talk when you keep sabotaging what I try to say?" She circles inside his hands to face him. There are tears on her cheeks. The kids thump their feet against the stroller.

"Sabotage? What do you mean by sabotage?" His own voice sounds softer.

"Burke. Please, would you please, please listen to what's happening?"

Then it is as if, in front of her, his clothes fall away. Naked, staring at her eyes, he is tilting in that direction. His hands on her are not hands grasping anything. It's like the beginning of a free fall.

"You say love and I feel muzzled, Burke."

He can say nothing.

All at once she breaks away from him and gives the stroller a big push forward along the sidewalk, then lets it go. The kids squeal with the uncontrolled speed. In several gazelle-like bounds she catches the handle and once more sends them motherless ahead.

Then she stops and waits for Burke to make his way toward her.

Once more they are walking side by side, step by step, and he is careful that in the old roundness of the world his feet don't trip in their own previous tracks.

"It's like this, Burke. We go along in a certain way, but we don't see enough. There's so much that could happen. I could die, you know, and you'd have to finish raising these kids—"

"Tiffany!" God, the things she comes up with!

"Let me finish, it could happen, these things happen all the time, and what I want to know, what I really want to know is how you would work it out. I mean, these kids, Burke, these kids of ours . . ." But she doesn't finish; her voice gets caught up inside itself.

In front of them the stroller slows on its own to a standstill beneath some locust trees. Over it the branches flex this way and that like roots searching for water in the sky.

"More, Mommy, more!" calls Lizzie's voice. The stroller rocks back and forth, jostled impatiently from the inside.

Before Burke can think how to answer, Tiffany runs from him and gives the stroller another hard push; the kids shriek and shriek.

Just ahead, close to the walk, is a place where the bluff curves in abruptly. Approaching, Burke can smell the swaths of burdock and other weeds that have recently been hacked down and left to decompose on the steep decline among the still upright honey-suckle and goldenrod, rank and sweet smells together, all famil-iar, like a soup of earth he has been living off of all his life but sometimes for long seasons forgetting to taste as essential.

Tiffany takes hold of the stroller again, but this time, pressing the handle down, tips it on its back wheels and whirls the kids around. "Again!" shrieks Lizzie. "Again! Mommy, again!" Tiffany whirls them around again and then again.

"Hey!" At first he's laughing: what spirit, what energy, with this great girl there's no chance things are going to wind down for either of them any time soon. But she keeps going around and around and around. Dizzily planted, he yet feels drawn toward the axis around which she has set the kids in motion. "That's enough now, Tiff."

Each time she turns, she bears down lower and lower on the stroller handle, raking more crazily the stage on which the chil-dren spin. "Okay, Tiffany, hold on here."

He wants her to stop; he wants nothing to stop; he wants everything to continue, on and on, because he can't be done yet, there have to be more chances.

Bear flies out. The kids squeal and giggle and shriek. Small bare feet churn the air. Chester bounds toward them and barks and whines in an anxious circling frenzy to nuzzle his way into the stroller. Woman and children and dog meld into a desperate, biological whirlwind, like creation itself dissolving, while Burke, in the tail of the spiral, gropes at air.

"For God's sake, stop."

You'd think by now her internal gyroscope might bring her around to him. Don't they both in the end want the same resolution?

"Tiffany!"

She stops. Chester leaps to the stroller and licks the kids as if they are lost pups, and Burke, in the echo of his own cry, at last can go forward with open arms.

Reunion

HER voice—could it be? He swiveled away from the computer screen and hunched over the telephone. Yes, it was Nissa, and she was calling from Minneapolis.

"It was your father's obituary—sent of course by Aunt Kit. I had no idea you were so close, Andy! I mean, *Chicago*, it's not like Atlanta or Houston or one of the coasts. You and I didn't fall very far from the old apple tree, did we?"

A tree big enough to cover the whole upper Midwest? Now he remembered how the budding scientist in him used to chafe over her lax verbal flourishes. "So how long exactly have you been been up there in Minnesota?"

"Oh, forever and ever. I'll tell all, but here's the main thing— I just happen to be coming your way."

Good heavens. Here he was in the final throes of writing another grant application. He looked at his watch. Today he also had to pick up his youngest child from day-camp, and with a boy like this you absolutely had to be on time and ready to hold on to him as he shot out of the maw of the bus. Thirty-eight years since he'd heard Nissa's voice, but there was no way he could stop for her today. Then he understood that she was suggesting next Wednesday, when she would be in town on a buying trip.

Had she said *furniture* store? He massaged his fingertips into his tight forehead. Was it possible that Nissa, of all people, whose early descent into tragedy might even have helped nudge him into his own sober course, had herself taken refuge in decoration?

Glancing around the closetlike lab office from where he directed his research team, he wished she could observe him in the devotions of his adult life. He'd have set himself up in an old packing box if he had to, anywhere, just to keep the postdocs happy in the best physical spaces. So much was coming together now in the research that he leapt up each morning as if his mind, as well as the experiments in the lab, had been incubating important data overnight, pressing to be decoded into conscious bits. But no matter how the momentum seemed to increase as you approached discovery, you still had to get there step by measured step.

"Do you think your wife can join us?" she was saying. "I'd like to meet her."

Nissa sounded sincere, always had. Teasing, yes, and also with that dangerous tendency to overstate, but he'd always appreciated back then the undertone modulating her voice, from her experience, he thought, with the resonant fact of death. Drawn to it, almost envying it, he'd determined even then he wanted a life that would earn him a parallel absolute note.

"Unfortunately, she'll have to miss it—that's one of the afternoons she teaches a lab course."

"Well, I'm delighted you can take off, Andy. I can't believe you've been so incredibly close all these years, and I do get down there to Chicago now and then. But I bet you never venture into the Merchandise Mart, do you?"

"You're right, I don't think I've ever been."

She laughed. "I'd have guessed as much. So, are we agreed on the Art Institute then?"

"Yes, twelve-thirty, I have it."

"Michigan Avenue side, be sure now."

"Yes." She must have children, too, he thought.

"Well, bye-bye for now, Andy. It'll be absolutely fabulous to see you."

"I hope so." He hung up. Why hadn't he answered that it'd be wonderful to see her, too? Absolutely fabulous.

He stared at the figure on his screen: he was requesting an additional ten million to carry the research into the next phase. This was his dedicated life, his scope, which he would probably never be able to impress on her. When you were racing to finish a grant, you wished you could expand every minute, but thirty-eight years of accomplishment, funny how they could collapse into the sound of a voice from the past.

Back then they'd both been seventeen years old, then eighteen, just good old-fashioned friends. Her heart belonged, she had told him quaintly, to this guy in the town from where she had just moved. By billing himself as a mere escort, Andrew had managed to spend a good deal of time with her during those two years after her parents had been killed in the crash and she'd come to live with her uncle and aunt. He'd been well over six feet already, awkward, sinewy, inflamed with acne, burning with his own intelligence and ambition. It had seemed to him that Nissa already contained a complete, fundamental knowledge, which she would simply have to uncover little by little, whereas everything he needed to learn he would have to acquire book by book, experiment by experiment, and no doubt mistake by mistake.

The last time he'd seen her had been the June dawn after their graduation. Up all night at a class party, they'd been saying good-bye on the front porch of her aunt and uncle's house. He was to go east that very day for a summer internship, then directly on to the university. She'd been laughing. Then she tapped him on his chest, sternum; his body could almost remember now that lightning spread of awareness. The waking birds were singing like crazy. She tapped him lightly with her fingertips, like a magician. Then he leaned forward and kissed her, not for the first time, but never before like that. She let it last a small moment, not helping him to define it, and then she pulled back and laughed again, not unkindly, and in her most teasing, fanciful voice said, "Oh, Andy, you do make my knees go weak."

He could remember no other specific words from those two years except *You do make my knees go weak*. He'd had no idea how to reach for anything she was not openly offering him. What he'd already embraced, he felt, was a future of obstacles and incremental progress and brief moments of insight or joy, the nature of science and of his own temperament, whereas he imagined, while knowing the idea to be irrational, that she might already have been initiated into all it was essential to know about mortal life.

She was late. He told himself to enjoy the novelty of standing still, waiting. Many other people were basking in apparent ease on the broad sunny entrance steps. Would he recognize her? Andrew scouted once more under the shadowed arches and back through the revolving door into the marble-floored lobby of the museum, where this time the enormous urn of flowers and corkscrewlike branches above the information island struck him as extravagant, in a world as needy as this.

Disgruntled, he took his lanky body back outside to his post at the top of the stairs. It was a challenge not to be impatient; he preferred for every minute to count for something. A dark-eyed boy jumping exuberantly around and around his relaxed parents several steps down reminded him of the youngest of his four children, the only boy, so energetic and prone to accidents Andrew worried about him almost as a reflex. He'd never felt this vulnerable until he'd had his boy; meanwhile, his calm wife kept trying to encourage him toward a calmer and more trusting view.

Her name was Anne. One September day, after he'd been called a bachelor for more than a decade, he noticed her in the laboratory, filling the microtitre plates, adjusting the speed of the centrifuge, focusing on the image illuminated by the light box. From then on he found he could only go toward her, trying to learn more, as if she were one of the great discoveries of his life, and this family-to-be-born had all that time been waiting for him like an entire field of meaning.

He spied Nissa. Yes, he was sure. She stood at the opposite cross light on Michigan Avenue, her face turned north where at that moment an ambulance was about to wail and flash through the intersection; then there she was again, Nissa, now facing east, toward the museum, not yet seeing him. He still had her to himself, had her even as she crossed with the others and approached the museum, just below one of the two great stone lions that flanked the entrance stairs. Without this plan to meet, would he have recognized her anyway? Yes, yes, even with the short gray hair. He didn't care any longer that she had kept him waiting.

He bounded down to meet her with some of that lilt of anticipation in his chest he used to feel going home before his parents had died—his mother some years ago, his father just this spring—the lilt of going toward a place of being known almost forever.

She was paying attention to the stairs. Under an arm she clutched an oversized leather bag. She wore slacks and an open jacket, in colors close to the stone of the lions, and flat shoes.

"Nissa."

She looked up, the sun glinting off her sunglasses and her silver jewelry. She shielded her eyes; her cheeks were flushed.

"Andy! Here you are! How marvelous!" She held her hand toward him.

All at once they were on the same step, and she was a tall woman facing him; he had almost forgotten the height of her.

"Andy. My goodness—I'd know you anywhere!"

"That's just what I thought when I saw you crossing."

She took his arm as they climbed. "Isn't this wonderful? It's so incredibly easy. Why didn't it happen years ago? I guess that's life for you."

He held his arm steady for her. Her chatter sounded giddy.

"Oh, it's so hot today! I've been looking forward to the garden restaurant all morning—I called for a reservation. Is that all right with you?"

"There's a garden?"

"A courtyard. My goodness, Andy, and you're the one who lives here."

"I've been a few times, but I guess never in summer."

"Oh, this museum is absolutely one of my favorite places on earth. I've had such *insights* here."

"You'll have to tell me more." They were in the lobby now, near that extravagant geyser of flowers and weeds and branches. Nissa removed her sunglasses, and he saw once more the intensely blue eyes he remembered.

"Oh, how lovely," she said to the flowers, fanning herself with her hand. "What an oasis. Let's go straight through to lunch, shall we? Maybe we'll have time for a gallery or two later—how long do you have this afternoon, Andy? You're looking a little preoccupied."

"Oh? I have some time."

"Well, I've been saving up things to ask you." He followed after her tripping voice. "Over the years you'd come in and out of my mind, and I'd wish I could talk over certain things with you. Does that surprise you?"

"You were always good at asking questions, Nissa." Why had she said *preoccupied*? He passed his hand over his brow and attempted to clear his face of whatever might have settled there from habits of thought.

"All these years, Andy, and I bet you never even thought of me."

"Not true—I did."

Now in a lofty space, they were skirting the branching flights of a central staircase, much grander and more light-struck than he remembered. Nissa led him briskly through a glass door, past a limestone Buddha on his stone lotus, past a tall gray stele of some sort, up a short flight of stairs between two oversized figures who seemed almost inclined to speak to the humans below— BODHISATTVA said a plaque—then into a long dark hall of porcelains, glass boxes of embroidered chasubles and suits of armor, a whole wall of antiquated weapons.

"My boys were very taken with this side of the hall," said Nissa.

He had to hurry to keep up with her, those long legs and flat shoes, striding past a blur of polearms, swords and rapiers, shirts of mail, jousting helmets, crossbows, revolvers, an ivory-stocked pistol in front of which he paused briefly before following her through another doorway.

"Do you have sons, Andy?"

"One. You have several, I take it."

"Three. No girls."

"Three! You with three boys! Well, what has that been like?"

"What has it been like?" They emerged from the swords and shields, and Nissa stopped before a brilliant blue wall, predominantly blue, stained-glass panels, another kind of light box, he thought, this one for purposes other than scientific. Andrew's eyes roved over the color for a moment and then returned to Nissa's smooth, flushed cheek. She seemed to be searching for an answer inside the wall of light. "Well, it's been, I guess you could say, in a word, extremely *physical*. No one's ever asked me outright before. Why should it surprise you that I have boys?" She turned her eyes full upon him. She wasn't giddy now, or brisk. And she really hadn't changed all that much: he still saw the willowy eighteen-year-old girl. And he remembered with a kind of pang the boy he had been.

"I guess I always considered you an expert on girlness."

She laughed and gave him a tiny poke in the ribs. "I'm glad you thought I was an expert on *something*."

"I'm the one with daughters—I have three, along with the boy."

"You do! Well, I suppose your sisters might have prepared you for that?"

"Oh, I don't know if anyone's ever prepared for children." He was thinking particularly of his son, the energetic, excitable voice, the bloody knees and broken bones, the concussion, the hairbreadth escapes. "Somehow the generations muddle along."

"I'm sorry about your father, Andy. But I'm grateful, too, because without the obituary we wouldn't be here today."

"True. It's funny how things happen."

She drew him down a ramp and closer to the luminous wall, and just then he noticed a small figure who appeared to be falling headlong out of the stained blue sky, a little boy perhaps, some-one's son, but Nissa was pointing elsewhere in the field of blue. "Look, Andy, do you see Chagall's angels here and then over here?"

"Is that what they are? I suppose I could do with one or two of those, if only there were such beings." He made his voice dry, but his own vision felt watery as he studied the figures, one in a wheel above the falling boy, the other in an orb of pale blue light above a desk, and he wished that he could dispatch both of them instantly to one small dark-eyed boy at day camp.

"Pine no more; I'm sure you have at least one. No, no, don't give me that old skeptical look—I refuse to debate angels with you so early in the day." She took his arm again. "Oh, how marvelous this is, Andy; it feels so familiar. Isn't this just the sort of thing we used to argue endlessly about—d'you remember? You weren't about to let me get away with anything."

"Then you have me to thank for the development of your reason." He peered closer at one of the wall labels and read a quote from the artist, I PREFER A LIFE OF SURPRISES.

"Oh, I do! I thank you very much indeed." Nissa nudged him into motion again. "This way, Andy, we're coming to my almost absolute favorite thing in the museum."

They passed more Buddhas, a smiling Ganesha whose elephant trunk and round sandstone belly Andrew surprised himself by wishing to stroke, more gods seated with consorts or dancing, dancing and dancing.

How tall he and Nissa were, tall and middle-aged and midwestern—what had they learned so far about the dance of life?

"Now stop here, Andy. This Indonesian sculpture is what I want to show you. It's very old. Well? Aren't they simply *darling*?"

A small mother monkey enfolded a baby on her lap. Andrew leaned closer to the forward-thrusting simian heads, touching ear to ear, the convex, pupil-less stone-ball eyes, the wide incised smiles. The eight limbs and two tails were so entwined that he found himself counting. "Hmm. Look how elongated those digits are." An image flashed through his mind of his experimental

monkeys in their laboratory cages, the treated ones, the ones held
for control, their eyes watching him when he entered the room,
their long fingers gripping the bars, rattling the cages. Sometimes he brought them figs or corn on the cob or other treats, or a
different video movie.

"Isn't it just completely endearing? Look at those *smiles*, Andy.
And look how their heads are fused. I'm simply in love with it.
Every time I see it, I melt."

"It's made of stone."

She laughed. "Yes, yes, it's made of stone." She drew him on
into another lobby, beyond which he glimpsed the park furred
with green, the toy rush of the outer drive, the constant blue
band of Lake Michigan, and then she took his arm and turned
downstairs to the lower level.

"Andy, I'll just dash into the girls' room here and repair
myself, if you'll excuse me—d'you want to go on through that
hallway and find our table?"

It was such a darkish, nondescript conduit that his emergence
into the square outdoor courtyard felt like an enchantment, of the
sort even he was willing at the moment to entertain. A sculpture
fountain and pool bathed the sunstruck center, the surrounding
tables and yellow umbrellas were dappled with the fine-leafed
shadows of the spreading crowns of locust trees, the strumming
of a guitar played over the plashing sound of water. Not for many
years had he landed in such a place in the middle of a workday,
yes, an oasis. All these people at their ease, this young woman in
narrow black pants gracefully leading him to a table, these
sounds of silverware and voices, water and music, was this what
everyone else did while each day he ate his sandwiches in his
cramped space? Well, hardly; he knew that well enough. Beyond

this great stone-surrounded space and these galleries of bartered, bought, and pillaged art was the seamless, inescapable, crying world to which he devoted his research in immunology.

Andrew thanked the agile young woman and sat where she had led him, a table beside a tree trunk trimly surrounded by a small hedge. He had to admit that he was grateful to let himself be still and do nothing but take in this cultivated ambience of sound and light and water. Here he was. One thing had led to another: the death of Nissa's parents, her move to his town and their friendship; then, after all these years, his father's death, the obituary and Nissa's Aunt Kit, all bringing him to this moment. It was life, his own long, brief life. He felt surprised how much emotion was welling up.

Was it true, as some people said, that girls were smarter about the emotions? Except for his breather as a bachelor, when he'd used almost all his time in the service of scientific vows, he'd never lived separate from a swirl of female voices—at first the trio of his mother and older sisters, and now his wife and daughters— all making a soft powerful center to his life that drew him close and closer but would never quite yield to his mind, as if they were of a substance just different enough to require perpetual research. But, strangely, what puzzled him most now, after all these girls, was the boy, the late baby, audacious Oliver. Andrew sighed and stretched out his long legs. How were they ever going to get this bundle of energies safely through childhood? The trajectory along which he was hurtling threatened never to land him in adulthood, where he might come to sit like this, an apprecia- tive man in a repository of civilization. Andrew dropped his head back and gazed up beyond the tilt of the yellow umbrella and the filigree of branches to the summer sky and the unseen interstellar clouds of deep space.

"Oh, this is lovely!" Nissa slid into a chair before he could even rise. "You know, sometimes when it's thirty below in Minnesota, I dream of this place, with the summer light filtering down and everything beautiful."

"Does it work?" He was still thinking about little Oliver.

"Somewhat. It's good to have experiences you can fall back on for reference points, don't you think, like people and places that have been good for you?" She sloughed off her jacket and took up her menu, but then lowered it. She touched his arm. "People like you, Andy."

"Like me? Well, if I'm a pleasant memory to you, then I'm glad."

"Oh, it's much more than that. You really were good for me. And it's partly *how* we used to talk that was so important—do you know what I mean? We were young but we talked as if we were old enough to take on the serious questions, and that was so good for me then, you know, after my parents had died, to find a friend who could be serious. I've wanted for years to thank you for that. I didn't understand then how rare it is. I thought I'd be meeting people like you all my life and talking like that, but I was wrong, Andy. I've only met a few, so very few." Again she reached over to press her fingertips on his forearm. Were there actually tears in her eyes?

"Nissa. Now you're making me lose my tongue."

She flashed him a challenging look. "Oh, I guarantee you'll find it in a minute, unless you've turned into a different person entirely. In those days *you* were the one who did most of the talking, you know that, don't you?"

"Me? Well, could be. I was just a nervous, brainy kid. And you, well, you—"

"I was a well-trained female who knew how to put the nickels in and stay quiet."

"Do I need to apologize for all my past errors?"

"No, and I intend to put a few more nickels in today. You know one of the things you told me once, Andy? I've never forgotten it—" Interrupted by the waitress, whose appearance was like an insouciant reminder of the age they'd both once been, Nissa turned her flushed cheeks, her blue eyes, the fullness of her matronly attention toward the ordering of grilled breast of chicken, asparagus, iced tea. "And could I have a bit of muffin or bread or something as soon as possible, dear? I'm finding myself quite depleted."

What could he have said back then that she had remembered for so long? Andrew gave his order hurriedly and waited for Nissa to resume her memory of him and of his long-ago words, but by now she had relaxed back in her chair and was casting her eyes over the courtyard, eyes that did look a little tired at this moment, hooded, above a smile that was almost wistful. Then she tipped up her face as if to catch a breeze only she could feel.

"So, you had a long morning?" he prompted in a moment.

"Furniture and more furniture, miles of furniture. But I'm pleased so far. Next month I'm going down to some remarkable workshops in North Carolina."

"This is a business you run with your husband?"

"Oh no, he doesn't care much about furniture, other than being comfortable in it. But I'm having fun. It's my little way of helping people take a load off."

"And so what does your husband do for fun?"

"Fishing! But when he's not beside the water or on the water or *in* the water, he's up in the air, piloting private planes, which he also buys and sells."

"A *pilot*?" Good heavens, he'd never have guessed such a man for her.

Nissa flicked over him a smiling glance that seemed to take him in entirely.

"I'm sorry, Nissa, I live too much in my own world sometimes."

"And I want to hear *all* about that world."

"My son seems out to prove that he can fly."

"Oh, do tell me about your son." Her tea came then, and she paused to drink and drink, her empty hand pressing flat against her chest, until she had nearly drained the tall glass. All at once Andrew saw how swiftly their lunch would be over; the light in the courtyard seemed already more angled from the southwest. The guitarist stopped just then and set aside his instrument. Near their table other voices sounded abruptly louder, less musical.

"I was parched!" Nissa set down her glass and tore off a segment of bread. "Now tell me, Andy. I want to know about your family and your work. I want to know if you have found out what you said way back then you were going to find out." She unwrapped a square of butter. He stared at her hands, the knife, the yellow butter, suspended in the rushing hour. He watched as she bit deeply into the composition of the bread. Somewhere to his left an object of some sort, like a spoon, clattered to the pavement. He reflected how gravity was the weakest of the forces of nature and how it was gravity that little Oliver seemed to be testing every day with his own miniature, full-body experiments in the dangerous laboratory that he created around himself.

In a kind of reverie he asked, "What was it that I said back then anyway?"

"Well. All right. But here, have some of this sourdough bread; it's fantastic. All right, what you said. One of the *many* things was that the reason you wanted to go into medicine and research was to find out about Life and Death, capital *L*, capital *D*. You said you wanted to get as close in to the big ones as you possibly could."

"*I* said that? Good lord, you must have found me insufferably pompous."

"No, Andy. I didn't. There've been times when I wished I could be in touch with you to hear what you really were finding out. To compare notes, I guess."

"Well, here we are. But this is funny because I used to feel that you were the one who already knew everything about life and death."

"Oh, I knew almost nothing then, and probably not so much now. But you, Andy, I always thought you'd find out everything important. I had absolute confidence in you."

"You did? Why didn't you say so then?" *It might have helped,* he didn't add.

"I did, I told you."

"No! Why don't I remember? But do you know the one thing I do remember your saying? Here it is: '*You make my knees go weak.*' "

"You're joking. I've never talked drivel like that in my life. It must have been some other girl who said that to you."

"No, no, it was you, there wasn't any other girl but you. Then." He stopped.

She observed him a moment. "You weren't in love with me, Andy, I absolutely know you weren't. Besides, think how incredibly young we were."

"What happened to that guy anyway, the one who gave you that ugly ring you used to hang around your neck?"

"Oh, poof, *him.*" Nissa took another bite of bread. Her eyes flashed their deepest blue. "I found I needed someone like Pete who could throw me around a little."

"Nissa!"

She laughed. "I just mean someone really active, who can pick me up and carry me around now and then."

"Is this meant for tender ears like mine?"

"I'm sorry if I disappoint you, Andy."

"Quite the opposite," he said carefully, as a plate of pasta was placed before him, the food he could scarcely remember ordering. But *was* he disappointed? Did he find her now a bit of a light-weight? He looked up again, to her eyes, that depth. No.

Nissa cut into her food. "I would like to hear about your children."

So he began talking not about his important professional work but about his three daughters, the thirteen-year-old and eighteen-year-old calm and serious like their mother, the youngest one musical, the oldest exceptionally studious, bound next year for college; the middle girl at fifteen sporty and easygoing, not an academic star by any means, but doing all right. "And then there's the boy, the one who thinks he has wings; he's only six." Andrew heard his own voice catch strangely, and he stopped talking.

"Only six! My boys are all in their late twenties and early thirties! You did start in on this parenting business later, didn't you?"

Andrew glanced across the fountain and saw that the guitarist was taking his chair once more, cradling his instrument across his chest and knees, bending his ear close to the strings, tuning. "How ever did you get your boys that far safely, Nissa?" he heard himself say just as the first plucked notes floated out and resounded in the court with a clarity that made him want to cry out, *Ah!* It was like a sound that had been plucked from somewhere else, almost too sweet to be contained, here.

"Andy? Are you all right? You have the most remarkable look on your face."

"What?" he demanded. "Tell me!"

She laughed. "Tell you about yourself? Yes, isn't that the great secret desire of all of us? I'd offer to read your palm if I didn't think it would put you off entirely. Well, all right, what you look like is sort of a cross between gastric deprivation and ecstasy." Nissa waggled her fork at his plate. "Eat something, Andy, I command you."

He took up his own fork. "When did you learn to be sassy, Nissa? This is something I don't remember."

"I told you, I had three sons to toughen me up. They taught me to be bold."

"I was thinking about my own son. I worry about him."

"He's a troublemaker?"

"No, not exactly. Everyone adores him, but from day to day the only thing that's predictable about him is that he'll be taking risks." Andrew zoomed his hand out into the air. "You know how you never know from one instant to the next if a quantum particle will measure like a tiny billiard ball or a wave? Well, Oliver's sort of like that. Anne's labor with him was so fast she hardly had time to do her breathing."

Nissa started laughing again. "Oh, I do want to meet your wife!"

"Listen, there's more. This little guy was climbing out of his crib before he was a year old. By the time he was walking, he had already learned to unlock doors."

"Where's you son today?"

"We all hope he's at day camp."

"What happens in school?"

"Well, so far he's only had kindergarten. He likes the sand table and the balance beam. He likes water. He likes wheels of all sorts. He loves speed. And as I told you, he's convinced that he's about one second away from knowing how to fly. *And* he's reading, too, did I say that? His sisters taught him to read when he was four."

Nissa was laughing very hard now. "This splendid boy is going to have his work cut out for him, trying to raise you."

"Nissa, I'm in parental distress and you're making fun of me." But, strangely, he felt a little less anxious. He took another bite of pasta. "Now you've got to talk to me about your sons."

"First I want to tell you something I learned when my boys were starting to go away and my heart was really getting torn out of me. The hurt was something terrible. Then I discovered that my job had turned into remembering who they are, essentially, and keeping that inside me all the time. It's like being pregnant in the heart. Of course I'd never tell *them* or anyone else about this." She stopped a moment and looked at him. "But I guess I have told you."

He'd been noticing her throat and neck, which was one place where she did look her age. It was fuller, softer, with a slight flush rising from the neckline of her shirt. He imagined a child's head nestling there, smelling the warm skin, feeling the creased softness.

"I was all right with the girls," he confided, "but when the boy came, something happened to me. In a way I lost a little of my confidence—I mean, not in other respects, not professionally, of course."

She studied him a moment. "I want you to tell me now about that professional life, Andy. The note from Aunt Kit just said you were doing something with genetics."

He smiled. "I always felt Aunt Kit trusted nothing too dangerous could happen to you with a nerd like me."

"Little did she know about our uncensored talk! So, start talking."

This was not how Andrew had imagined launching into a description of his research. So much more impressive would have been to show her the lab stocked with equipment, the dozens of other scientists at work, the list of hard-won grants. It took so long for them to label the proteins for the database, to clone and sequence the particular molecules for their study, to engineer the recombinant proteins to maximize their yield, but hardly any time at all to watch his words turning into the expressions on her face, which he was finding he couldn't exactly read.

"Is what you're doing safe, Andy?"

"You mean am I in danger?"

"Well, that, of course, but I mean safe for everyone, safe for the future."

"You haven't lost your lightning touch, Nissa. Well, what can I tell you? That I think about this every day? That I practically weigh risks and benefits with every breath? But the genie has been out of the bottle a long, long time—learning can't be forbidden."

"Hmm," she said. "So what comes next for you?"

Microsequencing, he told her, and tissue specificity studies, which was more or less where they were now. "What? Why are you looking at me like that?"

"Turn your head around a second, will you, Andy? Just look behind you."

He did as she said and saw their waitress serving dessert to another table, something yellow with red berries on glass plates. A man was lighting a cigarette—you didn't see that so often now. Unperturbed pigeons waddled from crumb to crumb on the pavement. What was he supposed to notice? The shadows were slightly longer. Then, as he watched, the hostess slipped one foot out of her shoe and rested it against her other black-trousered leg, like a dancer, like a bird.

Andrew turned back to Nissa. "What? What did you want me to see?"

"I wanted to look at the back of your head."

"What are you talking about?" His hand flew up to the back of his head, the top of the spine, the base of the brain; he had dissected heads, he knew the powerhouse he was touching. "Is something wrong?"

She smiled, radiantly. "The night of graduation I sat behind you, alphabetical order, you remember. And during that whole ceremony I couldn't stop looking at your head. It was like a revelation. All of you is good-looking, but the back of your head is really something wonderful. That night you looked like a distinguished grown-up man to me, as if I were seeing way into the future. It made me really happy, Andy." She stopped; there were tears in her eyes again. "And here we are. I was right about you!"

"Nissa." He was spinning in a kind of vertigo back through decades of experience to the youthful self who had talked hour after hour with Nissa beside the public tennis courts, or in the slow garden swing in her aunt and uncle's backyard, or on the bridge over the river, the bridge that Nissa had loved so much to walk at night, in and out of the segments of light, with the dark, flowing river always beneath.

"Do you remember the bridge?" he asked abruptly.

"Of course."

"Why did you always want to walk on the bridge?"

She shrugged. "That's true, isn't it? I always wanted to go across the bridge." Then she sat back and pressed her lips together. "Oh, Andy. Those years." Her hands covered her face for a moment, and silver bracelets slid down her arm.

They were both quiet.

Then he said, "You'd lost your entire home."

"I'm older now than my parents ever got to be. It's new territory. I'm going alone."

"You're all right? Nissa? I mean, in this part of your life?" He waited for her, and as he waited he remembered how he had felt driving home in March for his father's funeral, knowing with each approaching mile that no overseeing presence would be standing at the door to welcome him, never again. It had been the equinox, a day of blustery, damp wind, sweeping across the plain, as he overrode the past.

"Oh, Andy. It's so wonderful talking with you like this." She let out a great breath. "Yes, I'm all right." Then she went on in a rush: "I see how small my life must seem to you. I mean, you've done such great things. But I want you to know I have taken risks—interiorly, is what I'm saying, really looked at how I was living, made changes—oh, I'm no good at explaining." Her eyes passed over the courtyard and returned to him, swimming with tears.

"Nissa, no . . . Nissa, let me tell you something. Of all the people from my past, you're the one . . . I mean talking with you, listening to you, made everything—well, *bigger* for me. It's true. You'd already won victories when I hardly recognized the battles."

When she said nothing, just looked at him with those eyes, he went on, more playfully now. "You know you can believe me because it's a point of scientific honor with me not to exaggerate—do you remember?"

After a moment he asked gently, "Now will you tell me about your sons? I've just put a nickel in. I want to know about those physical boys who have made you so sassy and bold."

She pulled out her handkerchief and wiped her eyes and took another large breath. "Well, all right then, here's the story of my wonderful boys."

While she talked, Andrew ate the rest of his lunch. Hers was a very active family; that much was clear. A house appeared to him, a jumbled entryway of skis and skates and hockey sticks and fishing rods, a kitchen where large dogs threaded their way through a family of human legs, rooms of comfortable furniture, chosen by Nissa, filled by these men who had filled her life. Surrounding

this house, this family, he saw month after month of snow, then a
brief season of sun on a northern lake, a four-wheel-drive vehicle,
browed by overturned canoes, pulling into a camping spot and
disgorging one, two, three boys, a man, and then Nissa. He saw
her, at ease, at home, not as she would have lived if she had married him, but as she had chosen.

He saw her. He saw her face, caught in a blanching change of
light. Closing his eyes, he saw an afterimage, like an empty white
socket in a dark swarming sea of space in which he was suspended, as if between lives, hers, his.

"Andy? Are you all right? How was your pasta?"

He looked at his empty plate. "Good. I guess." If he could but
eat it again, he thought, he would pay more attention. Nearby
tables were being cleared. One of those iridescent pigeons
approached the understory of their own table and then retreated.
The afternoon was hotter now, and a large swath of the scene
seemed overexposed.

"I think all the blood has gone to my stomach," he said.

"Let's go inside. Let's just wander a little. D'you have time?"

"Some, yes. My son's camp bus comes at five."

He watched her push back her chair and take up that big
leather bag again. "I've got some chocolates here, Andy, courtesy
of one of the showrooms—want any?" He shook his head no, but
she still handed him two gold-wrapped coins. "Take some for the
road anyway." Then out of the bag came lipstick, and after a few
swift painting motions she grinned at him, in one flash both
mocking vanity and enjoying beauty.

"Nissa," he mused, as he slipped the discs into his shirt
pocket, "how was it that we lost touch with each other?"

"Well, you went east, Andy." She stood up. "And I went west.
And then I guess life took over."

They climbed upward, retraced their path past the smiling

mother monkey and her smiling baby, past Buddha, past the gods, the goddesses, past Chagall's blue window where Andrew located once more the boy who was still safely there, falling without really falling from the sky.

"Shall we go up to the modern galleries, Andy?"

"You lead."

On the way up broad marble stairs he caught a great visual expanse of blue on the landing above, something very broad and blue and white happening up there, like water. Their climb was like rising to the light-filled surface of water.

But it was not water: it was an enormous horizontal sky, audaciously viewed by the artist as if from above an ordered sea of many white oval clouds, all stacked toward the pink-and-blue distance like celestial building blocks, mortared by blue. Andrew stopped still. There was a lurch in his heart, as if his body in a dream of motion had fallen or swooped. Then the surprise spread out to a kind of broad weightlessness.

"You like this?" asked Nissa.

Andrew nodded. "I must bring my son here. It's meant for him."

"I think there's quite a story how O'Keeffe finally got that gigantic canvas stretched," said Nissa. "You can imagine the technical difficulties, the sheer heft of it. Oh, my goodness, Andrew! I've just had a brilliant idea! Why didn't I think of it sooner? Your boy must come up in one of the airplanes with Pete. Wouldn't that be fabulous? He'd have a chance to sit right up there with the controls, he'd be flying low enough to see everything, he'd be able to ask questions. Your whole family must come! What d'you think?"

Andrew felt as if his heart had melted into his son's, and he had just lifted directly off into free-floating wonder. "It would be fabulous," he said, "absolutely fabulous."

When they said good-bye in front of the museum, the sunlight was penetrating into the stone archway. "Give me your hand a minute, please, Andy." She held his open palm in hers and tilted it toward the strong light. "Hmm."

"Well? You can't stop now."

She traced a line or two as if they were runes. "It's just what I always knew. You have a lovely heart, Andrew."

"That's all you'll tell me?" He kept his palm open and insistent before her.

"You'll actually listen to more—you, the scientist? Well, all right, do you see these squares? That means the universe is taking care of you, and here, and here, like fingerprints, they're marks of God. And these triads? You've absolutely got to be of service to mankind, it's your mission, but you're already going in that direction." She folded his fingers over his palm. "That's enough for now. Your nickel has run out."

He caught up her hand and brought it to the center of his chest. Other people swished around them, other voices.

Andrew kept hold of her. "Where are you going now?"

"To one more showroom and then out to the airport—and then home where I'll start planning this brilliant meeting of our families. Talk to your wife about it, all right?" Nissa slipped her fingers from his. Then for a moment she was occupied with sunglasses; her eyes disappeared; her mouth smiled at him once more: she was a tall woman prepared to go back into the city streets. He did not have her; he had himself, his life, the rest of his life.

Alone in the summer crowd, he walked north past trees, artists' stalls, musicians, a hurdy-gurdy ice-cream truck from which he might have bought cones if he'd had his children with him. There were no clouds, only an astonishing blue. The leaves of the trees were of a green soaked with his surprise in simple sight. Gulls crossed the upper corridors of air against a backdrop of sky-scrapers, while to the open east along the distant stripe of lake the white sails of many small boats, all filled with wind from the southwest, curved into their course.

He had to leave the surface world to find his car, pass through a concrete tunnel that echoed with a lone fiddle player, into whose case he dropped a handful of coins, and then descend a flight of steps to the lower level of the garage, where dank walls oozed and the air reeked of urine and automobile exhaust. A child was crying somewhere out of his sight in the concrete bays of automobiles, an over-tired child probably, crying not monoto-nously, though, but in an acutely distressed way, a child who had probably fallen down and whose pain was compounded by this desolate underground eternity of cars. Then he heard an overpow-ering scream, words of some sort, an adult voice, female. Then silence. A slam of metal, like the trunk of a car.

It had been a false silence, a held breath. The crying burst out renewed with more than unhappiness: with terror. The scream-ing adult voice lashed out with an "I SAID STOP IT!" so hoarse and terrible and desperate in its own way that Andrew shud-dered.

"No, no, Mama, Mama, MAMA!" screamed the child's voice, hiccuping, convulsed, but the one called Mama screamed louder: "I SAID, I SAID STOP!"

Where were all the other people, the good citizens? He was alone with the voices. Where were the gods, the goddesses, where were the angels of that child? Andrew came to the end of one sec-tion of concrete and crossed into the next bay, identical except for the figures a dozen feet away, frozen in front of an open car door, the large woman with the raised arm, the small girl without recourse before her, beneath her.

The arm in the air was what he lunged at, his hand seizing the bare clammy flesh. "WHAT THE—" She whirled around to him, away from the startled child. He stared into an abyss of exhaustion in the woman's eyes that nearly sucked away his breath. "SON OF A BITCH!" She yanked at her arm, but he kept it buttressed aloft.

"My mother's name was Sylvia," he said.

"Who in the HELL do you think you are!" She pulled again to free her arm, and this time he let it go. The child was still crying, endlessly crying, though not as loud now. *Stop*, he wanted to implore, *stop crying now, please, if you know what's good for you, stop!* But the child couldn't stop. "SHUT UP!" the woman screamed. "GET IN THE CAR!" But the little girl could neither move nor stop crying. It was an endless underground world so cast in concrete and metal and the ceaseless mechanical roar of a huge grilled wall fan that nothing, nothing could change it.

A sweat broke out over Andrew; his shirt clung to his back and his heaving chest, where he felt the small weight in his pocket of the sweets Nissa had given him. He reached in. "Here, look!" he heard himself say to the child. "Look what I have here!" Swiftly he crouched and placed a gold circle in the small hand. "It's only chocolate," he said, rising to the woman. And before she could scream again he had offered her the second lozenge in his open palm, close under her chin. For a moment there was only the labored roar of the fan. The child was silent. The fury in the woman's face, surprised, did not know what to change into. "Please," said Andrew to the woman.

All at once she jerked her arm up against his and the chocolate flew out of his palm and rolled away. "Get in the car!" she said to the little girl, who whimpered as she was yanked by one arm up onto the seat, but she held fast to the chocolate, and she did not cry. The door slammed, and then all Andrew could see was the top of her small head, brown curls, bent over what she held in her hand. "You think you're smart, don't you?" the woman hurled at Andrew. "You think you're so goddamn smart! You don't know anything!" Then as she rounded the front of the car, she sobbed out *"People like you!"* and something else that he couldn't understand as she heaved herself into the driver's seat and started the motor and pulled out, backward, then forward with a screech. At the far end of the bay she nearly collided with an incoming car. Horns blared. And then it was over.

Andrew stood panting in the terrible air. The incoming car wanted the empty place where he stood. There were young people behind the windshield, a girl and a boy, seventeen, eighteen, maybe, laughing about something. He moved out of the way and went to his own car and got in. Sweat was still streaming down the sides of his face, down the runnel of his back. The boy and the girl hopped out of their car simultaneously, a choreographed emergence, two separate bodies that locked back together, hands in each other's denim back pockets, as they sashayed down the length of the concrete wall and through the doorway and out of sight.

Andrew started his motor and slowly pulled out of his parking space. He wanted to be aware of each thing he did. He joined another exiting car at the end of the bay, and then another and another in a line to the ticket booth, and then a stream of cars flowing up the ramp into a flash of sunlight and a low-sailing flock of pigeons. He glanced at the car clock. He was still in good time to retrieve his boy at the day-camp bus, and then together they would make their way mile by mile home.

Rain

I try as hard as I can. There's a lot to think about. This particular Friday we were trying to get ourselves down to the farm by eight-thirty. It's upsetting to my folks when we show up late with cranky children; it starts the whole weekend off on the wrong foot.

The plan was that I would leave the office early to collect Anne and Molly from school while Carol tried to get away from her projects soon enough to pack supper for the car. It's harder for her to stop working right on time. On a scale of one to ten, with ten being the most predictable in terms of scheduling and with a hospital emergency room ranking somewhere in the range of zero, my insurance company usually pulls a good solid seven or eight, but Carol's architecture office usually isn't much over three. This is one of the things we live with.

At the grade school there were already half a dozen yellow buses waiting out front, so I had to park down the block without a clear view of the front door. I felt anxious. What if my girls forgot I was coming and followed the herd mindlessly into one of the buses? I got out into the Indian summer heat, took off my suit coat and folded it back into the car, loosened my tie, and then went to wait near the arched stone entryway, well built in the twenties, now spray-painted with graffiti. Sirens blared through the intersection.

We're what the journalists call urban pioneers. I admit if it were my choice alone, I might be out in the sticks where I could grow decent vegetables and feel justified in having a large, energetic dog. But then, of course, I might not have Carol, which is unthinkable. She's committed to the city.

The bus motors idled and stank in the heavy air; one driver stood smoking by his open door. The weather forecast was for storms in southeastern Wisconsin tonight, another reason to get ourselves promptly on the road. I tried to picture Carol already home by now, laying out a double row of bread slices, building neat sandwiches. In her own ways she's orderly, as I am in mine. We fit together pretty well, I think, even though no one would call me artistic.

Actually, I don't mind being the prudent, plodding sort: I like looking after my family; I love having a wife and being a father. Flexing my shoulders to get the desk kinks out, I was suddenly so glad it was the end of the office week when I could start being a simpler, let's just say more physical man with his family. In a minute I would pluck my own daughters out of a tidal wave of children. I felt fortunate. I try to help people in the community as much as I can, and I work hard for my clients, but at times all I want is to quiet down and enjoy what I've got—my body, my wife, my two girls.

Ready as I was, I nearly jumped out of my skin when the closing horn blasted over my head. The bus driver who had been smoking leapt into his bus, motors revved, the school doors were flung open just as another siren wailed nearby, and the continuing story of me with my family was about to take up again.

Molly almost threw me off balance. She's a sturdy seven, and she still likes to hurtle herself at me and be swept off her feet, but that day she nearly knocked me off my own. She had a drawing to show me, which she pressed so close to my eyes I could barely focus, a tree, with its brightly colored leaves flying off in all directions.

Anne came along in another minute or so in a slow, hot scowl, dragging her red sweater in one hand and her backpack in another. Something must have upset her, and we might or might not hear about it eventually, depending on whether she felt like brooding or hashing things out. Anne is a temperamental child, opinionated, quick to pounce on injustice or faulty reasoning. Carol seems to be better than I am at asking the right questions, and I was glad that before long there would be a mother as well as a father with the two overheated children in the car. Sometimes I hear an age-old constriction in my voice, but I don't know what to do about it. Improving on your past isn't always so easy; habits get formed; on the farm no one said much or had much to say.

Carol's Volkswagen was already parked in the driveway when I pulled the Buick alongside our house.

"Carry in your own things, girls."

Why do I always end up saying the same things? Molly jumped from the backseat and raced around the corner of the house with her drawing; Annie was still hoisting up her pack in slow motion.

"Actually, Annie, will you carry my briefcase? I've got to get the garbage cart."

She took it with wordless annoyance. Something in me flared. Was this child appreciating her life? I work hard for her, I thought, both her parents do. Does she have any idea how we try to make things nice for her?

I felt very emotional as I watched her thin, leggy body lugging her pack and sweater and my briefcase to the back porch. She was only ten. I hoped things would get smoothed out when we were all together this weekend.

As I trundled the cart to the back of the house, I took note of various fall chores I'd need to add to my list. There's always so much to do. By now I've labored enough on this quirky Victorian to have made peace with it, but when we were first in the real estate market, I was very drawn to a modest, well-kept-up brick Colonial with a small central entrance porch flanked by two rows of healthy yew bushes and a nice foursquare quality to the rooms. Carol said she wouldn't even consider such a boring style.

This weekend my folks were sure to need help with their own chores. On a farm there's always too much routine upkeep— buildings, animals, land, machinery—not to mention emergencies. Most of the time humans get pushed way down to the bottom of the list. I think the whole package of always unfinished, dirty, repetitive, yet often reactive manual work would have been too much for me. For my sister Sharon, maybe it was the dirt that finally got to her. I never really wanted to farm anyway, and my mother always said she hoped I would get *out from under*, as she put it, though she did give me what I consider a country name, Cletus. I toyed with the idea of changing it when I first went to the university, but I didn't see how I could pull it off—I wasn't like an entertainer or a special religious person, just a business major from an Iowa farm.

My mother's views on my future prevailed so thoroughly that I don't even know if my father had other ideas. One thing is pretty sure: if I'd chosen to stay on at the farm, he'd still have his cows—cows that I'd be helping to take care of. Now my folks are even talking about selling the land, too. That part makes me uneasy; I know about investments, and land is land. It's funny, I've gone the farthest away from it, and yet I'm the one who's not sure about selling. Maybe I see things in more economic, less emotional terms than the rest of my family—or it might be the other way around.

I was surprised Carol hadn't put her own car away because we always take mine on trips. So I shoved the garbage cart into place and then rolled up the garage door and was about to swing into her little VW when she called to me from the porch.

"Thanks, Cletus, but just leave it. I'll tell you when you get in."

There was strong afternoon light on my wife. For work she usually wears her long golden-brown hair bound up in some professional way, and at that moment it was still coiled at the nape of her neck, but I nevertheless saw her as if in a loosened cascade of light. All I wanted was to be simple, and physical, with her.

"What do you mean?" I wasn't computing.

"Just come in. Please. I've almost got you packed." Even though she held the screen door open for me, I felt as if another door had been slammed in my face.

My throat tightened. "What do you mean?"

"Please come on in where we can talk."

We're both sensitive, perhaps overly sensitive, about the close proximity of our neighbors, but the happy truth is that we don't fight much at all, or even argue. We both enjoy the assurance that we're doing our work well and running a pretty trim ship at home. We cooperate.

I followed on her heels into the kitchen and was about to take her in my arms when her hands swiftly returned to folding the laundry on the table, the very batch I had thrown in the washer that morning while she made the breakfast. Her whole body could be read as an instrument of efficiency. Those neat stacks of folded clothes made me feel so mournful all of a sudden, as well as the row of wrapped sandwiches, the boxes of apple juice, the bananas, the cookies.

"What's wrong?"

"I can't go with you—there's been a glitch." She told me

details about a preliminary design and a presentation on Monday, but I wasn't computing.

"What presentation?" I had this stupid thought that if I refused to understand the situation, it would not have sufficient dimension to displace the substance of the two of us, my wife and me, standing within reach of each other in our own private house.

With a touch too much of patience, she explained.

"Why you?" But I already knew; her input was essential.

I don't ever let myself forget how proud of her I am. Proposing to Carol eleven years ago was pure brilliance on my part; ever since, I've sort of been trying to keep in step with my original inspiration.

"I warned you my plan to take off for the weekend was a stretch from the beginning. I told you how many deadlines are coming."

"Yes, but now my folks are expecting you." It wasn't what I wanted to say.

"They won't mind," Carol said briskly, as she snapped the last piece of laundry into submission and arranged the folded stacks back into the basket. "Molly!" she called up the stairs. "Your pink pajamas are down here, come and get the basket." Then she turned back to me. "Your mother wants to see *you*, not me. She wants to see you and her grandchildren."

At that moment I finally had the good sense to close the gap and get my arms around her.

"Listen to this—what if we just go for one night—we could come back tomorrow afternoon, I promise." I held on to her. It's true that sometimes I use my body as a sort of trump card with Carol. I wouldn't mind being a few inches taller, but the way I'm put together pleases her, I know that. She's another one, the original of Molly, who craves to be lifted, literally, off her feet. It's the wonderful flip side of all her discipline and efficiency.

She did let herself relax against me for a few long moments. "I really can't, Cletus. I'm so sorry. We need every minute we can get."

Molly bounded into the kitchen as we were still well fitted together. "Love! Love! Calla, walla, wuv!" she chanted loudly as she began rummaging through the folded laundry.

"No, no, Molly." Carol pulled away from me. "Take the whole basket up to our bed and sort things out the right way. Did you find your sweatshirt?"

"It's not anywhere."

"Of course it is. Look again. Ask Annie to help you."

"Annie's lying down."

Molly seemed small carrying the big basket, but how strong she was already, with the physical confidence to pick up a load and go with it.

"What's with Annie?" said Carol in a low voice. "I hardly saw her."

"Long face in the car. Didn't want to talk. I was counting on you to find out."

She glanced up at the clock. "I've absolutely got to get back down there." She pushed me toward the stairs. "Please go to her, take over, see that they're packed. Please."

"Aren't you even going to stay and say good-bye to us?" I asked over my shoulder. Even I could hear that I sounded about eight years old.

She just stood for a minute. It's sort of challenging to be looked at intently by someone like my wife. "You're really something else, Cletus—you know that?"

Was that good news or bad news? I trudged upstairs.

The sweatshirt was under Molly's bed. I said I'd be back to help close the suitcase. One down, one to go.

"Annie?" I stopped in her doorway. "What's happening?"

"Nothing," she said after a significant pause. She was lying down, a corner of her favorite blanket drawn up against one side of her face, her fingers nursing the satin binding. Talk about regression.

"Why aren't you packing?"

She didn't answer.

I entered the room and stood looking down at her babyish sulk. Suddenly I felt blinded. All day I had been trying so hard to make things turn out right for everyone. I yanked the blanket away from her. Her eyes were stunned but indignant.

"Answer me, Anne, why are you lying around?"

"I don't know." Her voice wavered a little, but her eyes held firm.

"Well, what *I* know is that you're going to finish packing right now. I will not leave this room until I see both your feet on the floor, and when I get back in here in ten minutes I want your suitcase zipped and ready to go. Are you planning to wear your school clothes in the car? Anne? Answer me! This is your father speaking to you."

"No." There was enough sass left in her voice to imply I had been a fool to ask.

"I told you last night how important it is that we get on the road on time today. Didn't I? Anne?"

I held out my hand to pull her, and in that moment, thank God, the blind anger passed out of me. "Come on, Annie, please let's get going. It's for Grandma and Grandpa, you know. It upsets them if we're too late."

She did start to sit up then, but rejected my hand, and so I was left only with myself and the rest of my own packing.

Twenty minutes later, as the girls were making their play house in the back seat, Carol and I stood together in the driveway. We had kissed inside; now we were saying our public good-bye.

Once more in her suit jacket, she was as much on her way as we were, and I could feel how this weekend was not going to be a sacrifice for her. Going to the farm, however, would have been. She feels that my folks, never having accepted her need to be a professional, try to sabotage her ambitions.

Then Carol surprised me. She embraced me. She kissed me. Out there in the world. "Thank you, Cletus. Thank you so much. I don't know what I'd do without you." Then she tapped on the backseat window and cheerfully blew more kisses. I got in and we were off.

We were behind schedule. It was nearly four-thirty, which would put us at the farm by nine-thirty, not a minute earlier. And if there were extra pee breaks, we could run as late as ten o'clock. In the middle of the elevated interchange, just as I was thinking I should call my folks to tell them we'd be later, I realized I'd left my phone in my briefcase. Well, I'd just have to do it from the road, maybe somewhere down in Illinois, after we negotiated the connections around Beloit and Rockford.

I glanced in the rearview mirror at the girls, who seemed content enough in their traveling nest, even Anne. They were whispering about something.

Well, kids are tough, I told myself. Nobody coddled my sensibilities when I was growing up. Which wasn't to say that I wanted my children to have my kind of childhood, when I often ached for attention and for talk that was affectionate or light-hearted. I keep trying to do better with my own kids.

"Are your doors locked?"

"Yes!" they both chimed and then started giggling as if I had just said something hilarious. Their laughter made me feel better. So what if they were making fun of me?

"Let me know when you get hungry."

"Now! We're hungry right now!" said Molly.

"We're not even out of the city," I said automatically. "We can't possibly eat yet."

"Why can't we?" asked Anne pointedly, her giggles abruptly cut off, a timbre to her voice that reminded me of Carol—the low, controlled tone designed specifically to cut through obstacles, but in a civilized way. I was taken aback. Fifth grade today, law school tomorrow. Watch out, world. I looked at her again in the mirror, with an amazed pride. "Dad? Did you hear me? This is your daughter speaking to you." And then both she and Molly doubled over in renewed snickering.

My father would have stopped the car, yanked her out by the arm, and spanked her by the side of the road, but I found myself smiling along with their laughter.

Why not? These were the free voices of the future.

"Well, all right then—go ahead. You've got the food back there. Dig in." But then I couldn't stop myself from adding, "Don't let me hear you in a couple of hours whining that you're hungry again."

They made a show of scrabbling into the picnic bag like famished beasts. "Do you want your sandwich now, too, Daddy?"

"Sure, why not?" I liked that it was Anne who had asked and that she had called me *Daddy*. Suddenly I had a sharp physical memory of how hungry I used to be as a kid at this time of day, a desperate, clawing emptiness. I unwrapped what looked like an excellent sandwich—turkey, Swiss, lettuce, sprouts, mustard, mayo—made just for me by my accomplished wife. The food didn't seem quite so mournful to me, now that I was actually biting into it. Soon enough the weekend would be over.

I turned on the radio: politics, politics, and money, money, money, which is supposed to be my interest; in a few minutes I turned off the contentious voices. The sun, having dropped beneath the lowering clouds, now flooded across my hands and the steering wheel. We hadn't beat the traffic; nothing to do but be part of it, streaming like metallic syrup through a constructed city world, side-lit from the west. My mother always commented on the number of church spires in the skyline of Milwaukee's south side, where so many of the immigrants first settled. My father's gaze was usually swallowed up by the vastness of the lake—not a barn or field or cow in sight. On my parents' rare visits away from the farm, I could never tell if they were enjoying themselves—not that it had ever been clear whether they were enjoying themselves *on* the farm.

I took another big bite of the delicious sandwich Carol had assembled for me. The city was amazing, really, how filled up it was with man-made shapes. And what did we all think we were doing here? From the elevated highway at this speed and in this light everything looked like a brief but extraordinarily interwoven play world. A gull flapped right in front of the windshield and sailed out over the industrial valley, in the direction of the harbor. For just a moment I could almost feel myself extricated from this mirage, sailing out, no longer in a body but still living.

I took another bite and then gestured with my sandwich toward the west. "Look over there, girls. It's going to storm for sure."

"When, Dad?" asked Molly.

"I don't know. Maybe we'll get far enough south before it hits."

"What'll we do if it lightnings?"

"We'd be okay."

"If there was a tornado, we'd have to get out of the car and go lie down in a ditch," announced Anne.

"Dad, would we?" asked Molly. "We'd get all wet."

"Oh, I've never had to do anything like that, and I've driven through some pretty bad storms."

"How bad, Dad? How bad?" Molly started poking the back of my shoulder with her bare foot.

"Well, let's see. I remember once when Annie was a baby." I glanced around to make sure Anne was paying attention. "We got flooded out in a terrific rainstorm on a back-roads shortcut north of the farm and had to detour all over the place before we could find a way to cross the Wapsipinicon."

"I was a baby?" asked Anne, cautiously alert.

"A babe in arms."

"Who was holding me?"

"That's just an expression. Your mother was taking care of you while I drove, and she wasn't very happy with me for getting us in such a pickle in the first place."

"Did I cry? Was I scared?"

"Probably not. You were a quiet baby, Annie—you seemed more interested in watching the world."

In the rearview mirror I saw her looking now with a kind of dreamy self-awareness out her window toward the setting sun and the oncoming storm. What I had just said was the truth but not the whole truth: she had been a quiet baby, but not exactly an overjoyed one. Serious, yes. Extremely observant. Sometimes we called her The Judge.

"Was I quiet, too, Dad?" asked Molly. She prodded her toes urgently into the back of my shoulder. "Dad, was I a good baby?"

"Well, you had colic for a while, Molly. You kept us up nights. Then you got over that and you were a peach."

"Am I a peach now?"

"Most of the time you are." I pressed my shoulder back against her kneading foot. It felt good. "You're both peaches."

We all went back to eating. That wasn't a bad conversation, I thought—anyway, not for me. With Carol in the car, responding to the girls' questions, distributing the food, pointing out things for all of us to notice, I could easily slide by wordlessly for mile after mile, as if getting us there safely, and on time, was my part.

Some crows, lifting off from a harvested cornfield, then sharply veering, indicated how much the wind was picking up. Now we were angling to the southwest, toward the narrower and narrower band of light between earth and the lid of clouds. Often around this stretch of road I would see hawks circling, but tonight there were none.

Earlier than I had planned, I stopped at a plaza near Beloit and insisted we all use the toilets before the rain started. In the men's room, midstream, I was suddenly fearful for my girls, out of sight, vulnerable; my feelings felt as whipped up as the weather. I hurried out and was relieved when they emerged from the women's room together, giggling and bumping their hips against each other. Their T-shirts instantly flattened against their flat chests, and they screamed into the wind as they scuttled back to the car.

Everyone else was driving a little too fast. Friday night, I thought, seemed to bring with it an anxiety to pursue pleasure, just when people should be slowing down and relaxing. The cloud layer had clamped down completely over the west. Now it felt like a more dangerous highway.

"Is it going to lightning now?" asked Molly.

Almost immediately a bright bolt jagged down the sky to our right. My daughter the prognosticator. Both girls screamed again at the thunderclap.

The rain hit. I strained to see. There were greasy blurs in the fan-shaped swipes of the wipers. Then I remembered I'd forgotten to call my folks at the plaza. Well, in the hours of Illinois ahead of us there'd be time before it got too late.

I kept on and kept on but couldn't get beyond the swath of the storm. Molly fell asleep. Anne asked if she could turn on the car ceiling light to finish her book, and when I said absolutely not, she scrunched down into her corner of pillows. I turned the radio on again, very softly, and scanned the stations for weather reports. In a few more days it would be the autumnal equinox.

One hundred and fifty–odd years ago my pioneer ancestors went around this particular stretch of land by way of water. They drove the Conestoga wagon and ox team onto a barge near Pittsburgh, made their way down the Ohio River to the Mississippi, and then disembarked up the Mississippi at what is now Muscatine. They purchased their first forty from the government for a dollar twenty-five cents an acre, then mortgaged the land again and again over the years to pay for more acres and for the equipment to farm it. They tried hard to hold on; now what was left of the family was talking of letting go.

Both girls were asleep and sheets of rain still swept across the highway. I didn't want to wake them, and I didn't want to leave them unattended while I ran in somewhere to a telephone. I drove on and on through the dark flat farm country beyond Dixon, a segment of Illinois that has always appeared so bleak to me that I sort of dread going through it—and I'm supposedly a country boy. Here something terrible seems to have happened, or be about to happen, maybe the ghosts of Indians rising up to reclaim land that never should have been bought and sold in the first place. On a clear night I would at least have been able to see the spaced lights of farms and small towns, reassuring distant constellations.

I like picturing how the journeying pioneers, on clear nights, might have slept outside their wagons under quilts with stars sewn into them and a whole dome of stars flung overhead, out in the prairie, completely uninsured. Did my ancestors enjoy them-

selves? I hope there were moments when all seemed well. Sometimes when Carol and I make love, I imagine we are outside, pioneers ourselves in the wild grasses, and then I feel simpler, less
conditioned, more chancy and creative, more my real self. As a
kid I daydreamed, of course, but I never came up with pictures
that let me feel the way I feel when I'm with Carol.

It was nine-fifteen as we came down to the Mississippi. Even
in a heavy night rain the great river still looked silvery; if you
were a bird flying you could follow it like a pale road. I wished I
could stop the car in the middle of the bridge and lean for a few
minutes against the railing, getting my tired face wet and looking out at the stippled water.

On the Iowa side of the river there were plenty of places to
stop and call, but it felt too late for that now. It felt too late to do
anything but push on and make every minute count. Anne woke
up in the brightness of the highway lights around Davenport.

"Where are we?" It was more complaint than question.

"We just crossed the Mississippi," I told her softly, so as not to
wake Molly. "Half an hour more." I didn't want her to ask to stop
for a bathroom, and I was grateful when she didn't, even though
by then I was uncomfortable myself.

We passed the town and were once more in dark countryside,
though in the lessening rain I could now detect the intricate,
spread-out network of light nodes. There probably wasn't an inch
of Iowa left, I thought, that hadn't been meddled with in one way
or another.

In a little while Anne's voice came forward to me, "Why
doesn't Mom like the farm?"

I was startled. My daughter the psychoanalyst. "She didn't
come this weekend because of her work, Annie."

"But anyhow she doesn't like it."

"How do you know?"

"I know."

Nothing, I thought, can remain hidden. "I guess basically she'd rather be doing other things. How about you—are you glad to come to the farm?" I glanced around. I could make out that her arms were folded over her stomach, her hair mussed. Again I wondered if this child was happy in the life we were making for her. I felt exhausted. I try hard, but I can only do so much.

"It depends."

I kept my eyes straight ahead. There was a sensation on the right side of my neck, as if Anne were staring pointedly at me. Judging me. I wanted to tell her that it wasn't my fault, at least not in any way I knew, that her mother wasn't with us.

The farmhouse looked wide-awake—lights in the living room, on the high pole between the garage and the barn, at the back door, in the kitchen. I stopped just in front of the old cement hitching block and cut the motor. My ears were ringing. My neck and shoulders ached.

This east side of the house needed paint even more than it had the last time we were here, at the beginning of June. As I was growing up, any big job required that we do without in some other area. But this time it wasn't so much a question of the money. Ever since the cows went, there seemed to be less and less impetus for Mother and Dad to keep things up—as if the cows had been their most important judges.

A stubby figure was coming through the kitchen now, into the back entry porch. Mother. I felt so tired; tonight I just didn't want to go back into this childhood. There would still be time, just a split second in which I could start the motor, slam the car into reverse, and peel out of there, five hours back home to my beautiful wife.

Molly woke up and instantly started to cry. My mother was shielding her eyes to peer out beyond the porch light. Her vision is poor right now; her cataracts seem to be taking forever to be ripe enough for surgery. "Molly, Molly." I got out quickly, grateful that at least the rain had stopped, and opened her door and lifted her from the back seat. It'd been a long time since she'd wakened from sleep howling.

"What is it, what is it?" I stroked her dampened hair. She felt sweaty all over, and it was a lot cooler outside. "Annie, come on sweetie, get yourself out, there's Grandma at the door."

"Del!" I heard my mother shrill back into the house. "Delbert! They're here!"

Molly weighed a ton.

"Oh, what's wrong?" said my mother as we reached the door. "Oh my, why is she crying like that?" She gave Molly's back an awkward pat, and Molly hid her face in my neck. "Your beds is all ready," Mother said to me. Her gray hair looked newly and painfully crimped. She was still wearing her apron.

"Hello, Mother." I bent with difficulty, Molly still wailing and clinging, to give my mother's cheek a kiss. She smelled vinegary; so did the whole entry porch. "Sorry we're late—it was unavoidable."

"Your wife called." Not Carol, but *your wife*. But she had called, that was good. Why hadn't I imagined that she might? "It's a shame she works so hard, Cletus. She ought to take it easier."

"She knows how to rest, Mother." I looked behind me and saw that Anne was trying to carry too much from the backseat. One book and then another spilled from her armload onto the wet grass. Just then my big father appeared in the entryway, walking stiffly, the top of his bald head white, his face red, his eyes bleary.

"Hello, Dad." I reached around Molly to shake his huge paw.

"Shush, now," I whispered into her ear, "You're almost in bed, you're all right."

"She sick?" asked my father. He's three inches taller than I am and probably sixty pounds heavier. Once, when he was angry, maybe over the way I'd cleaned the combine or let a battery go dead—something like that, funny I can't remember exactly—he clamped his hands like a vise around my upper arms and threw me against the side of the barn. Coming down, I hit my tailbone on the nineteenth-century creek-stone foundation, laid by my great-great-grandfather and his son, my father's grandfather. That place on my tailbone still occasionally gives me trouble.

"She's just overtired—sorry we're so late—I'll take her straight up to bed. And here's Anne, good girl, Annie, you brought a big load." For some reason, maybe just the wailing child in my arms, it seemed too much to ask Anne to retrieve the books in the grass. Carrying Molly up the steep stairs, I asked myself if we gave in too much to our children's moods. Ruin is always possible, at any stage. What I worked so hard for was just the opposite.

I knew every tread on the staircase, the rust in the old upstairs washbasin and toilet, the lavender soap, the way light broke into colors here and there in the old beveled mirror. As she was pee-ing, Molly shuddered once all over and then stopped crying. I cleaned her teeth with some paste on my finger. She shuddered again and spit, and then she drank two whole glasses of water. Trouble in the night, maybe, but the kid had been parched.

"Your pajamas are in the car, Molly. Let's just take off your shoes, okay?"

The bed was beautifully made, the blankets smelling of cedar, the pillow plump and covered with an ironed, crochet-edged case. Molly sighed and settled her cheek into it. I felt as if it was my turn to cry now, but I kissed her forehead and smoothed back her hair. "Are you all right now?" She nodded. Her eyes were closed. "When you wake up, you'll be here, you'll be at the farm." She nodded again.

Ten-twenty by farm time is the middle of the night. Downstairs all the lights were still on. I had expected to see my mother giving the counters one last wipe, my father punching a final remote surf through the TV channels. And I had thought that Annie would probably follow me and Molly directly upstairs. But what I found was the three of them sitting at one end of the kitchen table eating pickles. Mother had been canning. Red and green battalions of finished jars stood on the counter by the stove.

"What do we have here," I said.

Annie looked up at me. Her lips were stained bright red. On the table were two dishes of pickles: beets, and a yellowish green mound of something else. Also a deck of cards, the sight of which soothed me a little, cards being one of the few things beside work and meals that our family used to do together; the card games sort of filled the awkward spaces. At the other end of the table, arranged on a towel rag with the cleaning kit and oil, were the disassembled halves of my father's pump-action Winchester Model 12.

"Have some pickles while they're still warm, Cletus," said Mother. "They're awful good that way."

My father pinched up a limp mess of the yellowish green kind and lowered it into his mouth.

"What're those?" I pointed.

"Sweet zucchini and onion," said Mother. "It's Sharon's recipe. Calls for lots of turmeric. Your father has taken a shine to them."

"I like the red ones best," said Anne.

"Annie, you never eat beets at home." I saw how this pleased my mother. I sat down with them at the pickle end of the table. Pickles now, trouble later, I thought, but I started tasting anyway. Growing up, I had eaten enough pickles to put a few wrinkles in any personality.

"Did you find everything all right upstairs?" asked my mother.

"Yes. You make the best beds in the world."

"She sick?" asked my father as he chewed.

"No, Dad, just worn out. So, how's the Winchester?"

"Getting to be that time of year—you coming down this fall for the pheasants, Cletus?"

"You know I'm a lousy shot, Dad. Sharon's probably still better than I ever was."

"Can't get Sharon out to hunt no more, now she's a mother. Everybody's giving up on me." He stared hard into the bowls of pickles, grinding his jaw. "Couldn't even get your mother out to the barn to help do the cows."

"Oh come, Del, we all know the story. You could have hired someone and you know it. You was pretty near wore out yourself." My own mother's eyes looked mysterious behind the smeary clouds of cataracts. What did I really know about her? It surprised me to hear her so outspoken. Maybe these days she was picking up more than recipes from her daughter.

"My troubles all started when I married *her*," said my father in a jokey voice, nodding in Mother's direction. Then, to my shock, he actually winked at me.

"Giving up that barn was the best birthday present I ever did give myself," said Mother, as if what Dad had just said was of no account. "I don't regret it, not for a minute. You can't keep on the same way forever."

"Why not?" said my father, and I saw Anne perk up her ears at a method of arguing straight from her own ten-year-old book.

She reached down the table and stroked the tips of her fingers down the metal barrel and then up along the ringed wood pump on its bottom. "I'll go hunting with you, Grandpa."

"Oh no you won't," I said swiftly, and then before she could protest I added, "and the reason why not is that your mother wouldn't let you, either—you're way too young."

"If I was a boy, would you let me?" Her high, quavering voice was a sure sign of exhaustion. She rose from her chair and lifted the barrel with both hands.

"There's no need to hunt," I said lamely, and my father snorted. His face got redder, but he said nothing.

Everything rushed back to me: the intense cold as I tramped after him on the frozen bumpy earth between rows of corn stubble or through thick stiff grasses of ditches and swales, wearing boots and lumpy jackets that always seemed inadequate. Yes, I had been frightened to death—of his impatience, his jerkiness, his appetites. The actual killing would send a shudder through me and leave me colder than I was before: the bird plummeting from the sky, Dad's whoop; the only part I enjoyed was watching the dogs rush forward. Would my father have liked me better if I had been more like a dog?

"Where's Tricks?" I said suddenly. "I didn't see her when we came in."

My mother pressed both hands down on the table, as if she were about to push herself up. Annie was using the gun barrel as a scope upon various points of interest in the kitchen. Now the gleaming shaft swung around to me. My mother did get up then, brought the pickle jars back to the table, and nervously started forking into them what we had not eaten from the bowls.

"Had to put her down," said Dad. "Arthritis so bad she couldn't hardly walk. Good dog. Last of the good hunters."

I gestured to the handle of the gun on the table, and my father nodded.

I pictured where he had probably tied her up and done it, out behind the barn where the smartweed and buttonweed took over in high summertime, where on hot afternoons you could count on a large angular shape of cool shade, where I had once come across my father jerking off, facing the old cement silo, his back partly turned. I don't think he saw me, I walked right away, I was only a few years older than Anne. I walked quickly around the corner of the barn and across the blazing barnyard, and it wasn't long after that, weeks maybe, another scorching afternoon, when I made my own way into the machine shed, clear to one dark end behind the old cannibalized Chevy pickup, and I opened my pants and tried it myself, first time, dirty hands and all. The amazing thing was how primed I already was, without exactly knowing it.

I wondered where Tricks was buried. Black Lab, big amber eyes, a way of looking at you—of course, is there a dog that *doesn't* have a way of looking at you? Tricks's mother, Roxy, who had been my special dog, used to follow me everywhere. She'd gotten run over, pretty far down the road, they told me, a few weeks after I'd left for the university. I guess she'd waited as long as she could and finally just started out to look for me, a dog's odyssey.

"It's so shiny in there!" said Anne.

My father guffawed in rough pleasure.

"What's the wood part for, Grandpa?"

"Pumps the new shells in and the spent ones out."

"I want to do it," said Anne in that reedy, unsteady voice.

My mother screwed the caps on the pickle jars and carried them to the refrigerator. She took off her apron and hung it on its hook, turned out the pantry light, then stood on tiptoe to pull the chain of the bright light over the sink. It struck me then that my father should have been able to foresee, with his eye for breeding animals, that if he married someone as short as my mother, he might end up with a runt like me.

"Lay down the barrel now, Annie. Maybe you can help Grandpa put it back together tomorrow."

"But I want to *shoot* it."

I rubbed my hands down over my face. "Isn't anybody else around here tired?" Then I remembered the suitcases still in the car, the books still in the wet grass. I said I was going out for the luggage.

"Do you want your father to help you?" my mother said.

"No thanks, there's hardly anything."

I felt like a dead man as I banged out the door into air that was much clearer and must have been twenty degrees cooler. Everything was changing very fast. I thought of the coming winter, of my list of fall chores, all the things I wouldn't be doing at my home in the city while I worked here in the country, for my parents. To my surprise, someone had already retrieved the books from the grass. Breathing deeply, I threw back my head. Backlit clouds raced over a brilliant moon deep in a blue-black sea. It was so spectacular I wished someone else was seeing it alongside me.

Annie's flushed cheeks looked as if they, too, were stained with beet juice; getting her to simmer down enough for bed wasn't going to be easy. She had insisted on carrying all her own things upstairs. I followed, observing her struggle.

"Were you the big girl who brought in the books from the grass?"

"Of course."

She was telling me she was competent—yes, Dad, enough to handle a shotgun. In the moonlit bedroom she found her pajamas and swished assuredly past me to the bathroom.

But after a minute alone, she stuck her head out and whispered loudly, "Dad! Can you come stand outside?" She waited until she saw that I had taken my station, and then she closed the door with its translucent glass panel, patterned in a starburst design. I glanced through it at the unrecognizable blur of my eldest daughter. My child. The toilet flushed. Water ran. I thought about being human; I thought about fear.

My father entered the stairwell and began toiling up, leaning heavily on the banister. Each time we visited him, his arthritis seemed worse. What had he felt like, I wondered, as he tied up old arthritic Tricks and aimed the gun at her and fired? A shudder went through me. Now my mother came along behind him. She, also, took the steep stairs one at a time.

At the top, Dad stopped for a minute on the next to the last step to breathe heavily, blowing out through pursed lips. "Too bad your bride couldn't be here."

"Yeah, too bad." The way he'd just spoken recalled a hot afternoon at the swimming quarry years ago, right after Carol and I were engaged, with my father in a folding chair, his overalls rolled up his white legs to his knees, his eyes under his cap brim following Carol everywhere as she dove from the ledges, pulled her sleek body up out of the water, lay herself out to sun, like a taut mermaid in comparison to the flopped walrus shapes of my mother and Sharon.

Then Mother piped up from halfway up the stairs, "I'm sure she has better things to do."

"It's not that, Mother," I said, knowing that actually it was, partly.

"Well, good night then, it's late," said my father, and he made his stiff-legged, swaying way into his bedroom and closed the door.

"Good night, son." My mother patted my arm dolefully. "I hope you're able to sleep." It felt like a malediction. She started to turn away, but on second thought added, "You know, Cletus, I never thought you would live to grow up. I thought you might die as a little tyke."

"Really! Why?"

"It was just a terrible thought I couldn't get out of my mind. I prayed to God, but it didn't go away. I swear I saw you dead."

"But here I am—your prayers must have worked."

"The worst thing that can happen is for a child to die before the parents, especially a son."

"Didn't you worry about Sharon?"

"Not that way. Sharon was like somebody else's girl—tough from the beginning."

Annie opened the door from the bathroom. She looked so much like Carol at that moment, with her thick, golden hair and her serious, smart expression, that I felt an enormous relief over how the gene pool had gotten so obviously improved. And I had done it; I had gone out into the world and found a wonderful bride.

"Here's my girl." I opened my arms.

"You like Grandma's pickles, all right, don't you?" said Mother.

Annie nodded. She was shivering, one bare foot curled on top of the other. I kept my arms around her.

"Yes, it's a terrible thing when a child is the first to go," continued Mother. "Believe me, there's no worse thing in the world."

I glanced at Anne, whose brow had knitted as she scrutinized her grandmother. Inside the circle of my arm she felt to me like a quivery sapling.

"Well, it's off to bed for this healthy little one," I said quickly, steering my daughter around. "Good night, Mother, sleep well."

"What was Grandma telling?" said Anne as I unsealed her bedcovers and held them open for her.

"She was saying children should live long lives," I whispered.

"But why?"

"Because that's normal."

"But why was she telling about it?"

"She didn't used to think I'd live to grow up."

"But then I couldn't have gotten born to you, could I?"

"That's right."

I pulled the covers up, but she right away undid the tight envelope and searched under the sheet flap until her fingers found the satin binding of the blanket. In the next bed Molly slept on.

"I'd have to have a different daddy then."

"Well, maybe, but I'm glad you were born to us; I'm very glad."

"Did Grandma have a baby die once?"

I watched my ten-year-old working her fingers along the blanket binding as I searched the past I knew. "I don't think so." I had never considered the idea before.

"Dad, you're not going to die now, are you?"

"Not by a long shot."

"You can't because you haven't finished with me yet!"

"That's right—we're not finished." I kissed her forehead. "Do you want another blanket?" She shook her head, no, and then her brow eased, as if more than just my lips had passed over it.

My body, as I undressed in the moonlight, had a spectral sheen. The body I wished I could be seeing instead was Carol's. It felt unsettling to be here, in my own childhood home, without my wife. We were supposed to be together. I rummaged in my duffel for sweatpants and shirt and then went over to the window that framed the moon and the ongoing scud of clouds. Up the road to the north was the farm of the neighbor against whom my father has held a grudge since before I was born, for buying the eighty acres between us out from under Dad, who had already put down a deposit check; our neighbor then offered cash, and the seller, a

city person, the grandson of a dead farmer, not caring a fig which
country guy got the acres, had only seen the ready dollars. It'd
been unethical but not strictly so because nothing had yet been
signed. This, and many other disappointments over the years,
Dad has taken in such a way as to sour him.

The land tonight looked subdued and almost indeterminate
out there beneath the swift clouds. I seemed to see it and not see
it—the rolling, ancient seabed land that has been so briefly
touched by my family. What did they think they were doing,
those pioneers? And what did I think I was doing when I left the
land for a life of paper investments?

Then I had an absurd thought, in my exhaustion, that the
right thing now might be to return the land, to return to that
warm night on the prairie before the first land purchase, when the
man and woman lie joined together, their liberated imagination
mirroring the figures of the stars, content not with ownership but
with their vision alone. Could the time have come, I wondered, to
travel backward and give the land away? But to whom? And who
am I to be thinking these thoughts? Just someone who has sur-
vived his childhood, who now has children of his own, who has
used up tremendous energy all his life, trying in anxious human
ways to feel secure when the world is in truth indeterminate and
not to be held.

Then I remembered something, like a moon disk rising from
the deep, I had seen years ago from this very window. It had been
midsummer, one of the years I was home from the university.
Waking abruptly one night from a heavy, farm laborer's sleep, I
felt pulled to this window. There was a bright moon that night,
too. I looked to the south, and I thought I saw my mother walking down the road in her light-colored nightgown. Yes, it was my
stocky fifty-one-year-old mother, walking away from my eyes
down the public road, her gown ballooning gently. I couldn't

move. Just then a screen door slammed and the figure of my father in his bathrobe and work boots lumbered down the lane and out onto the moon-bleached blacktop road. She continued walking as if she thought herself alone, and he continued his heavy striding behind her, closing the distance between them relentlessly. But then, before he reached her, she herself stopped and turned slowly around. She faced him: I couldn't really see their faces, or hear any words. Instead I heard the shrill of insects, crickets, katydids. Don't, I whispered from my watching place, don't strike her. He didn't. He aligned himself with her on the pale road, and they both started walking in this direction. It was a hot night, the fireflies swimming upward through the humidity. I watched until my mother and father disappeared around the back of the house.

And then what happened? What did I make of it? I don't remember. I must have just gone back to sleep. That's how I was then, strong young man, tired out from labor, full of myself, thinking I knew who I was and where I was headed, and pretty sure that I'd all but gotten away from the farm for good.

I pried my way into the bed my mother had made for me. As I lay chilled and flattened between her ironed sheets, I wondered if it was possible there really had been a baby who had died before my time, a ghostly sibling who all this time had been watching me survive. I yawned, conscious of myself yawning. We live with a lot of strange wonderfulness, I thought, and act as if it isn't much of anything. I yawned again.

Tomorrow was Saturday, next day Sunday. Nothing earthshaking would probably be decided about the farm this weekend. We'd all be two days older. Some chores done, meals eaten. I'd have to entice Annie away from the shotgun.

A dead child, could it possibly be? My mother had spoken as if from experience—my own mother, like a stranger.

I shivered, really wishing Carol were in here with me. She was the part of earth I had gone out into the world and been inspired to find, and did I ever want to hold on to her. She'd said she couldn't do without me, which was good news, but I knew in truth she was mine and not mine. Everyone has to live like that, I thought: holding and not holding.

Gradually I got warm enough to relax, and in a few more minutes I hardly felt the dimensions of my ironed-out body; I was no size, just alive, myself.

A ghost brother: I could question him. I could ask: What more can I do? I could catch hold of my little boy and beg to be told why I care so much how I live if it is all to end anyway.

And then I was very surprised to receive an answer. I hadn't gone to sleep; I hadn't gone anywhere. It was an intimate voice, as immediate as if it had been right here talking all along and I had just gotten warm enough to fall into step with it: because, it said, because it does not end.